Murder on the Moorland

Helen Cox is a Yorkshire-born novelist and poet. After completing her MA in Creative Writing at York St John University, Helen wrote for a range of magazines and websites, as well as for TV and radio news. Helen has edited her own independent film magazine and penned three non-fiction books. Her first two novels were published by HarperCollins in 2016. She currently hosts The Poetrygram podcast and works for City Lit, London. Helen's new series of cosy mysteries stars librarian-turned-sleuth Kitt Hartley and is set in York.

Helen's Mastermind specialism would be *Grease 2*, and to this day she adheres to the Pink Lady pledge. More information about Helen can be found on her website: helencoxbooks.com, or on Twitter: @Helenography.

THE KITT HARTLEY YORKSHIRE MYSTERIES

Murder by the Minster
A Body in the Bookshop
Murder on the Moorland

HELEN COX

Murder on the Moorland

Quercus

First published in Great Britain in 2020 by Quercus
This paperback edition published in 2020 by

Quercus Editions Ltd
Carmelite House
50 Victoria Embankment
London EC4Y 0DZ

An Hachette UK company

A CIP catalogue record for this book is available from the British Library

PB ISBN 978 1 52940 228 5

Print

Papers used by Quercus are from well-managed forests and other responsible sources.

For the doctors and nurses at the Whittington Hospital
who have shown my husband and I such kindness
and ceaseless care.

ONE

Detective Inspector Malcolm Halloran jammed his foot down hard on the accelerator of his black Fiat Linea and sped past a road sign for Esk Valley prison.

Three miles.

Three miles of rugged moorland between here and the fusty visiting room where he would once again look his wife's killer in the eye.

If he could do that then he would know for sure whether somehow, even from behind bars, Jeremy Kerr had managed to murder again.

Halloran tried to breathe through the many ways in which that thought stung him. This was all supposed to be over. Had Kerr really found some way of killing again, even if only vicariously? If so, how would he get Kerr to confess to it now that he was disgraced and incarcerated? There was no hope of a get-out-of-jail-free card for the likes of him, no matter how much information he offered. Regardless,

Halloran had to find a way of squeezing out the truth. Last time, Kerr had taken seven lives before Halloran noticed a book about Anglo-Saxon gods sitting on his bookshelf one night. If he hadn't been so desperate to close the case after the death of his wife, maybe he wouldn't have spotted it amongst the number of other innocuous volumes about moorland walks and military history. One of the runes on the spine of the book had matched a symbol carved into the hand of Kerr's third victim and it was the first breadcrumb in a trail that would lead to the conviction of a ritualistic killer and once-close colleague. If somehow Kerr had been responsible for ending yet another innocent life, Halloran had to do whatever it took to make sure the body count stayed at one.

Desperate to dismiss the swarm of questions hazing his mind, he tried instead to focus on the purple heather scrolling past the windscreen, fixing his eyes on the point where the bracken met the pastel blue of a dawning June sky. Not even the ravishing colours of the midsummer moorland could hold his attention, however, or help him forget the scene that had played out at York Police Station a little over three hours ago.

Halloran let out a weighty sigh. Today wasn't supposed to be like this. He was scheduled for a Sunday off this week for a start. But not just that. He was supposed to be spending the morning in bed with Kitt. The night before had been special. After six months of proving himself worthy of her trust, she had given herself to him, completely. Before he could even think of showing her the desires he had kept hidden from others he'd been intimate with, it was important to him that Kitt knew how tender he was at heart. Thus, when they had started sleeping together a couple of months ago, he'd made sure their encounters had been slow and gentle. That they were purely about connecting with this new, extraordinary person in his life. Last night though, for the first time, he had been able to do what he had wanted to do with her since they'd met – or at least make a start on the list.

He remembered the sultry smile on Kitt's face as he had looped his belt around her wrists. He should be with her right now, whispering a few more suggestions in her ear and watching her eyebrow rise in mock outrage. Instead he was out here on the moorland, hunting ghosts from a past life.

Halloran shook his head, trying to shake off his thoughts. He had left a note on his pillow letting Kitt know how much the night before had meant to him and that he had been summoned to the station. But at the thought of all they had shared he wanted to call her. To hear her voice and let her in on what was happening. Giving in to this urge, however, would probably force him to think twice about what he was about to do and he couldn't afford that. No matter the cost, he was determined to face Jeremy Kerr once again.

The car crested a small hill and the Hole of Horcum, a 400-foot-deep hollow in the Levisham valley, opened up by the roadside. Local legend told that the depression had been forged by a giant who, during an argument with his wife, had scraped up a handful of earth to throw at her. In truth, the chasm had been formed by water welling up from the hillside and wearing the rocks down slowly over thousands of years. The feeling of being hollowed out, of a primal force welling up inside and eroding what you once were, was one Halloran was more familiar with than he ever wanted to admit.

He had never cried publicly over the death of his wife. Not even at her funeral. There had been many nights, however, where the whiskey bottle had called and in solitude he had allowed himself to mourn. Before this morning he had managed to convince himself that he had finally left those dark times behind, but he had been wrong.

Skirting around the abyss cut into the heart of the moorland, the car climbed another hill. This time, Halloran found himself staring across the short stretch of road ahead to a long, sandy-coloured building less than a mile in the distance. He frowned and felt his heart quicken. Could he smell Kamala's perfume? He breathed in deep again. No. That was impossible. Any last traces of her scent had long since drifted out of his life. In fact, save for a wedding ring packed away in a box of odds and ends in the attic back in York, there was no physical evidence left that he had ever had a wife. And yet right now, in this moment, there was no mistaking the gentle hint of jasmine and peach that seemed to hang in the air. Winding down the window, Halloran welcomed the cool breeze and rubbed his hand over his face as though trying to wake from a bad dream.

He looked at his watch: 7.40.

The message to get down to the station had buzzed through to his phone just after four. Kitt had been sleeping so soundly, he wouldn't have awoken her for the world. When he got to the nick, they had all been waiting for him: Chief Superintendent Ricci, Detective Sergeant Banks and Detective Sergeant Redmond. He would never forget the look on their faces when he walked into that room, the news they broke to him, or the reckless manner in which he had reacted to what Ricci had to say. He was sure he'd seen a flash of fear in Ricci's eyes as he had raved and ranted. He couldn't blame her for being unnerved. His behaviour had frightened him too; he needed to get a grip before he faced Kerr again.

Halloran overtook a group of cyclists already making a start on whatever epic ride they had planned across some of the steepest terrain in England. He'd never understood the draw to cycling steep hills, to him it seemed borderline insane, but then Kitt thought the same about his morning jogs.

'What are you running from, I wonder?' she would say with a wry smile whenever he pulled on his running shoes.

'Definitely not you,' was all he could ever bring himself to tell her.

After a minute or so Halloran indicated left down a side road full of potholes that led to a tall black fence built of reinforced steel, strong enough to keep criminals in and strong enough to keep anyone who wanted revenge on them out. Usually, if an officer wanted to visit a prisoner there would be forms to fill in and several other bureaucratic hoops to jump through. If you were a high-ranking police officer with connections in the community, though, it was possible to pull in a favour. If Kerr refused to speak to him, there was nothing he could do to force him, but something told Halloran that Kerr wouldn't pass up the opportunity to confront, and likely taunt, the man who had put him away.

Halloran pressed the security buzzer to announce his arrival to the officer at reception and a moment later the iron gate began to swing open. Somewhere inside this building, amongst the maze of long white corridors that echoed with the footsteps of wardens and sometimes the wails of a tormented convict, Kerr was shovelling down a prison breakfast, unaware of the fact he was about to be visited by the man whose life he had tried to destroy. Exactly what Halloran would do when he once again came face to face with his wife's killer, he hadn't yet decided.

TWO

Halloran's stomach clenched as the door to the west wing interview room creaked open. Slowly, he raised his eyes. Kerr almost swaggered towards him in his prison-issue tracksuit. Burgundy, Halloran noted, the colour of congealed blood.

Halloran knew Kerr would be accompanied by two officers but he didn't even glance at them. He couldn't just now. He was too busy taking in the cut of the man responsible for upending his life five years ago.

The prison diet didn't suit Kerr, that much was for sure. He was slimmer than he had been when he had worked alongside him as a DI at Eskdale station. It had been a tranquil existence: closing workaday cases and living in the quaint moorland village of Irendale with Kamala, before Kerr strangled her to death. Kerr's hair had been shaved short during his time inside, making his big ears stick out even further than they once did. But those grey-green eyes were still as cold and empty as they had always been, even before Halloran had unmasked him as a serial killer.

Kerr sat down across the table from Halloran with a faint smirk on his lips. Though he held the prisoner's gaze, Halloran tried not to focus on that. It was the sort of expression that made him want to punch Kerr's lights out but, satisfying as that would be, getting himself locked away on a GBH charge wasn't going to achieve anything. If Halloran wanted to get to the truth he was going to have to keep his cool and stay focused on one thing only: luring Kerr into giving something – anything – away that spoke of his connection with the body that had been found early yesterday evening.

'Just give us a knock when you're done with him, sir,' said one of Kerr's chaperones, before turning her back on them and walking out of the door, her colleague in tow.

The pair stared at each other in silence for a moment. Kerr probably thought Halloran was using the same interrogation tactics they had once used together. Waiting a suspect out. Forcing them to speak first just so you could interrupt them and show them who was in charge. In fact, Halloran was merely taking the time to size him up. Looking for some telltale sign that indicated just how surprised, or otherwise, Kerr was to see him. But his ex-colleague's face remained cryptic. That smirk could indicate he had been waiting for Halloran to call but it could just as easily be a sign he had no clue what was going on. Either way, Kerr probably sensed he had the upper hand in this conversation. He was smart enough to understand that Halloran wouldn't come to him unless he had no other choice.

''ave you missed me then, Malc?' said Kerr.

Halloran's innards tightened another notch. It wasn't just the reminder of how much Kerr's raspy voice grated on him. Since he was knee-high, everyone had always shortened his name to Mal, except Kerr. He had to have his own special pet name. In all the nights Halloran had obsessed over what had passed between him and Kerr, he had wondered if even this had been a manipulation. A way of tricking him into thinking they had a unique bond, and thus allaying his suspicions. Was Kerr really mad enough to believe any residue of that friendship remained? Or was he just trying to rile him?

'Been counting the days.'

'I bet you 'ave. I bet you're going to be there the day those gates open and I walk back out into the sunshine. But you've got a long wait for me to get out of 'ere. You saw to that.'

'Don't flatter yourself. I haven't thought about you in years.'

Kerr leered. ''ad other things on your mind, ave yer? Or other people, perhaps? Got yerself another woman already? That didn't take long.'

Halloran resisted the urge to argue but under the table his fists flexed. He had waited several years longer than most other men would have before moving on. The insinuation that he thought the women in his life in any way disposable stung nonetheless. Kerr was baiting him, then. He mustn't bite.

'I did think of you this morning, though,' Halloran said, somehow managing to keep his tone casual.

'Whatever floats yer boat,' Kerr said. 'I always thought you maybe had a dark side yer kept to yerself. If thinking of me and what I've got away with gets you through the day, satisfies some need, I'm happy to help.' His leer broadened but Halloran could see from a flash in his eyes that a curiosity had been ignited. Was he feigning to create an air of innocence? Or just curious over how much Halloran knew about the murder?

'I looked through your visitor records just now and a familiar name jumped out.'

'Aye, we worked together for three years, Malc. It's not like you don't know me friends and family. Or the ones who are still willing to call themselves that.'

'Since when were you such good friends with Kurt Goodchild?'

Halloran fixed his eyes on Kerr's face, searching for a twitch or a tell, but mentioning Goodchild hadn't ruffled him.

'Ah, Kurt, 'e always was a bit of a lost little lad.'

'You know it's worse than that.' Halloran was trained to remember important details such as the defining features of a person's face, but Kurt Goodchild's was particularly distinctive. It was his eyes. He had the eyes of a startled rabbit: wary and cowering. It wouldn't take much to intimidate him.

'Aye, well, when yer live in a small village like Irendale word gets round. Schizophrenia, isn't it? Terrible thing. Can make people—'

'Impressionable.'

Kerr eyed Halloran. 'Aye. I suppose.'

'So you're admitting it?'

'A man in my position never admits to anything, Malc, you know that.' Kerr leaned back in his chair. 'But I've got time on me hands, thanks to you. So, go on. Tell me a story.'

'You've been talking to Goodchild.'

'When people make the effort to come and visit you in prison it's a bit rude to sit there in silence, where's yer manners?'

'You better get serious,' Halloran said. 'Right now.'

'Being in prison puts things in perspective, Malc. When you don't 'ave the personal freedoms you've become accustomed to, you don't sweat small things. I've got more disturbing characters to deal with on this side of the fence than the likes of you. So if you want me to take you seriously, you're going to 'ave to give me something to get serious about.'

'You know better than to test me,' Halloran growled.

Kerr's leer only widened. 'Maybe testing you is an entertainin' way to pass the time.'

'What did you and Goodchild talk about?' Halloran said, doing all he could to ignore Kerr's jibes.

''is ma, most of the time. Difficult to get 'im to talk about anything else, if you remember. She's really the only friend he's got, besides me, of course. So he likes to talk about her quite a bit.'

'And if I asked Goodchild, would he tell me the same?'

'I 'ave no idea what a kid like that might tell you under the duress of interrogation.'

Halloran could feel his temper shortening by the second but couldn't afford to give Kerr any outward sign he was getting to him.

'All right. Let's play it your way.' Halloran's tone was easy but he stood, placed both palms on the table and leaned towards Kerr. 'Here's what you want to know: a woman was found dead in Irendale last night. According to current information the investigating officers believe the murder took place on Friday night.'

'Murdered? 'ow?' Kerr licked his lips.

'Why don't you tell me?' Halloran stood up and began to circle around the table, arms folded.

'I don't think I understand what you're getting at there, Malc.'

'What I'm getting at is I know that one way or another you're involved in this woman's death. It's only a matter of time before I find out exactly how, but of course, you could help yourself by just confessing now.'

Kerr frowned. 'I was very good at what I did, my son. Took you a bloody long time to piece together what I was up to an' all. But even I 'ave to admit I'm not good enough to commit a murder from behind bars in a village twenty miles away. Flattered you think I'm that creative though.'

'Someone like you would find a way.'

'With all the ne'er-do-wells between 'ere and Teesside, what makes you think I 'ad owt to do with it, eh?'

'Let's just say this body had some things in common with the bodies you left strewn across the village five years ago. Only difference is, you didn't do it yourself this time,' said Halloran. 'You got Goodchild to do it for you.'

Kerr started to laugh. He had a quiet huffy laugh that sounded as though he couldn't quite catch his breath. 'If that's the best theory you've got, I don't like the odds of you solving this one, lad.'

Halloran glowered. 'Underestimating me hasn't done you any favours in the past. You might as well be out with it and come clean about what you said to Goodchild.'

'I already told you. Nothing about a murder. If Kurt 'ad anything to do with it, it weren't because of anything I said to 'im.'

'So it's just a coincidence that Goodchild visits you and three days later a woman is murdered in the village you used to live in, using your MO?'

'And it couldn't be a copycat, eh?' Kerr said. He shook his head at the inspector. 'You didn't even entertain that thought, did yer? Jumped straight to the assumption this case was about you. About what I did. That's always been your problem, Malc, you always take things too personally. When I killed K—'

'Don't you dare say her name,' Halloran spat, trying not to imagine wrapping his own hands around Kerr's throat. Squeezing hard enough to let him know the pain and sheer terror his victims would have felt right before the end. Kamala included.

As if able to guess at Halloran's thoughts, Kerr stared at him. His face was more serious than Halloran ever remembered seeing it. 'Well, this *is* a sorry state of affairs. After all these years, you still think that what 'appened was all about you, don't yer?'

Halloran remained silent and folded his arms.

'Malc, the killing I did was never about the victims or their families. I was just doin' what I was told to do by a voice in 'ere.' Kerr tapped the side of his head and let out a hollow chuckle. 'It was like a hunger I 'ad to feed. There was nowt personal about it. I thought a copper as bright as you would've clocked that by now.'

Halloran frowned at Kerr for a moment, digesting what he had said. Whilst he was killing, Kerr had claimed he was under the instruction of Woden, an ancient god of death. Halloran had never known whether Kerr really believed this or was just using it as a way of distancing himself from the atrocities he'd committed. Five years in a high security prison might have afforded him that level of reflection on his crimes; to reassess his own psychological make-up. But Halloran had been played by Kerr once before and he wasn't going to let it happen again.

'What do you want, understanding? Some kind of gold medal for philosophizing what you did?'

'Just tellin' it 'ow it is,' said Kerr. 'A small part of me was relieved when I first got banged up. The choice about whether I submitted to that voice was taken away from me. After the cases you've worked over the years, some part of you knows what I'm talking about. You just don't want to listen to that part of yerself right now. Too busy making this girl's murder about you and pointin' the finger. It's not what you want to hear, but I'm innocent, Malc.'

'Innocent,' Halloran said bitterly through gritted teeth. 'Not a word I'd readily choose to describe you. I don't know how you're involved in this woman's death but mark my words, I am not going to stop until I find out.'

THREE

A fresh breeze ruffled Halloran's dark hair as he stood on the gondola of the Tees Transporter Bridge. The 'Tranny', as it was known to the local people of Middlesbrough, had carried workers and residents across the river to Port Clarence, and back again, for more than a hundred years. Consequently, its blue, geometric outline had become a symbol of resilience to those who lived in the region. Halloran stared over at the north bank and noticed a familiar figure with long red hair sitting on a bench. Though he was too far away to make out the title, he could see she was reading a book. Halloran might have guessed. He wanted to smile at the warmth and familiarity that always stirred in him at the mere sight of Kitt Hartley but after all that had passed that morning, he couldn't quite manage it.

Besides, after his confrontation with Kerr, he hadn't been able to get hold of Kitt via mobile, at the cottage or several other places he'd gone in search of her. Seeing she was safe was a relief but it was unlike her to cut herself off. Was she angry at him for not being there when she awoke? Had she heard about the murder on the news and made the connection with his disappearance? If so, perhaps she was cross that he hadn't let her know what was happening. Whatever the issue, something was definitely amiss.

This particular area of Middlesbrough had once been packed with chimneys, factories and blast furnaces, almost all of which had been stripped away by Thatcher's government. The sparseness of the landscape somehow made Kitt look even more lonely than Halloran imagined she felt just now. If she was angry with him for leaving her to wake alone, he could only hope she could forgive him for ruining what should have been a very special morning after.

Once he had disembarked the gondola, Halloran made his way down a small, grassy path that ran along the riverside and in minutes he was just a few feet away from where Kitt was sitting. She raised her head from her book before he was within speaking distance, a frown fell over her face, and she froze. She made a few awkward gestures as though she was trying to figure out just what she would do with herself but a moment later her eyes dropped back to the page, her safe space, even though Halloran could tell she wasn't reading. Despite his first thought being about how best to open this conversation and quickly get to the bottom of whatever was troubling Kitt, he was only human and it hadn't escaped his notice that she was wearing a green polka dot sundress that clung to her in all the right places. It was not the kind of garment Kitt would have worn when the pair had first crossed paths but she had become increasingly daring in her clothes choices over the past six months. Halloran liked to think he had a little something to do with that. The dress she wore today emphasized the way her waist pulled in, which in turn accentuated the ways in which the rest of her jutted out and reminded him of the warmth and comfort he found in her soft curves. Something about that thought made the horror of this morning fade. It was replaced by an ache to be close to her.

Slowly, he sat down on the bench.

'How did you find me?' Kitt said, her tone neutral. 'You didn't track my phone, did you?'

'I don't need to do that to find you.'

'That's not what I asked.'

Halloran shook his head. 'I didn't track your phone. Once I'd been to the cottage, to the library, to your favourite bookshops and to Evie's, this was the next stop.'

'That's the problem when you let someone in,' said Kitt. 'You tell them about all the songs and books and places that're special to you and then they can always find you, even when you don't want them to.'

'Kitt . . .' Halloran went to take her hand but she pulled away. 'Talk to me, what's wrong?'

Tears rose in Kitt's eyes. 'How can you even ask me that? I deserve better treatment than this, you know, and I don't have to put up with it. If I walk away from you it won't be my loss, that I can tell you.'

'Don't say things like that, pet,' said Halloran. 'I know having to go into the station this morning wasn't ideal but it's my job, and I left you a note to explain.'

'A note? No you didn't,' said Kitt with a frown.

'Oh God,' Halloran said, the realization hitting him. 'You didn't get my note?'

'No,' Kitt said. Her voice had softened but her eyes remained narrow enough to let Halloran know he still wasn't completely off the hook.

'I wrote a note explaining I'd been called into the station,' said Halloran. 'And I may have included one or two details about how much last night meant to me.'

'Oh really,' Kitt said, 'and where did you leave this alleged note?'

'On my pillow. I wanted it to be the first thing you saw when you woke up.'

Kitt's frown deepened. 'There was no note on your pillow. But . . .'

'But what?'

'Well, when I woke up Iago was sitting on your pillow, purring away, and now that I think about it he was looking a little more smug than usual.'

'That bloody cat hates me,' said Halloran, leaving out that he didn't have a lot of love for Kitt's feline friend either.

In spite of herself Kitt chuckled. 'No, he doesn't, he's got used to it being just the two of us, that's all, and he's taking some time to adjust.'

'What do you think he did with it? The note, I mean.'

'I don't know,' said Kitt. 'I'll have another hunt when I get back to the cottage but either way I don't think he was deliberately trying to sabotage our relationship. He can't read, after all, at least not as far as I know. For years he's snuggled up on that pillow on cold mornings waiting for me to wake up. He probably saw an alien object there and took it upon himself to move it out of his territory.'

The inspector nodded, though despite Kitt's insistence to the contrary he was fairly sure the 'alien object' Iago would like to remove from his territory was Halloran himself.

For the first time since he'd arrived, Kitt looked deep into Halloran's eyes. 'So, what was so important that you had to leave like that after . . . what we shared?'

'I drove out to the moors, near Irendale, this morning.'

Kitt's head jerked backwards and she glared at him. Perhaps given the village's association with his ex-wife, that wasn't the best piece of information to open with.

'There's been a murder there,' he quickly clarified.

Kitt frowned. Her voice softened even further than it had before. 'That's awful. Was it someone you knew? Someone you were close to? Did you have to go and identify them or something?'

'No, it was the nature of the murder, not the victim, that drew me there.'

'What do you mean?'

'A young woman was strangled on Friday night and the killer had carved a runic symbol into her hand.' Halloran paused and then added, 'That's how Kamala died, and the others Kerr killed.'

Kitt's breath caught in her throat. She spoke slowly then, still trying to make sense of what Halloran had just told her. 'I'm so sorry, I didn't know that Kerr had . . . I didn't know that was how Kamala died.'

'I was hoping you'd never know, that I could spare you that kind of detail. After I found out about this new murder I spent most of the morning behaving . . . well, like a bit of a madman, truth be told. Went straight out to Esk Valley prison to interrogate Kerr . . .'

'Oh, Mal.' Kitt shook her head. 'This must be just horrible for you after all this time. And what, you think the killings have started again? But how? Kerr's in prison. Is it a copycat?'

'Just because he's behind bars doesn't mean he hasn't had some part to play. As for whether it's a copycat, I don't know. I'm not supposed to try and find out, either.'

'What do you mean?'

'I mean I didn't take the news well when Ricci broke it to me this morning and she's put me on stress leave effective immediately. She expects me to rest for two weeks and lie low; she's probably hoping an arrest will be made in that time and that will be enough to calm me down. After two weeks there'll be a meeting when she decides whether or not I'm fit to come back. In the meantime, according to her, I'm not to go anywhere near this case.'

'I know we had a few initial reservations about Ricci but from what you say she's proven to be firm but fair over the past few months. I'm sure she's only thinking of what's best for you, and the team.'

'I know.'

'When you say you didn't take the news well . . .?'

'Honestly, I don't quite know how I'm going to face her again after the way I went on. She was trying to do me a favour. On the way here I already listened to a news report about the murder on the radio. It's likely all over the TV stations and the internet too. She called me in as soon as she heard about it to make sure I didn't hear it on the news or that some reporter didn't come knocking in the early hours because I was the one to close the last case like this in Irendale. Unfortunately, the favour she did me backfired.'

'How so?'

'You have to understand, we'd just had this incredible night together and I was really starting to believe this was all behind me. So when I was called into the station and Ricci told me, all the grief came surging back and . . . I took it out on them.'

'I do understand,' said Kitt. 'And I'm sure your colleagues will too.'

Halloran shook his head. 'I don't know. About three

seconds after Ricci told me what had happened I was planning my own investigation. The others tried to reason with me but I wouldn't have it. I wasn't listening. Then Ricci said the case was out of our jurisdiction. She was right but . . . I totally lost it.' Tears formed in Halloran's eyes. 'Kitt, I don't know what happened to me. I was shouting and mouthing off. It was like something inside me just burst.'

'Poor old thing,' Kitt said, running a hand through his hair.

'Crackers old thing, more like.'

Kitt was quiet for a moment, seemingly mulling something over, while Halloran noted with a wry smile that she didn't immediately jump in to contradict the idea he was crackers. 'So, let me get this straight: you've been told not to work the case?'

'Yes.'

'Even when you were instrumental in catching a killer with the same MO last time?'

'If I'd been able to keep my cool, Ricci might have got in touch with Eskdale, and suggested a consultation. But nothing I said or did in that room this morning was calm or collected, and now she thinks I can't be objective.'

'Well, she's probably right on that point,' said Kitt.

'Thanks for the vote of confidence.'

'We wouldn't be together if you were the kind of man who could stay objective after something like that.'

Halloran slid a little closer to her on the bench. 'So, we are still together?'

Kitt stared at him and then looked out at the river with half a smile.

'Given Iago's part in this morning's misunderstanding, yes. Besides, finding out that there's been a murder identical to your ex-wife's has to rank somewhere amongst the top excuses of all time for not indulging in a lie-in.' Kitt looked back at him. 'I'm glad we've got it sorted. When I woke up and you weren't there I thought—'

'That I'd left you,' Halloran said, pushing a stray strand of hair out of her face. 'But I would never, ever do that. If there is ever a time where you don't hear from me, it's because something is stopping me from getting back to you. I'm not Theo, I'm never going to do what he did.'

Kitt stroked Halloran's beard. 'He said he'd never hurt me, too.'

'I'm afraid that's not the promise I'm making,' said Halloran. 'I can't promise I won't hurt you. When you let someone in pain is inevitable at some point.'

A mischievous glint surfaced in Kitt's blue eyes. She opened her mouth to speak but Halloran cut her off.

'And no, before you say it, I'm not just talking about what we got up to last night.'

'I do hate it when you step on my jokes,' said Kitt, the glint still in her eye. 'I have so few of them. Can't you let a girl have her moment, once in a while?'

'My point is,' Halloran had a faint smile on his face but corrected himself before continuing, 'if I hurt you in some way, I will be here to iron it out with you, to talk it through, to make it up to you in any way I know how.'

Kitt took a deep breath, looked at him quietly for a moment and then nodded. 'That's probably the most honest thing a boyfriend has ever said to me. All right. But in the spirit of making things up there's something else I want you to promise.'

'What's that?'

'Before, you said you wanted to spare me certain details,' said Kitt. 'Please don't. If you are going through something, I can only be here for you if you let me in. If you let me share the pain with you. Keeping me at a distance will hurt me more than any truth about what you're thinking or feeling ever could. I want you trust me, completely.'

Not one to give his word lightly, Halloran closed his eyes for a moment, thinking. 'I want to, pet,' he said, opening his eyes again so they could look into hers. 'I really want to and I'm trying. Last night was a big step, I've never shared my wants with someone the way I have with you.'

'Neither have I.'

'I know. All I can tell you today is, I will do my very best to let you in. Is the fact that I'm working on it as hard as I can good enough, for now?'

'Good enough,' said Kitt. 'Now, how shall we go about this investigation?'

'What?'

'Well, you drove all the way out to the moorland this

morning to interrogate Kerr so I assume you're not taking Ricci's warning very seriously?'

'I . . . well . . .'

'Were you not planning to find out who committed this crime under your own steam?'

'Yes, emphasis on "my own steam".' Halloran had unsettled himself that morning by responding to the news of the murder the way he had. If that was day one of the investigation, who knew where he'd be by day three?

'Now, Mal, you just promised to do your best to let me in and I think if you're planning a covert investigation it's only fair that you allow me to help.'

'I don't know . . .'

'Mal . . . you said you trusted me. This is the moment to prove it.'

'It's not you I don't trust, it's myself.'

'I've got enough trust in you for both of us,' Kitt said.

'And that means the world to me, but I don't think it's very practical for you to join me on this. I'm going to need to be up on the moorland most days and you're in at the library.'

'Oh, that's easily solved,' Kitt said with a dismissive wave. 'How could anyone deny me annual leave when you've surprised me with a last-minute holiday in a quaint little cottage on the moorland?'

'You . . . think we should go away together?'

'I had hoped our first getaway might not be as part of a

covert investigation related to the death of your ex-wife, but a gal can't have everything now, can she?'

After the morning he'd had, Halloran shouldn't have been in the mood for Kitt's dry humour but there was something about it that never failed to uplift him. Her matter-of-fact summary of the situation made that whole catastrophic experience seem somehow more normal; a digestible part of life to be accepted like any other. After five years maybe it was time to start accepting that's just what it was.

'And you think Michelle will buy that story?'

'No, but luckily my oh-so-cynical superior is on holiday herself this week so I've only got to get it past her much chirpier boss, Maureen. Besides, it's the summer. Most of the students are either at home or on holiday. Anyway, never you mind about library politics. By midday tomorrow I'll have my bags packed for a week away.'

'And you really want to be part of this, even though it relates to Kamala?'

Kitt ran her fingers through Halloran's hair and looked into his blue eyes. 'Kamala is part of your story. We can't just ignore that chapter of your life, or erase it. Besides . . . loving someone means loving every bit of their story too, because every chapter led them to you.'

'And your curious streak has no part in this, I suppose?'

'I might be vaguely intrigued,' Kitt said, avoiding his eye.

He chuckled but then something struck him. 'Wait. Loving

someone . . .? You said "loving someone" . . . We haven't said "I love you" yet.'

Kitt smirked. 'I still haven't.'

'You're a terrible tease,' Halloran said.

'I resent that description. I'll have you know I'm a perfectly competent tease.'

Smiling, he held her face in his hands, and nudged her nose with his. After looking into his eyes for a long moment she slowly parted her lips, inviting him in. The second their mouths met, she made the most unexpected and delectable moan. After their unwelcome separation earlier that morning, it was a sound that left Halloran with a singular need: to be as close to her as possible. He pulled her body up against his so he could feel the softness of those curves and breathe in the lavender in her perfume. Her fingers tugged at his hair in a way that made him want to find some quieter place where they wouldn't be disturbed . . . but then a thought came to him and he broke off the kiss.

'Hang on a minute.'

'Mmm?' Kitt's voice had a dreamy husk to it that left him wondering why the hell he'd stopped kissing her.

'Are you really willing to forgive and forget the misunderstanding this morning, or do you just want to be in on this investigation?'

Kitt pressed the back of her hand to her forehead in the style of a Shakespearean damsel and looked off into the distance. 'Alas, you will never know. Even a seasoned investigator like yourself will never uncover the truth.'

Slowly, Halloran took the length of Kitt's hair in his hand and wound it around his fist until her head tilted back and she was once again looking into his eyes.

'I do have ways of getting the truth out of you, you know.'

'Sounds like fun,' Kitt replied.

FOUR

Halloran had seen the name of the village marked on the occasional road sign during his journey to Esk Valley prison the day before, but after all this time nothing could have quite prepared him for once again driving past the words 'Welcome to Irendale' painted in an all-too-familiar italic script. At the village boundary line, the drystone walling stopped. Instead, the approach to the village green was verged with an array of flowerbeds. Poppies and pansies bobbed their heads in the low summer breeze. Behind them stood a procession of stone cottages with red-tiled roofs, and behind those was a seemingly endless patchwork of moorland fields and untameable stretches of heather.

To the eyes of an outsider touring the quaint villages of the moors, hopping between Hutton-le-Hole, Rosedale Abbey and Grosmont, Irendale would look like just another sleepy settlement cocooned in a quiet valley of the North York Moors National Park. They would imagine no greater drama here than James Herriot-inspired animal emergencies on the surrounding farmland. But such events were hardly the darkest secrets in Irendale history.

Halloran glanced at Kitt. Her eyes were narrowed as though she were examining every doorway, chimney pot and garden wall scrolling past the car window.

'It's not along here,' said Halloran, his voice as gentle as he could make it.

Kitt's shoulders tensed. 'What?'

'The house, where me and Kamala lived. It's on the other side of the village.'

'Give over, I was only looking to see if the village had a bookshop,' said Kitt and then half-smiling, added: 'Oh, all right. I might have been keeping a lookout. Just on the off chance. Silly, really. It's not like I'd have any way of singling it out from any other house here. Still, it's not very fair to use those inspector-strength observation skills on your girlfriend, you know? Will we pass it?'

'No.'

'Do you . . . want to? Go back, I mean. To, well, to see it, I suppose?'

Halloran glanced at Kitt and put a hand on her thigh. 'There's no need, pet. If we end up in the vicinity on some other day I'll let you know, and we'll cross that bridge when we come to it.'

Kitt put her hand on top of his and sighed in what he interpreted as relief. He was glad to be able to set her mind at rest. Just being back in the village was difficult enough all on its own without making a special visit to the house he had once called home.

Pulling into a parking space in the small square at the centre of the village, Halloran turned off the ignition, exited the vehicle and took a look around. The familiar scent of cut grass was the first thing he noticed. Even though it was Monday and everyone was probably at work, rather than mowing lawns, it seemed to Halloran that that fresh earthy smell had always lingered in this place and probably always would. Five years had passed and yet in this quiet, blink-and-you'll-miss-it nook of the moors, little – if anything – had changed. A red telephone box still stood outside the small post office-cum-corner shop. Mobile signal was not spectacular up here so unlike the disused units in the cities it no doubt still had a working phone inside. Across the perfectly mown village green, he spotted the same old garden furniture rusting outside the Wold's End – the village pub where most locals whiled away their evenings, and some of them the afternoons too. Halloran was pleased to see the smattering of local-goods shops were still in business, selling everything from fossils and minerals combed from the north-east coast to handmade pottery.

After he had made this quick assessment of their surroundings and ensured nothing was odd or out of place, Halloran noticed Kitt was also staring across the village green. He followed her gaze and smiled to see her sights set on the small library and archive.

'Not sure that the little library here will have much on the Vale of York University, pet,' said Halloran.

'Worth a look anyway though,' she said. 'If we get time, I mean. You'd be surprised at the little treasures you can find in local libraries.'

Halloran was about to retort when a familiar voice came from somewhere behind them. 'Now then, sir, it's good to see you again.'

Halloran turned and smiled at the sight of his old colleague. At the time he left Irendale for York, DI Damian Bailey was a young DC just learning the ropes of basic detective work at Eskdale station. Until Kerr had struck, this had largely comprised of apprehending sheep rustlers and being vigilant over exactly what kind of crops were being grown in the surrounding fields after the owner of a local caravan site was caught growing marijuana.

In the years Halloran had been away the once bright-eyed fledgling seemed to have grown into a somewhat more seasoned detective. His dark hair was much shorter and thinner than it had been when he'd first joined the force, and in place of his uniform he now wore a dark blue suit and tie which must have been stifling given the warm June weather. One small mercy of being in Irendale in an unofficial capacity was that, for the most part, Halloran could probably get away with walking around in jeans and a T-shirt.

'Good to see you again too, Damian,' Halloran replied. 'A very belated congratulations on your multiple promotions.'

'When the best DI we 'ad left for the bright lights of York, they 'ad no choice but to promote the likes of me.'

Halloran smiled at Bailey. The lad was joking, of course, he hadn't got where he was without a lot of hard work. But there was more to his humour than jolly self-deprecation. He was trying to tactfully skirt the fact that the only other DI working in the area at that time had been locked away on a serial murder charge. Something in Halloran's chest tightened a notch at the unwelcome thought of Jeremy Kerr.

Kitt cleared her throat.

'Oh, er, sorry,' said Halloran. 'This is Kitt Hartley, she's . . . assisting me.'

'So I suppose in a roundabout way that means you're assisting me,' DI Bailey said, reaching to shake Kitt's hand and holding onto it a moment longer than Halloran would have liked him to.

'I suppose it does,' Kitt said with a chuckle. 'Halloran told me about your little Sherlockian arrangement.'

Bailey frowned then and looked at Halloran, confused. Halloran replied with only a gentle shake of the head.

'We help solve the case without taking any of the credit,' said Kitt, reading Bailey's confusion. 'Those were the terms Sherlock Holmes struck with the London police.'

'Kitt's a librarian by trade and has a . . . fondness for

mystery books,' Halloran clarified. 'This probably won't be the last you hear about fictional detectives.'

'Good to 'ave a learned person on the case,' Bailey said with a glint in his eye.

'Flattery of that nature will get you everywhere with me,' said Kitt.

'Praise where it's due. I'm not sure anyone down the nick, myself included, 'as made the time to read a book in the last decade. Well, maybe *The Da Vinci Code* but that's 'ardly highbrow.' A rueful expression crossed Bailey's face. 'Besides, DC Enders spoiled the ending for me before I finished it. I've never really forgiven her.'

Kitt sucked through her teeth. 'There should be some kind of law against *that*. Still, even if it's not highbrow, you can't fault the plot. And at any rate, it's not as though the Sherlock Holmes stories were considered highbrow when they were first released.'

Sensing that this was about to turn into a book club meeting, Halloran interjected. 'Yes, well, that aside, I'm really grateful to you for letting us in on this investigation, Bailey.'

'It's not exactly protocol and you'll have to keep a low profile if you don't want word getting back to your gaffer, but given your experience in a related case, I can't think you'll be anything other than an asset. Besides, looks like I might get some stimulating conversation thrown into the bargain.'

Bailey looked at Kitt with a broad smile and suddenly Halloran found himself wishing he had introduced Kitt as his girlfriend. Just so everyone was clear where they stood. The problem was, at the age of forty-four the word 'girlfriend' sounded a bit secondary school.

Bailey's eyes drifted from Kitt. 'Eyup, looks like your arrival has caused a bit of a stir – not that it takes much round 'ere.'

Halloran turned his head back towards the village green to see a number of locals staring at them, and they weren't even trying to be covert about it. Most were faces he recognized, like Jerome Harrison who owned the Wold's End and stood on the step of the pub smoking his pipe. Reverend Sykes glanced their way as she crossed the square. There were one or two faces that weren't familiar. In particular, a man with long sandy hair and a tanned face, whom Halloran was sure he'd never met, stared over at them with more than average curiosity as he left the post office. Though Halloran could have done without their attentions, the fact that everybody was into everybody else's business here was likely to be an asset when it came to tracking down their murderer. Whoever was responsible for this latest murder, be it Kerr, Goodchild or another person entirely, the odds were that someone here knew something about it.

'Come on, we'd best get inside before the lace curtains start twitching at the windows . . . Follow me,' said Bailey, nodding in the direction of the old mill.

Halloran looked away from his not so discreet audience to where Bailey had indicated. The old mill was a large red-brick building, topped with a defunct chimney. It dominated the west end of the village and had been converted into flats some twenty years ago. With its unparalleled views of the moorland and a small weir running down the hillside beyond, it was mostly occupied by tourists wishing to stay in quaint short-let quarters while they explored the wilds of Yorkshire. There were, however, one or two local residents who lived there long-term, those blessed few who could find jobs either in Irendale itself or in the surrounding towns. From what Halloran had understood from his prior phone call with Bailey, the victim, Amber Downing, had been one of them and late last Friday night, in flat twenty-one, that woman had breathed her last.

FIVE

Bailey unlocked the door to flat twenty-one and as it swung open Halloran couldn't help but notice Kitt's eyes widen. She had seen quite a few things he wished she hadn't had to in the time they'd been together. The sight of a dead woman's personal belongings strewn callously around the space she had once lived in was another one for the list. Though hardly the most gruesome thing she'd ever had to digest, it was undeniably sad to see the many ways in which a killer can strip a victim of their dignity. Perhaps he shouldn't have brought her along, but then, she had insisted that they were in this together and in his experience once Kitt had made her mind up about something it was very difficult to persuade her otherwise.

The trio stepped inside a long, narrow living room and at once Halloran's eyes darted around the layout and entry points, making a swift analysis of his surroundings. Sunlight streamed in through tall windows on the opposing wall but the flat was on the fifth floor, so the odds of anyone entering that way seemed unlikely. The whole room, presumably the whole flat, had been tossed. The coffee table at the centre of the room had been turned over. Papers of every imaginable variety were scattered all over the hardwood floor. Every drawer had been pulled out, every cupboard opened and gutted of its contents. Fragments of ornaments and picture frames were scattered across almost every available surface.

'The other doors just lead to bedrooms and bathrooms?' Halloran said at last.

'Aye,' said Bailey. 'This door is the only entry point as far as we can tell.'

'And there was no forced entry?'

'No,' Bailey confirmed. 'At this stage we're working on the principle that the victim either knew the murderer or trusted them enough to let them in.'

Halloran's gaze landed on a photograph in a cracked frame lying on a nearby shelf. He recognized it as the victim after studying her Facebook profile the night before. It was a graduation photograph taken some years ago. Amber's smile in the picture looked to Halloran like that of a young woman who was ready to take on the world. Her long brown hair fell in thick waves beneath her mortar board and there was an optimistic gleam in her brown eyes. Somebody had cruelly dashed for good whatever hopes were shining in that girl's eyes and in his heart Halloran made a promise that he would do everything in his power to hold that person to account. 'Do we know what the killer was looking for when they trashed the place?'

Bailey shook his head. 'Not yet. We obviously don't have a complete list of Amber's belongings before the murder but there's plenty of jewellery left behind so it doesn't look like they were after that. We've been through all her financials and it doesn't look like there was much to take there either. She was comfortable, don't get me wrong, but there was no secret bank passbook to some hidden fortune. From what we can see, no major purchases of expensive art or property. Her statements are full of the kind of transactions you'd expect to see. Cafés. Supermarkets. Petrol stations. Transport hubs. There was only one weird little blip we're still trying to get to the bottom of.'

'What's that?' asked Halloran.

'The week before she was murdered she made a cash withdrawal almost every day of £250,' said Bailey.

'At cash machines?' said Halloran.

'Aye,' said Bailey. 'She could've got more out in one go if she'd gone in t' bank in person but for some reason she didn't do that.'

'And these withdrawals didn't match her usual behaviour?' asked Kitt. 'It does seem like a lot of money to take out all at once.'

'Yeah, far as we can see, like most people she used card transactions for almost everything, only taking out the odd tenner or twenty here and there.'

'So she needed cash suddenly for some reason, and plenty of it,' said Kitt, tugging on the ends of her long red hair as she thought.

'Maybe to pay someone off?' said Halloran.

'Maybe,' said Bailey. 'Or maybe someone she knew was in trouble.'

'Or maybe she was in trouble herself and was planning to run away, go off the grid?' said Kitt.

'All possibilities,' said Bailey. 'As yet, we don't have a scrap of evidence to support any of these theories. But we've only made a small dent in the data available to us. We're going to keep digging into her phone records and financials. There's maybe some clue further back in her transaction history we haven't got to yet.'

'Who found the body?' asked Halloran.

'We did, the day after the murder took place,' said Bailey. 'She was due in to work a Saturday shift at the local archive. When she didn't clock in and wasn't picking up her phone or answering the door, Pippa Swithenbank, who works on the reception desk at the archive, called and reported it to us. By the time we came round late Saturday afternoon, well, we 'ad an idea before entering what was waiting for us behind the door. The body had clearly been there for some time.'

Kitt frowned and then seemed to catch Bailey's meaning. It was quite rare for an officer to discover a body – often a friend or neighbour would get there first. But Halloran had found one or two during his years on the force and if the body had even been sitting overnight it was a smell you would never forget. He was fairly sure some remnant of it lingered in the air even now.

'Amber worked at the archive, then?' asked Kitt.

'Aye, and you could tell. The number of papers she kept on her finances for someone with a bog standard current account and a couple of shares in the Pickering Pie Company is staggering. We're still wading through it all two days later.'

'Pickering Pie Company?' said Kitt, her face lighting up at the mention of something pastry-related. 'Don't think I've heard of them.'

'Aye, they're a new start-up and have made a bit of a splash. Do a good corned beef and potato that'll set you up till teatime.'

'Did her colleagues have any idea about who might have done this to her?' said Halloran, trying to steer the conversation away from pie. After books, food was one of Kitt's favourite things to talk about and as much as he was happy to indulge her appetites on any ordinary day, there wasn't time for in-depth pie chat just now.

'We interviewed the people who worked closest with Amber,' Bailey explained. 'Pippa, who reported Amber as missing, her colleague Meg Crampton, and the chief curator of the archive and library Sebastian Mountjoy, but they all sang Amber's praises and couldn't think of anyone who might want to hurt her.'

'I remember Mountjoy from when I lived here,' said Halloran. 'Seemed to run a fairly tight ship, to put it politely. I think he'd know if something was out of place with one of his employees.'

'Oh, nothing gets past him, from what I understand,' said Bailey. 'Since Amber doesn't have any obvious enemies, we've started looking at people in her personal life. Her parents live up in Northumberland so I sent DC Enders out there to interview them. They said the same thing as Amber's colleagues: they couldn't imagine anyone wanting to hurt her.'

'Siblings?' said Halloran.

Bailey shook his head. 'Amber is an only child. Her parents aren't keen on her current boyfriend, Liam Long, however. The Downings are not short of a bob or two and gave Enders the impression that they thought she could do a lot better.'

'They think Liam might have had a hand in what happened to Amber?' said Kitt.

'Doesn't really matter if they do,' said Bailey. 'We've already checked into Long. He was away in Amsterdam on a stag do when Amber was murdered.'

'So he's got an alibi,' said Halloran.

'Yeah, he left Thursday night for a long weekend. That's why we found her first. He doesn't live 'ere but he still would have found her before we did if he'd been around.'

'And there are no other suspects?'

'Not yet. Although since you've discovered Kurt Goodchild visited Kerr we will be taking Goodchild in for questioning.

I'm not sure if Kurt would go so far as to kill anyone, or if he's physically capable, but voluntarily spending time with a serial killer who committed similar murders does make him a person worth talking to.'

'I wonder if the cash Amber was drawing out had anything to do with Kerr or Goodchild,' said Kitt. 'If she was involved with something illegal or even just a bit dodgy, that might link her to Kerr somehow. Through someone he knows in the prison or through someone he locked away during his policing days but is now back out.'

'The cash is a chief concern, I agree,' said Bailey. 'But if she was into something shady, she hid it well. As far as we can tell Amber lived a fairly quiet life. She 'ad a few friends around the village and started seeing Liam a few months back. She doesn't seem to have 'ad any issues with anyone and according to her work colleagues she was absolutely fine on Friday afternoon, which is the last time anyone saw her alive.'

'Do you have a time of death?' said Halloran.

'According to the pathologist she was strangled between eight and ten p.m. on Friday.'

'Strangled with what?' Halloran pushed.

'A Brew Hound brand guitar string – the killer used one out of a new box and left the box behind.'

'Ms Downing played guitar?' asked Halloran.

'We can't find any evidence that she did. At least, there's no Fender sittin' in't' corner of her bedroom.'

'So the strings most likely belong to the killer,' said Kitt.

'It seems odd they'd leave that behind when it's obvious the police would then be looking out for anyone who recently purchased that brand. Almost like the killer wants the police to find them.'

'Or, they're just not very bright,' said Bailey.

'Suppose we can never rule that out,' Kitt said.

'If the strings do belong to the killer it's a detail not in keeping with the last set of murders,' said Halloran. 'Kerr always strangled the victim with something that belonged to them.'

Halloran noticed a curious look cross Kitt's face which she was trying hard to correct. He could guess at what she was wondering: what possession had Kamala been strangled with? He could only hope Kitt wouldn't want to talk about that later. It was still a source of deep pain to him that he had provided the weapon Kerr used to end his wife's life: a black silk scarf embroidered with silver stars he had bought for her the preceding Christmas.

Perhaps in an attempt to make out like she had other things on her mind, Kitt's eyes riveted on the mantelpiece or, more specifically, on a small golden trophy lying on its side. She tilted her head to read the inscription. 'First place, North-East Scrabble Championship.'

'Aye, Amber was part of a local Scrabble club that take the game pretty seriously. According to Liam she was very fond of puzzles.'

'An archivist with a love for puzzles,' said Kitt, her face

falling. 'Amber sounds like the kind of person I'd get on with famously. I'm sorry not to have known her when she was still here.'

'Aye,' Bailey said. 'Murder is always tragic but from what Amber's friends and family tell us she was an incredibly intelligent woman with a real playfulness and altruism about her. It's a real loss. Mind you, when she left us she also left a puzzle for us to solve for ourselves.'

'What do you mean?' asked Kitt.

'We found a strange note in an envelope tucked in the back pocket of her jeans.'

'What did the note say?' asked Halloran, wondering why a note written by the victim hadn't been the first thing the officer had mentioned.

'I don't think there's owt to it. At first I thought it was gibberish. It was just one word. I'm not sure how you pronounce it. The note itself is in evidence now. But 'ere, I've written it down in my notebook.'

Halloran and Kitt leaned in to look at the page. To Halloran, it looked as though someone had tried to write a word in English, but it had somehow gone wrong, as though maybe the person writing it had had one too many pints before putting pen to paper. He wasn't even going to attempt pronouncing the bugger.

'*Hwæt!*' Kitt said with a note of triumph in her voice.

'Is that how you say it, then?' said Bailey.

'Well, there is some debate about it, actually,' said Kitt.

'Some pronounce it hwait, hwat or even hwayet, but I would pronounce it hwæt.'

'Right . . . well, apparently, it's Old English. Amber specialized in the Anglo-Saxon era and worked with documents written in Old English all the time. The original note is in her handwriting so we know she wrote it herself.'

'It's not just any Old English word,' Kitt said. 'This is the opening word to *Beowulf*.'

Bailey nodded and frowned simultaneously in a way Halloran recognized as an attempt to mask his ignorance.

'What does it mean?' asked Halloran.

'Taking it in the context of *Beowulf*, in the Seamus Heaney translation it just means "so",' Kitt explained.

'Amber's colleagues don't specialize in Old English but said to the best of their knowledge it meant sort of "well" or "now",' said Bailey.

'Yes, well, the thing about translating Old English into modern, as with any translation, is that there are a number of possibilities. But I imagine the *Beowulf* link has to be significant.'

Halloran half-smiled. 'Of course you do, it's to do with literature.'

'Ooh, give over,' Kitt said, administering a playful nudge to Halloran's arm. 'You're telling me it's a coincidence that a specialist in Anglo-Saxon documents has the first word of the longest epic poem in Old English in her pocket at the time of her death? I don't think so.'

'If anyone was going to die with an Old English word in their pocket, surely an expert in Old English is more likely than anyone else? It could have been just a note she wrote at work,' said Bailey.

'I have to side with Bailey on this. Even though it was found on the victim's body it's not necessarily significant,' said Halloran. 'I mean, it's a bit odd, isn't it? From what both of you say, it's not like it's a deeply meaningful word.'

'But it was meaningful to Amber for some reason,' said Kitt. 'She took the trouble to write it on a piece of paper, put it in an envelope and keep it in her pocket. That's got to mean something, hasn't it?'

'I know what you're saying seems to make sense, but we're not really convinced, to be honest,' said Bailey. 'The envelope the note was kept in was already opened, probably by the killer. If they saw it and left it behind they can't 'ave been that bothered about the police seeing it.'

'But they left the guitar strings behind,' Kitt countered. 'Maybe the note is significant somehow but the killer just didn't realize how significant.'

'Maybe. I mean, yeah, you could be right, I suppose. The note is just one of several weird things about this case,' said Bailey. His eyes, all of a sudden unable to hold Halloran's gaze, fell to the floor.

'The runic symbol carved into the victim's hand,' Halloran said, so that Bailey didn't have to.

'Aye. Do you . . . want to see it?'

Halloran nodded.

'This is what it looked like.' Bailey turned another page in his notebook and showed Halloran and Kitt a small symbol that looked a bit like two arrows pointing away from each other. They were set slightly askew and thus interlocked almost in the fashion of a zigzag.

'It isn't one that Kerr used before, but then, he used different symbols on each victim,' said Halloran.

'Apparently it's called *jera* – I think I'm pronouncing that right,' said Bailey.

'Perfect pronunciation,' said Kitt. 'Though it's spelt with a J it sounds like a Y.'

'Does this feature in *Beowulf* too?' asked Halloran.

'No, the runic alphabet is very different to Old English,' said Kitt. 'I've just read one or two things about runes over the years.'

'When we find a subject you haven't read one or two things about I'm going to die of shock,' Halloran said with a mocking smile, though in truth her boundless knowledge was one of the many things he adored about her.

'Not exactly an incentive for me to ever let you find one,' she returned. 'Better double down on my non-fiction volumes when we get home.'

Bailey, who had been watching this exchange like a tennis rally, cleared his throat. Both Halloran and Kitt returned their attentions to him.

'According to the internet it's a rune associated with

reward,' Bailey explained. 'And if it's anything like last time, the runes will be significant to the killer in some way.'

'Definitely worth looking into it a bit further,' said Halloran. 'I'm trying to keep an open mind but given past experience I hope you'll forgive my suspicions that Kerr has had his part to play in this.'

'I know it looks like it, sir, but you've already highlighted a key difference in the MO – the guitar strings not belonging to the victim – so between that and Kerr being behind bars there's a strong likelihood we're looking at a copycat rather than a repeat of what's gone before.'

'That's true but just because it's a copycat doesn't mean Kerr isn't involved,' Halloran argued. 'If he's manipulated Goodchild or anyone else into doing his dirty work for him then there will be variables.'

'Regardless,' Bailey said, seemingly unwilling to concede the point, 'if we want to get to the truth we've got to look at the case from every possible angle.'

'I call dibs on checking into the *Beowulf* angle,' said Kitt.

Bailey smiled at her. 'We'll probably need to do a bit of homework ourselves now you've brought that to our attention but I can't see any harm in a specialist like you doing some research of your own. You might uncover something we don't know how to.'

'Not that it'd surprise me, but got a copy of *Beowulf* on your person, have you?' Halloran said, raising his eyebrows at Kitt.

'There'll be Wi-Fi at the let,' said Kitt. 'The anonymous *Beowulf* poet has not been heard from in about a thousand years so it's pretty firmly out of copyright. It'll be easy to find online.'

'All right. But I don't want you to get your hopes up too far about this note. The killer was looking for something, he turned the flat upside down looking for whatever it was. Clearly, it wasn't that note. Like Bailey said, if it was significant I doubt he would've left it there.'

'Your point has been acknowledged.' Kitt smirked. 'But murderers slip up all the time, that's how we catch them.'

'"We"?' Halloran said, and even though there was an amused note in his tone Kitt had the decency to look a little bit shamefaced at her brag.

'I like your spirit,' Bailey said with a chuckle.

'Yes, well, I can probably put my familiarity with the people here to some use,' said Halloran. 'I'll ask around the village to see if there're any other potential suspects the initial financial and phone records haven't spat out. Naturally, if I dig anything up that's worth your time I'll let you know straight away.'

'That's fine. If you can point us in the direction of anyone acting out of character in any way we'll appreciate it,' said Bailey, his voice taking on a more formal tone than it had before. 'But, sir, just so you know, when it comes to Kurt Goodchild I think it's best that you let us handle his interrogation.'

Halloran paused for a moment, his jaw tightening. 'I respect the fact that this is your investigation but if there's any chance of me being involved in Goodchild's questioning, I'd appreciate it.'

'I'm not stopping you from going near him in general, sir. I'm sure you're experienced enough to make the right call on how to coax out any information he might have,' said Bailey. 'But as you say, I'm the lead on this investigation so it's important that we have a go first in an official capacity. As agreed, it's fine to have you helping on the sidelines where possible but we have to follow protocol. Besides, we're less – it's less personal for us. We've got to get it on record anyway and if we get a confession we might be able to spare you from a difficult conversation. If we get something concrete out of Goodchild we'll be able to confront Kerr with it then.'

Halloran nodded. He knew it was important for Bailey to follow procedure and thus it made sense for him to talk to Kerr first. Once they'd started work, no DI would want to give an investigation away to another officer anyway. Halloran couldn't help but wonder, however, if Bailey also doubted his ability to question Kurt Goodchild objectively, given the history.

A buzzing in Bailey's pocket interrupted the silence growing between them.

'Sorry,' he said, answering his phone. After the opening pleasantries a frown fell over his face. 'What? When?'

Kitt and Halloran mirrored Bailey's frown as he continued.

'Get DS Lister down there straight away,' said Bailey. 'I'll follow on and be with you asap.'

With that, Bailey hung up the phone. Halloran's throat closed up to the point he could barely speak. Had the worst really happened? Had another body been discovered? Was this nightmare starting all over again?

'What is it?' Halloran managed, trying to take a deep breath at the same time so that he might temper his anxiety.

Bailey shook his head. 'They've found something in Amber's papers down t' nick – a last will and testament.'

Halloran relaxed a little bit though Bailey's face was still a picture of concern.

'Was there something in there that helps with the case?' said Kitt. 'A list of assets that you didn't know about, for example?'

'Or does the will name some chief beneficiary? If someone benefitted from Amber's death that might lead us to a new suspect,' said Halloran.

'I don't know the full details yet but DS Lister is on his way to Amber's solicitor and we'll be looking into it. At present there is one detail that stands out above all the others: the date the will was drawn up,' said Bailey.

'What do you mean?' said Kitt.

'The will was only drawn up two days before Amber was murdered,' said Bailey.

Halloran's eyes widened.

'Oh good grief,' Kitt said. 'Amber knew her life was in danger.'

SIX

Before driving back to the cottage Halloran had rented in Castleton, Kitt had insisted they stop in at the village tea room to see if they had any Lady Grey in stock.

'Ee, Mal 'alloran, is that you?' said a familiar voice as he opened the door of the tea room and took in the rich scent of brewing coffee.

'Moira, lass, how're you doing?' Halloran said addressing the pinny-wearing tea-room owner with a measured smile.

'Fair to middling, fair to middling,' Moira replied, but her beady green eyes had already fixed on Kitt. Until this moment he hadn't given much thought as to how the people he had known in his old life would react to his new life. With the usual Yorkshire-bred lack of subtlety, he imagined.

'Oooh, she's a beauty this one, in't she?' said Moira, squeezing Kitt's hand while Halloran tried not to smile at just how accurate his estimate had been. 'I knew it wouldn't be for ever before some lucky lass snapped 'im up. If I were twenty years younger I might 'ave given you some competition.'

Halloran tried to suppress a cringe. Moira had a crop of soft auburn curls and an alluring edge to her smile that some men might be drawn to if they had a taste for older women but she wasn't known for her discretion. One night with her and the whole village would know about his darkest proclivities.

'Now. I want to hear the full story,' Moira continued, barely pausing for breath. 'Where did you meet? Who asked out who? How long have you been going out? Is it looking serious?'

Kitt smiled a tight smile and looped her arm through Halloran's in a manner that was at once both protective and reassuring. 'Nice to meet you,' she said. 'I'm sure you do have a hundred questions, seeing Mal after all this time. But—'

'Eeee, a lot more than a hundred, love,' said Moira. 'Closer to a thousand.'

'Yes, well. Sorry to cut to the chase but I am gasping for a cuppa and I see you serve speciality teas. Not got any Lady Grey, have you?'

'Mmm,' said Moira. 'We've got over fifty blends but not that one, I'm afraid. Earl Grey's the closest.'

'That'll do in a pinch,' said Kitt. 'I'll have a pot and a scone to go with it. Mal takes his coffee black with an obscene amount of sugar, and you better bring him a scone too. He's a growing lad, you know.'

'Oh! Right-o, love, right-o. Put wood in't hole and take a seat. I'll be reight back with you,' said Moira, bustling off to the kitchen.

Halloran followed Moira's instruction to close the door behind them – an instruction surely given more out of habit than to keep the cold out on a day as hot as today – and then smiled over at Kitt. She was adept at navigating most situations but her handling of the ultra-nosy tea-room owner was nothing short of artful. She had remembered that there is always one thing that trumps Yorkshire curiosity: the desire to do good business and keep customers happy.

'Let's sit in the window, shall we?' said Kitt.

Halloran was about to suggest sitting somewhere else – he didn't much fancy being perched on display for the whole village to see – but then he realized what Kitt must have already clocked. The only other remaining empty tables were very near to the kitchen, which meant they would be sitting in earshot of Moira. The window seats, though exposed to the village green, were as far from Moira as the pair could get.

Turning to the table in the window, which just like all the others was covered with a red-checked tablecloth, Halloran pulled out Kitt's chair before sitting down himself.

'I know this isn't an ideal location but the alternative is—'

'Even less ideal, I understand,' Halloran said. 'Sometimes I worry you've got so good at reading, you can read my mind.'

'I can,' said Kitt. 'It's filthier than your average bodice-ripper.'

A laugh bubbled up in Halloran that he wasn't expecting at all, given the situation. He reached across to Kitt and held her hand. 'How is it you can always make me laugh or smile when a moment before it's the furthest thing from my mind?'

Kitt shrugged and then flashed him an impish smile. 'You've brought out a certain playfulness in me since we met and it only seems fair to repay the favour to the very serious detective inspector.'

Halloran laughed again and squeezed her hand. 'Thank you for doing this, for coming up here with me.'

'Of course,' Kitt said. 'I promise not to rub it in too much when I crack the case before you. *Beowulf* is so obviously the key and I've read that text many times over. You've got no chance of outdoing me.'

'And with your infamous modesty at play, arrogance will at no point trip you up,' Halloran teased.

'Oh yes, that's right. A man can exude confidence in his abilities but a woman should never dare. How arrogant I am to believe in myself. I honestly don't know how I forgot my place. Silly little me,' said Kitt, her blue eyes sparkling.

'All I'm saying is, I'm not sure that *Beowulf* is going to be much help. It's more likely someone in her personal life threatened her enough that she was convinced she might not see next year. Or, like you said back at her flat, she was involved with the criminal element somehow and that ended up being a link to Kerr.'

'I agree with you that those are the most likely scenarios,' said Kitt. 'But if she suspected she was going to die, and she knew who was going to kill her, then that makes the note in her pocket even more significant. It's obviously a clue to who her murderer is.'

'Obviously,' said Halloran. 'It couldn't be the silly superstition of an Anglo-Saxon specialist to keep the first word of *Beowulf* on their person. It couldn't be a note to herself of some personal significance or something she was going to give to a friend because it was a joke between them. It couldn't—'

'All right,' Kitt said, holding up her hand. 'Yes, fine. There are other possibilities. But I'm sticking with my theory that the note will somehow reveal the identity of the killer, thank you very much.'

'Here you go, loves,' Moira said, returning from the kitchen, tray in hand. With deft efficiency, she set out an assortment of cups, saucers and side plates on the table. Halloran hoped that would be the end of it but once she'd arranged everything Moira continued to hover.

'Now then, am I right in thinking you're back in town more on business than pleasure?' she said, looking at Halloran over her spectacles.

Halloran cleared his throat to buy a moment of thinking time. He was supposed to be on stress leave, not solving a murder case outside his jurisdiction, and besides that, Bailey had been clear that he wanted them to stay on the sidelines of the case. Best to keep the number of people who knew their true agenda down to a minimum. 'We're staying in Castleton for a few days, just the two of us. But I have heard about the terrible incident over the weekend, so I'm not surprised you'd assume that.'

'What a coincidence that you should be staying nearby,' Moira said, her tone knowing. 'Well then, of course, you won't be interested in who everyone 'ere thinks done it.'

Halloran shrugged. 'I don't know. Even off-duty, an inspector couldn't be blamed for taking a passing interest in that kind of information. Especially given the nature of the case.'

'Thought so,' said Moira. 'As far as folks round 'ere are concerned, this situation 'as been brewing for quite some time.'

Halloran paused for a moment. Was that Moira's coded way of saying that they somehow knew that Goodchild had been visiting Kerr and forming lord knows what manner of unsavoury relationship with him? 'What do you mean?'

'Don't get me wrong. I don't think any of us thought it would go this far. But, from an outsider's perspective, trouble has been brewing between Amber and Max Dunwell for a few months now, and word is 'e finally snapped.'

'Max Dunwell?' Halloran repeated. 'I don't think I know him. Did he know Amber well?'

'You could say that. Truth be told, Amber could be a bit of a flirt at times. You don't wish stuff like this on folk but it were only a matter of time before it came back to bite 'er.'

Halloran noticed Kitt's hand, which was still resting under his, clench in response to Moira's words. As the librarian in charge of the women's studies section it was perhaps no surprise that Kitt was quick to pick up on victim-blaming. Halloran only wished everyone else practised the same vigilance on the matter.

'Are you saying Amber was having some kind of secret relationship with Dunwell behind Liam's back?' Halloran said. If that was true then even in his absence at the stag do, Liam definitely came back into the frame too.

'That might be a bit of an overstatement,' Moira said, shaking her head. 'From what I've 'eard, he tried it on with 'er while she was with Liam. She told him to sling 'is hook. And apparently he didn't take it well.'

'How do you mean?' asked Kitt.

'Well, you overhear a lot of chatter in my line of work and I heard customers gossiping a couple of times about Max going round to Amber's flat and trying to slime 'is way in whenever 'e knew for sure that Liam was elsewhere. Far as I know she never let him in, but there's been speculation, like, that last Friday night she made an exception.'

Halloran looked at Kitt and she stared back at him. Both resisted saying anything in front of Moira; this was only hearsay, after all, and as yet there was no proof there was any substance to these rumours. Still, it was obvious Halloran and Kitt were thinking the same thing: Liam had been away from Thursday, giving Max Dunwell ample time to wear Amber down into letting him into the flat. The question was: if he did get inside, was Amber Downing alive when he left?

SEVEN

Back at the cottage on the outskirts of Castleton, Halloran blu-tacked a final photograph up to the mantelpiece. In the hearth stood a whiteboard he'd brought along from home. On it he had scribbled Amber's time of death. Usually, the somewhat grubby whiteboard sat in his kitchen and was used only for shopping lists and other little domestic reminders. This week, though, it would serve as a place to record the timeline of the murder and any relevant activities of all known suspects.

If it had been winter he would have lit the fire and probably found other more pleasurable ways to pass the time between now and the meeting he'd arranged with Bailey at eight o'clock. As it was, Kitt was sitting over at a small desk by the bay window that overlooked an endless stretch of rugged moorland, marbled green and purple and bordered by a drystone wall. Having decided she needed a short breather from thinking about the case, her concentration was entirely focused on writing a letter to one of her correspondents – she was the only person in the world he knew who still wrote letters by hand. With just over an hour before the pair were meant to meet Bailey at the Wold's End, however, Halloran thought it best that he at least tried to stay focused. After all, the sooner he resolved the case, the sooner he and Kitt could go home and move on with their lives together.

When Halloran had called Bailey to update him on what Moira had to say for herself on the subject of Amber's murder, Bailey had relayed that Monday nights were karaoke nights at the Wold's End pub and every Monday, without fail, Max Dunwell turned up to belt out his own special rendition of 'I'm Too Sexy For My Shirt' by Right Said Fred. By Halloran's reckoning, he should be behind bars for that alone and it was with regret that he noted this would be stretching the limits of the Public Order Act.

Bailey's team were still looking into the details of Amber's will and so they had decided the easiest plan was to intercept Dunwell at the pub and ask him for his alibi. Moira had certainly made it clear that he had been persistent when it came to Amber and in Halloran's experience, persistence could so easily evolve into obsession.

The desktop printer in the study at the cottage had just enough ink left to print some poor quality images of the key people who might be involved in Amber's death, collected during a hasty online search. Halloran looked along the line of faces. Amber's was the first in a series of four photographs. Even in patchy greyscale, it was difficult for Halloran to look at the smiling profile picture he'd downloaded off Facebook. Amber stared at him with a certain coyness over her thin-framed spectacles. Thirty-two was no age to die. Especially at the hands of a murderer who would go on to mutilate your body. Halloran winced at that thought. He wanted to believe, as the others had suggested, that this was a copycat case. That this murder had nothing to do with the ones he'd put an end to five years ago. But something deep in the pit of his stomach nagged at him. Some empty ache insisted that he had failed to fully put a stop to Kerr's depravity, and that meant Amber's death was on him.

Kitt's phone rang then, jolting Halloran out of his thoughts.

'It's Grace,' she said, looking at the screen. 'I asked her to do some research on that word, *hwæt*, and see if she could unearth anything.'

Halloran's body stiffened. Grace Edwards was Kitt's assistant at the library. She had proven an asset on a couple of cases on which Kitt had assisted but she was, to put it politely, a bit giddy at times. Halloran didn't like the idea of her knowing just how personal the case was for him and hoped Kitt had found a way of being discreet about the finer details.

Kitt swiped the handset and hit speaker phone. Grace's thick West Yorkshire accent echoed out. 'Hello, Kitt, hope I'm not interrupting anything intimate.'

'Yes, thank you, Grace, it's still quite early in the evening and we're not animals,' Kitt said but raised an eyebrow at Halloran. He couldn't help but offer her a little smile. 'And just so you know, you're on speaker, so Halloran can hear everything you're saying as well.'

'Oh.' Grace, who had been giggling at Kitt's response, paused and continued in a much smaller and more sheepish voice. 'Hello, Inspector Halloran. Just wanted to call and let you know that the word you texted me – I'm not even going to try and pronounce it – I think I've found another interpretation of it.'

'Well done. That was quick work,' said Kitt. 'What did you dig up?'

'Apparently, as well as all the other suggestions you mentioned, the word can also mean "listen". I thought out of all the interpretations, that seemed like more of a meaningful word than the others.'

'"Listen",' Kitt repeated. 'Definitely more significant than "so" or "well". Did you uncover anything else?'

'Not in terms of the language, there is some disagreement over how the sentence should be spoken, i.e. whether the opening line should be an exclamation or not, but other than that nothing came up that you hadn't already outlined to me before I started research.'

'Well, it's another thing to consider at any rate,' said Kitt. 'Thanks for this, Grace, I'm not sure what significance the word has yet but you never know, this might come in really handy. Although,' she added, her tone sharpening, 'it does seem like the kind of thing you might have texted me rather taking the trouble to call. I would've thought you'd be too busy for phone calls with me and Michelle out of office this week. Have you run out of journals to catalogue? If so, that's a first in the department's history.'

'It would have been quicker to send a text, it's true,' said Grace.

'But let me guess,' said Kitt. 'Over a phone call you get to enjoy the effect your comment about interrupting something intimate far more than you would via text.'

'Something like that,' Grace said with a nervous little laugh.

'Well, you've got the luck of the devil, there's no phone signal round here but of course you managed to reach me.'

'Is that any way to thank me for my above and beyond brand of assistance?'

'I suppose not,' said Kitt. 'I am grateful, Grace, but I probably shouldn't keep you too long and we've got a meeting with another officer soon. I'll be in touch if there's anything else.' The pair said their goodbyes before Kitt hung up the phone and looked at Halloran.

'Well, I don't know about you but I'm one step closer to solving the case. All I've got to do is figure out if the word "listen" has some bearing on what happened to Amber.'

'Good luck with that.'

'Finished your makeshift murder board, have you?' asked

Kitt, emphasizing the word 'makeshift' as she stood up from the desk and joined him in front of the fireplace.

'For now. It's highly likely there are more potential suspects than the ones I've got up here,' said Halloran.

'It's a starting point. Who's that man?' said Kitt nodding at the second photograph in the row, depicting a man with shoulder-length hair and dark bushy eyebrows.

'That's Kurt Goodchild,' said Halloran. 'Why?'

'I saw him, through the window when we were having a cup of tea earlier. He was walking past the library on his way out of the village square. He looked a bit skittish.'

'Are you sure? I didn't notice him. But skittish is how I'd describe his demeanour.'

'I'm sure. He was one of many people milling about outside and you weren't looking out of the window just then.'

'Would you say he was panicked?'

Kitt shook her head. 'No, he had a bit of a funny, jerky walk, though. And he stood out to me because his hair is longer than most other men. Otherwise I wouldn't have noticed him above anyone else.'

Halloran sighed. He would have liked to get a look at Kurt's conduct for himself.

'I recognize Amber but who are the men in those other two pictures?' Kitt asked. 'None of them are Kerr, are they?'

'No, I couldn't stand to have his face leering at me for the next week.'

'That's understandable,' said Kitt, pulling Halloran's hand

to her lips and giving him a quick peck on the palm. 'I suppose one of them must be Max Dunwell.'

'He's the third one along,' said Halloran, nodding at a man with hair that was a dome of tight dark curls. It had been cut in a similar manner to how some people cut their hedges.

'So who is the other one?'

'Liam Long.'

'You think Liam might have had a hand in Amber's death even though he had an alibi?'

'Initially, when Bailey said he was away, it seemed more or less that he could be ruled out,' said Halloran. 'But if there's anything to this rumour about Max Dunwell, it's a possibility that he is somehow connected to his girlfriend's death. That he killed her out of jealousy or possessive nature. When I printed off his picture, I realized he was one of the gawkers when we arrived at the village green earlier today. He might just have been curious but maybe he was paying us more than our due attention for a reason. Bailey didn't elaborate on what Liam's relationship was like with Amber. He just said he happened to be away when she was murdered and that her parents didn't think much of him.'

'So you want to speak to Liam personally?' said Kitt. 'Will it really do any good to talk to him? Hasn't Bailey already questioned him?'

'Yes. Bailey talked to Liam over the phone on Saturday night. He flew back from Amsterdam on Sunday and they spoke to him in person then. Apparently he behaved as you'd expect him to.'

'But that doesn't satisfy you? You still want to speak to him yourself?'

'I don't think it would hurt to swing by the garage he works at . . . see about that rattling sound in the car.'

'What rattling sound in the car?' Kitt said, and then, catching on, smiled. 'We do have a journey back to York and we don't want that old banger giving up on a hill in the middle of the moorland.'

'Hey, enough with the old banger remarks. Just because I haven't had a mid-life crisis and bought a red Ferrari.'

'Yet,' Kitt said, raising her eyebrows in a manner he recognized as baiting. Seemingly she'd still rather be thinking about other things besides the case. They would likely spend the whole evening talking shop once they met with Bailey, so maybe it wouldn't hurt to indulge themselves now, just a little.

Halloran took a step towards Kitt. Her eyes widened in anticipation and her body arched gently in his direction. He turned her head just a touch and leant forward to murmur into her ear. 'Keep up the cheeky comments and I'll have no choice but to put you over my knee.'

Halloran heard the breath catch in Kitt's throat. He smiled, remembering how much they'd both enjoyed themselves last time they'd played this particular game.

'Mal . . .' The tone in her voice jerked him out of the haze.

It had none of the husky quality it usually did when he made such advances. There was an unmistakable note of distress.

'What is it?' he asked. She pointed at the window, her eyes even wider than they had been before. 'Look.'

Halloran frowned.

All the air left his lungs.

He couldn't quite believe what he was seeing. Walking towards the window, he blinked. But what he'd hoped was a mirage didn't disappear. On the stretch of drystone wall right outside their cottage a large symbol had been drawn in dark red spray paint. It was the same symbol that Bailey had shown them in his notebook just hours before. The symbol that had been carved into Amber's hand.

Kitt clung to his arm. 'This has to be some kind of sick joke or something,' she tried, but she didn't sound as though even she believed it.

Halloran swallowed hard, the red icon completely filling his field of vision. He craned his neck, trying to see if there was anyone outside, but the lines of sight weren't good enough. Quickly, he strode out into the passage and opened the front door. Kitt followed close behind and watched as he looked up and down the road that ran alongside the cottage.

But there was nobody there.

'This isn't a joke,' said Halloran, his instincts working overtime. 'It's a message.'

'A message to say what?'

'The killer knows we're here.'

EIGHT

The Wold's End, like many pubs found on the moorland, boasted dark wooden beams and an open fire around which customers huddled in winter to put the world to rights over a pint and a roast – complete with a Yorkshire pudding, of course. In the summer, however, people were most drawn to the tables nearest the long, leaded windows where warming shafts of bright sunlight bled through to the otherwise murky interior.

Halloran and Kitt managed to secure the last table by the window before ordering drinks and a meal apiece at the bar. The incident back at the cottage had been disturbing and they had done nothing but turn it over and over between them in the last hour. Ultimately, they both decided that food, as well as keeping their strength up over what was proving to be the longest day either of them could remember, would give their minds and bodies a shift of focus. Bailey professed he was too busy preparing to apprehend Dunwell to be hungry, but Halloran suspected otherwise. Halloran might have felt guilty about tucking into a sumptuous meal in front of the lad if he himself hadn't forgone so many good feeds over the years while on duty.

'I'm afraid there aren't any cameras exactly where you're staying,' said Bailey. 'There are some traffic cameras near the surrounding villages, though, and whoever it was would 'ave needed a car to get to you and to make such a quick getaway, so I'll put a PC to work on the footage asap to see if anyone related to the case passed by the Castleton area between six and seven.'

'I'd appreciate it. Half the village watched us roll in earlier on, so our arrival didn't exactly go unnoticed,' said Halloran, before taking a sip of his Coke. 'I know you released the fact that a symbol had been carved into the victim's hand to the press, but did you tell anyone what the symbol was?'

'No,' said Bailey. 'That information was supposed to be for members of the investigative team only. There's only one other person likely to know exactly which symbol it was and that's the killer themselves.'

Halloran nodded. There were a few things he could say in response to this but it was unlikely Bailey would welcome any of them. He wished that he could discount the idea of a corrupt police officer in the ranks but after the betrayal he had suffered at the hands of Chief Superintendent Percival, his former boss, and of course Kerr, he wasn't going to dismiss the possibility so quickly. Perhaps Goodchild wasn't

Kerr's patsy after all. Perhaps it was someone who worked with Kerr or was somehow beholden to him?

'Is it possible someone at Eskdale station let something slip about the symbol?' He made sure he sounded doubtful enough that his question didn't seem accusatory. If he was going to crack this case, he needed to keep Bailey onside.

'I doubt that,' Bailey said with a frown. 'I suppose there's a chance of a bit of pillow talk. Compartmentalizing any information in small villages like this is an almost impossible task.'

Halloran remembered having the same challenge when he was a DI in the area but he'd managed it. He wasn't convinced this potential leak was as innocent as Bailey would like to believe.

'Steak pie and a chicken parmesan?' a waitress said, interrupting their conversation.

'Yes, that's us.' Kitt beamed, as enthusiastic as she always was when a plate of food arrived. 'Parmo here, and he's having the pie,' she said, indicating Halloran. The waitress set the food down alongside some cutlery and then tottered off back to the bar.

'Have you had any luck questioning Goodchild?' Halloran had managed to wait until the food arrived before asking this question but couldn't put it off a moment longer. Especially after what had happened at the cottage. Kitt had seen Goodchild in the village square earlier. Was there a chance he had also seen them? If Bailey hadn't taken him into custody that afternoon as promised he might have been the mysterious vandal.

Bailey shook his head. 'Not yet. We did go round to his house. He lives with his mother but she didn't know where he was. He's left his phone at the house so we can't track him that way.'

'Isn't that a bit suspicious in itself?' said Halloran. 'Maybe he left it at home because he didn't want to be tracked?'

'I don't think so but of course we will be asking him about that when we get hold of him. According to his mum it's touch and go as to whether he ever 'as it on him. He 'asn't been seen around the village since early this afternoon. He can't 'ave gone too far. We'll check at his mum's again later tonight and see if he's come home to sleep.'

Halloran tried a polite smile on for size but felt his fists tighten around his cutlery. Was Bailey being deliberately contrary? Refusing to join the dots on purpose? 'Shouldn't we go a bit further than that if he's essentially missing and a potential suspect in a murder case? It's a bit convenient that he went missing at just around the time the wall near the cottage was vandalized, don't you think?'

'He's not a well man, and I'm afraid he regularly goes walkabout of his own accord. It's not out of the ordinary. Also, he's not really a suspect. I mean, we've got no physical evidence placing him at the crime scene and as far as we know his visits to Kerr weren't suspicious. While he was an officer, Kerr did a lot to look after Goodchild – drove him home when he got himself lost and such. Goodchild 'as never forgotten it. It could just be a coincidence.'

'If Kerr looked after him, that makes it more suspicious,' Halloran snapped. 'He's probably been grooming him all this time. He knew he wouldn't get away with it for ever and wanted someone to continue his work. Had you thought of that?'

Halloran paused, realizing his voice had become louder than he meant it to. He was short of breath, almost panting. When he did breathe in, it was there again: jasmine and peach; the scent of Kamala's perfume. Bailey looked at him with what looked like a mixture of pity and incredulity. The atmosphere between them grew thicker.

'I can't believe they serve parmos this far south of Middlesbrough,' Kitt said after a moment, in an attempt to break the awkward silence. Halloran looked over at her and she offered him an awkward smile as she tucked into her first bite of the pride of Teesside: breaded chicken slathered in a rich cheese sauce and served with chips.

Bailey turned his attentions to Kitt and nodded, probably relieved that she had changed the subject. 'They seem to be becoming a bit of a delicacy round these parts, actually. Lots of pubs along the coast around Saltburn 'ave them on the menu. It was only a matter of time before someone round here followed suit.'

'I—' Halloran began, but faltered.

I'm sorry. That's what he should say. He should say he

was sorry that he couldn't be calmer about the fact that his ex-wife's killer might have killed again. That he couldn't look at the evidence objectively, as was expected and required. That he just wanted to get to whoever did this no matter the cost. But Halloran did not apologize or admit to any of these things. Instead he met Bailey's eye, who gave him the faintest of nods, a tiny sign that the officer understood why Halloran couldn't take the topic of Goodchild lightly. In his relief that he still seemed to have Bailey's confidence despite his outburst, Halloran looked down at his steak pie and said: 'I didn't know how hungry I was until there was food put in front of me.'

'Mm. That's where we differ,' said Kitt. 'I always know how hungry I am.'

Halloran and Bailey chuckled, lightening the mood further.

'Well, I'm not surprised you've worked up an appetite. You've only been 'ere a few hours and you've already dug up a new potential suspect.'

'How reliable the information is, given the source, is another matter,' said Halloran.

'True, but there's no smoke without fire.'

'That phrase reminds me of Moira,' Kitt said. 'You should've heard the way she was going on. Talking about what a flirt Amber was. Respect for the dead clearly isn't her number one priority. As if there's anything wrong with flirtation anyway.'

'There certainly isn't,' Bailey said, smiling at Kitt.

It was then that Halloran saw an opportunity to do what he had wanted to do before: clarify to Bailey, and anyone else for that matter, that Kitt was his. Pointedly putting down his cutlery, he reached his arm around Kitt and gave her a squeeze. 'That kind of attitude is one of the many reasons I snapped this one up for myself.'

Bailey's smile remained. 'Thought you'd made a smart decision the moment I saw you together. As long as you know,' he said, leaning into Kitt in a mock-conspiratorial manner, 'that he's punching above his weight.'

'Oi!' said Halloran. Part in jest, and part to distract himself from how silly he felt for indulging in his own special brand of mild paranoia. Why hadn't he realized that Bailey would have known they were a couple? He was a detective, a younger detective, but a detective all the same. It's not like he couldn't have deduced what was going on, especially given the way he and Kitt flirted. Was this just another way of his recalcitrant mind convincing him that whenever he stumbled across something good in his life it would somehow be taken from him?

Kitt laughed at Bailey's comment before sobering again. 'I don't know if I'm supposed to be asking this, or what you can tell us, but I'm still intrigued about that will you found earlier. Did anything more come out of that?'

Bailey looked into his drink for a moment and then back up at Kitt. 'There's something a bit weird about the will.

Amber left some choice sentimental items to her parents. Other than that, everything else was to go to Liam.'

'Is that so unusual?' said Kitt. 'To name a partner as the beneficiary?'

'It is a bit strange in this case,' said Bailey. 'Remember, Amber and Liam had only been together a few months.'

'Yes, but, if you haven't found anything of substantial value in her effects is it really a motive? I mean, I've seen people kill for some pretty twisted reasons but is it really worth going to all that trouble for a few shares in the Pickering Pie Company?' said Halloran.

'She left the flat to him, which her parents bought for her outright when she left home. Amber had excelled in academia and they didn't want worrying about rent or mortgages to split her focus. So they bought her a flat, and now that flat belongs to Liam. When I told the Downings about the will over the phone I got a right earful. They're livid about it.'

'Hm. Those flats are worth nearly half a mil, now,' said Halloran. 'Do you think Liam knew about the will?'

'I don't know, but we're going to have to question him again, even if he was in Amsterdam at the time she died and you can bet we'll be digging into his phone records and finances too. Oh, eyup,' Bailey said. 'Max Dunwell's already arrived for his preparatory pint.'

Kitt and Halloran started to turn their heads.

'Don't both of you look over at once! He might be soft in

t' head but that might spook even him if he has been up to something he shouldn't.'

Kitt and Halloran corrected their positions and looked back at the table.

'Ladies first,' Halloran said to Kitt.

Smiling, Kitt subtly turned her head in the direction Bailey had been looking. 'I see him. No real chance of him going incognito in that Hawaiian shirt, is there?' she muttered.

'It is difficult to miss,' said Bailey. 'But to be honest he won't be wearing it for long. He always tears it off during the first verse.'

'I might close my eyes for that bit.'

'Sounds like you've been studying his routine rather closely there, Bailey,' Halloran said with a glint in his eye, trying to recover more of the officer's goodwill after his earlier outburst.

'Give over. Like there's anything else to do round here but come to the pub. You end up seeing the same thing week in, week out. Could probably do 'is routine for meself.'

'Thanks for that mental image. All right, Kitt, come on, my turn now,' said Halloran. Kitt averted her eyes and Halloran took pains to look right along the bar before pausing momentarily at the man in the Hawaiian shirt. He was joking with the barmaid and seemed at ease. No suspicious glances over his shoulder and he wasn't exactly keeping his voice down either. Halloran could hear his bawdy cackling even from this distance.

'Right,' Halloran said, pulling his chair back from the table. 'Obviously I'll let you lead, Bailey, but—'

'We're not going over there right now, are we?' said Kitt with a pleading look on her face.

'Why not?'

'Well for one thing, we've only just started on the food.'

'And for another?' Halloran said, a smirk forming on his lips.

Kitt paused before speaking. 'And ... for another he's only on his first pint. Do you think he's going to be more talkative after one pint or after three pints?'

Halloran examined Kitt's face. 'You want to see his karaoke performance, don't you?'

'What? Don't be absurd.'

'You do. You want to see him tear his shirt off.'

'Now, that's unfair. You know the only person I'm interested in seeing with their shirt off is you.'

Bailey cleared his throat. A slight blush rose in Kitt's cheeks but Halloran couldn't care less what Bailey overheard. He wasn't working directly with Eskdale station any more so it wasn't like it could damage him in a professional capacity.

'I just ...' Kitt was still trying to explain herself. 'We've heard so much about his performance – it doesn't sound like the kind of thing you see every day.'

'That's still not the truth. And I thought we were going to be honest and open with each other?' He was teasing but also sensed that her hesitation to be upfront hid some tantalizing fact she didn't want everyone to know about her.

'Oh all right,' Kitt conceded. 'I like watching karaoke. Even bad karaoke. There's something . . . moving, I suppose, about someone standing up in front of everyone and putting themselves out there even if they sound awful. There's a sort of enchanting vulnerability to it. And it's not like he's going anywhere till he's finished his song.'

Halloran shook his head at her. She was the one mystery he knew he'd never solve. 'All right, pet,' he said with a smile. 'I'll let you have your fun, you deserve it.'

'I can't believe you two are going to make me sit through this again,' said Bailey, staring into his lemonade and probably wishing it was something stronger.

Once the karaoke began, the trio sat through a warbling rendition of 'My Heart Will Go On' by a lady who, by the whiteness of her hair, must have been somewhere in her eighties. She was followed by a pair of twenty-something lads who rapped a song Halloran had never heard of. In truth, the word 'rapped' might have been a bit generous. Neither of them seemed to have a natural rhythm and lyrics written by American artists inspired by their life on the rough streets of the Bronx did not come across well in a broad Yorkshire accent.

Kitt was nodding her head and laughing along to these questionable renditions but Bailey looked as relieved as Halloran when Max Dunwell was called up to the microphone.

After they had suffered through his performance, they could find a quiet room and sit down with Max for a word about his whereabouts on the night of the murder.

Not long into said performance, Halloran was certain that if Max Dunwell was a murderer, he had masterfully disguised himself as an utter buffoon. The second Right Said Fred's jaunty beat began, he started cavorting, crotch-first, up and down the corner of the pub where the microphone was hooked up to a crackling amp. His head tilted this way and that in time to the music and much like the 'rappers' who had preceded him he was having difficulty keeping time. Halloran cast a pained expression in Kitt's direction, which only seemed to make her laugh harder. Given how amused she was, however, Halloran didn't mind too much that it was at his expense.

Unfortunately, the view of his vivacious girlfriend temporarily disappeared when Max, as billed, tore off his Hawaiian shirt to mock coos and screams from the women in the crowd. He swung the shirt around by the sleeve and cast it into the audience where it landed squarely on Halloran's head. Halloran swiped the sweaty garment away to see both Kitt and Bailey covering their mouths with their hands, doing all they could not to openly lapse into hysterics. Halloran glared towards the stage as Max strutted, posed and leapt around the small performance area, running his fingers through his dome of dark curls, the only thing about him that wasn't bouncing around due to the amount of gel he used.

Mercifully the song, and Max's gyrating, did eventually come to an end.

'Thanks, fans, see you all at open mic on Friday,' Dunwell said, with a bow.

'Oh, booked for two performances a week, is he?' said Halloran.

'Yeah,' said Bailey. 'He brings his guitar along every Friday and slaughters a selection of Oasis songs. Funny, I've sort of gone off Oasis in recent years.'

'Guitar?' said Halloran.

'Oh no . . .' said Kitt, and then Bailey's eyes widened as he joined them in the realization.

'Eyup, mate, can I get my shirt back?'

Halloran, Bailey and Kitt all turned to see Max Dunwell standing next to their table with an overly-wide grin on his face. Halloran stared up at Dunwell and wondered. Could this man have murdered more than the Oasis back catalogue last Friday night?

NINE

Slowly, Halloran handed Dunwell his shirt.

'Thanks, mate.'

'Sit down with us for a minute, will you, Max?' said Bailey.

Dunwell shrugged and made himself comfortable across the table from Halloran. Then Bailey took a notebook out of his jacket pocket and in an instant Dunwell's face hardened. ''ey, what you need a notebook for? If this is official police business you have to take me down the station for that. Caution me and stuff. I've seen it on TV.'

'Oh, I see,' said Bailey, making a show of closing up his notebook, 'so you're saying that I should question you formally? That we can't just clear a couple of things up quickly here? Got something to 'ide, have you?'

'No . . .' said Dunwell, though he didn't sound sure. 'What do you want clearing up, like?'

Bailey opened his notebook again and sat poised to write. 'Just a small matter. We want to know where you were between eight and ten on Friday night.'

Dunwell swallowed hard and it was obvious from his expression that that was the last question he wanted to be asked. He tried to offset whatever was going on inside his head with a nervous little chuckle. 'You know where I was, same place I am every Friday night. Open mic. Singing "Champagne Supernova" to my adoring fans.'

'And you were here for that whole window?' Halloran said, in no doubt whatsoever that there was more to Dunwell's story than he was letting on.

'Yes,' Dunwell said, his tone defensive.

'And if we asked around, the people 'ere would vouch for the fact you didn't leave the bar before ten?' Bailey pushed.

Dunwell looked down at the table. 'I might 'ave gone for a walk out on t' village green around the nine o'clock mark. Just to get a bit of fresh air, like. It can get reight stuffy 'in 'ere later on.'

'And did that walk take you up to the old mill?' said Bailey. 'To Amber Downing's flat?'

Dunwell sat in silence, looking between Bailey, Kitt and Halloran like a child who was in trouble and didn't know how to get out of it.

'In my limited experience in these matters,' Kitt said, her tone soothing, 'you're always better off telling the truth than you are hiding anything. Best just to tell DI Bailey what you know, whatever it is; it always comes out in the wash.'

Halloran tried not to dwell on those last words. Kitt had asked him to be completely honest with her, and he wanted to be. But did she really want to know every detail? Like the fact this case was getting to him so much that there were moments when he could smell his ex-wife's perfume? He shook his head, trying to shake the thoughts off at the same time. Right now he needed to focus on questioning Max.

'If I tell you the truth, you'll think I did it,' said Dunwell, shaking his head.

'If you tell us the truth we 'ave a better chance of finding who did do it,' said Bailey. 'And now you've let slip that there's something you 'aven't told us anyway. So come on, no point pretending: out with it.'

Dunwell sighed. 'All right. I did go to Amber's flat that night. I knew Liam was away and I wanted to . . . talk to her, like. So I pressed t' buzzer for 'er flat. I pressed it over and over again for about ten minutes but she didn't answer so I came back to the pub. I tried again on me way 'ome, about eleven. She didn't answer. I thought maybe she was out but when I 'eard that her body was found on the Saturday, I realized that maybe she didn't answer because she were already dead.'

Halloran sighed. If Dunwell was telling the truth that narrowed the time of death window to somewhere between eight and nine. But then, the tossing of the flat would have taken some time. Meaning that the killer might have still been there when Dunwell tried to call.

'If you were just going round Amber's flat to talk, why did you try twice? Was it something urgent?' asked Kitt.

'No,' said Dunwell. 'Just fancied talking to 'er, that were all.'

'Hadn't Amber already told you, several times over, that she didn't want to . . . talk?' Halloran asked, with a clench of his jaw. Halloran had seen this kind of story play out too many times. One person gets obsessed with another person and won't leave them alone. Next thing you know, something terrible has happened to the object of their affection.

'Who's been talking about me and Amber?'

'Come on, Max,' said Bailey. 'This is Irendale. You don't think you can keep something like that quiet, do you?'

Dunwell tutted. 'All right, Amber was with Liam but whenever I saw them out and about she didn't look 'appy. 'e was a proper waster. But I knew I could make her 'appy. So I told her. Only she wouldn't listen. 'ad this idea that Liam were going to make something of himself. But I knew she'd see through him eventually, she just . . . needed some persuasion, like.'

Halloran shook his head. 'When a person tells you to back off, the right thing to do is respect their wishes. But you didn't do that. Did you?'

'No.' Under the ferocity of Halloran's stare Dunwell's voice had become small and quiet.

Bailey raised his hand and looked around the pub. 'I'm going to stop you there, Max, I think we'd better go outside.'

'Why?'

'Because, Max, I have to caution you and I don't want to do it with the whole village watching on.'

'What the— Caution me? What for?'

Bailey sighed. 'You've just admitted to motive for Amber's murder. You had opportunity, you went to her flat not once, but twice on the night in question.'

'But I didn't go in!' Dunwell whined.

'I know that's what you say, but there's too much going on here for us to ignore. You didn't just have motive and opportunity, you also had means.'

'Means?'

'You play the guitar. Amber was strangled with a guitar string.'

'Half the bloody village plays the guitar, are you going to take them in too?' Dunwell tried, his voice getting squeakier in its panic.

'Half the village didn't knock on Amber's door last Friday night,' said Halloran.

'Max, I'm trying to do this quietly. Like it or not, we need to bring you in for further questioning. We need to check the guitar strings you've got at home against the guitar string used to strangle Amber. If they're not a match that'll help you but you're going to need a lawyer.'

'A lawyer! But—'

'Don't make a scene, eh?' Bailey said, and Dunwell quieted. With a nod he got up and walked towards the door of the Wold's End. Bailey and Kitt followed closely behind him while Halloran watched Dunwell's every move.

TEN

It was nearing midnight and Halloran had just finished his rounds of the let cottage, checking that all of the doors and windows were locked and secure. Twice. Perhaps they had less to worry about, safety-wise, given the circumstantial evidence now stacked against Max Dunwell. After Dunwell had been properly cautioned and interviewed, Bailey felt he had no choice but to put the suspect under arrest and detain him until the morning when a warrant could be processed to search Dunwell's flat. Bailey feared if he released Dunwell, he might destroy or dump the guitar strings they knew were in his possession and they might be the key to unravelling this whole case.

Though Dunwell was still in custody, when it came to protecting the people he loved Halloran didn't do things by halves. Max claimed he had been at work in a homeware shop in Guisborough that afternoon and if that checked out it meant he couldn't have been the person who painted the rune on the wall outside their cottage. From what Bailey said about Amber's will, Liam Long might be in the frame, and he was still very much roaming free. Thus, whoever did it might still be out there and for all Halloran knew it was more serious than a sick prank; whoever it was might wish Kitt and him genuine harm.

On returning to the bedroom after his checks, Halloran was greeted with the most alluring of sights: Kitt sprawled on the bed wearing nothing but a silk nightgown. The garment exposed a pleasing amount of creamy cleavage and rode up at the hem enough to show off the curve of her thighs. She was oblivious of how tempting a prospect she looked, however, because all of her concentration was focused on a small pile of papers on the bed, and whatever webpage she was looking at on her phone.

'Still hard at work, pet?' said Halloran, closing the door of the bedroom behind him.

She didn't look up from what she was writing. 'Just rereading the opening to *Beowulf* and making a few notes. There's got to be some kind of clue in here somewhere that explains the significance of the word "listen" to Amber. I'm obviously missing something. I just don't know what.'

'You're not still on that, are you? Evidence is mounting against Dunwell, and if not him, Liam. Goodchild is also suspiciously missing – in my book anyway – so, I'm really not convinced *Beowulf* is going to be of much help in sending the true culprit down.'

Kitt stared at Halloran. 'So you think Max Dunwell actually did this?'

'Right now, Max Dunwell is the prime suspect, yes.'

'If it's as simple as all that, why did he go to the effort of carving the rune on Amber's hand?'

'We don't know the whole story yet. Perhaps there's a link between Dunwell and Kerr, or Dunwell, Goodchild and Kerr that we've yet to uncover. Or he might be trying to make it look like a copycat murder to throw the police off his trail.'

'All right, what about the fact that Dunwell allegedly used guitar strings to strangle Amber, carefully leaving the box at the scene, when half the village watches him at the open mic night every week and, given the rumours about him and Amber, it was only a matter of time before someone put two and two together?'

'The man sings "I'm Too Sexy For My Shirt" on a weekly basis, voluntarily. That doesn't show a lot of self-awareness and it's obvious he's not exactly the brightest crayon in the box.'

'But that's exactly my point, see?' said Kitt. 'How can he be both smart enough to make it look like a copycat murder and stupid enough to use a weapon that would implicate him? Contradictory behaviour.'

'Maybe, or maybe even the likes of Max Dunwell are allowed one cunning idea per year.'

'That's not the only thing that doesn't add up,' Kitt said.

'You saw the state of Amber's flat. The whole place had been turned over. If Dunwell's motive for killing her was that he couldn't take no for an answer, why do that? Why turn over her flat?'

'Again, probably for the sake of appearances. He wanted it to look like Amber had been killed for something valuable, to disguise his motive.'

'If he was smart enough to do that, why didn't he take some jewellery or something else of worth to really make it look like a fake burglary?' said Kitt, gathering up her papers into a neat pile and resting them on the bedside table.

Halloran nodded. 'I hear what you're saying. I suppose in some respects I'd just rather it was this straightforward so the nightmare was over. But I've got my doubts too, you know I have. So what do you want to do?'

'Keep looking. Maybe talk to the people Amber worked with for ourselves. They were the last people to see her alive, by the sound of things. Maybe we can press them harder about her behaviour leading up to the murder. There's still the question of that cash she took out the week before she was killed. Bailey questioned them before he found out she had a will made up just days before it happened. Maybe we could question her workmates from a different angle, using this new information somehow?'

'We could do that, if you are absolutely sure you want to keep pursuing this strand of the investigation.'

'Bailey's team will have their hands full trying to gather

physical evidence against Dunwell and Liam who, based on the evidence, are the most likely suspects. But I still can't believe that Amber had that note on her person by accident. It's not a police priority so I think it's something we could look into without interfering too much in the main investigation. Besides, this is a case I'm not letting go of until every last loose end is tied up,' said Kitt.

'And that's different from the other cases you've worked on because . . .?' Halloran tried to tease her but for once she wouldn't be drawn. She went quiet for a moment before speaking again.

'There's a lot riding on this.' Her voice was small, timid even. 'Making sure this is all completely squared away is our best hope for a real future together.'

Halloran took a sharp intake of breath. He could hear the pain behind her words and her pain became his pain. 'I didn't mean to go off like I did before, at Bailey.'

'I know. But I know something's really up. It's not like you to let things get to you that much. You're usually good at staying in control,' she said with a small smile that faded as quickly as it had appeared. 'But this case is really affecting you, even more than you're letting on. Isn't it?'

'Yes,' he said. 'I used to love my work. But after what happened with Kamala, that changed. Sometimes, it's like a weight hanging around my neck. Or something like that . . . I don't know. The truth is, it's a difficult thing to talk about. I haven't really found the words yet.'

'I understand,' said Kitt. 'But when you do find the words?'

'You'll be the first to hear them,' said Halloran. 'In future, you'll be the first to hear anything important I've got to say.'

At these words Kitt's posture seemed to soften a little bit. He noticed her eyes travelling from his, along the length of his arms and down his bare chest. Since the unfortunate misunderstanding of Sunday morning, the pair had kissed but nothing more and now that he was standing here he couldn't help but wonder if what he wanted to do with her would be pushing it. Whether, despite her longing looks, their bond would need time to heal from the damage it had sustained. Slowly, he reached towards her feet; her toenails were painted a rich purple and he ran a thumb over the smooth colour before grazing her skin lightly with his fingertips. He wrapped his hands gently around her ankles and looked back at her, waiting to see how she reacted. She answered by parting her lips as her breath deepened.

Without needing any further invitation, Halloran gave a swift, sharp pull that made her gasp and giggle all at once. He hooked her feet over his shoulders so she could be in no doubt about how far he intended to take this and again paused to gauge her reaction. A small, coy smile formed on her lips.

Revelling in the sudden warmth of her skin against his, he rubbed the softness of his beard against her ankle and began to kiss her pale, perfect skin, being careful to hold her gaze as his lips moved up along her calf, past her knee and along her inner thigh.

'Oh, Mal,' he heard her moan in that soft husky tone she only ever used when she spoke his name. In the space of those two short syllables, Halloran knew there was going to be little sleep for either of them between now and dawn. His hands stretched upwards, reaching out for the softness of her curves as his mouth continued its journey.

ELEVEN

By midday the next day Halloran and Kitt returned to Irendale as she had suggested. Halloran wasn't sure if Kitt genuinely thought Amber's workmates might be able to provide a lead Bailey and his team hadn't thought of, or whether she just missed being in the library environment and wanted an excuse to visit one. Dunwell's flat had been searched earlier that morning after he had been arrested. In his bedside drawer the police had found, amongst an assortment of other oddments, a handful of guitar picks and a box of Brew Hound guitar strings, the same brand that had been coiled around Amber Downing's throat.

Halloran had expected to feel relief when Bailey told him he had secured some concrete evidence against Dunwell. Part of him had even imagined that once Bailey made an arrest he could pack his bags and go home. But he should have known better. Dunwell was the most likely suspect but they still didn't have any forensic evidence linking him to the crime. On top of that, they still didn't know if Dunwell was linked to Goodchild or Kerr. Kerr was wily and over the course of almost five years in prison he would have had a lot of time to plan something intricate if he was still taking instruction from that voice in his head. Bailey had made it clear he expected Halloran to stay on the fringes of the investigation, so for now all he could do was look at the case from all possible angles and hope the truth surfaced.

The pair pushed through the double doors into the library and archive to find a woman sitting behind a reception desk, tapping away at her computer. The spectacles perched primly at the end of her nose and the long, drawn shape of her face might have fooled some into thinking she was older than her years. However, Halloran could see from the smoothness of her skin that she was probably only in her mid-twenties. The name on her badge was Pippa. Bailey had said she was the one who had reported Amber as missing.

Halloran hadn't been sure how cooperative people at the library would be when it came to talking about Amber so just in case he'd brought his ID along.

'Excuse me,' he said, holding up his badge. 'I'm with North Yorkshire Police and wondered if you could help me. I'm following up on the death of Amber Downing.'

At this, Pippa's bottom lip quivered and without a word she started wailing. Loudly. Unashamedly. She grabbed a tissue from a box on her desk and blew her nose.

'Oh Amber, poor Amber,' she whined as she buried her face in her hands.

'There, there now,' Kitt soothed, patting Pippa's hand before rummaging in her satchel. 'Here, have a Glacier Fruit.'

Halloran frowned at Kitt. Although he knew, like most people of the north, she believed food was some kind of miraculous all-healer, he wasn't convinced this woman mourning the loss of a co-worker could be placated in the same way one might placate a child.

To his surprise, the girl reached over the counter and, between sniffs, took a sweet from the bag.

'Oh, go on, take two,' said Kitt.

The girl did as she was instructed with a faint smile and seemed to calm a little at Kitt's kindness. Maybe the badge had been too hard a line after all.

'I'm sorry,' Pippa said, unwrapping one of the sweets. 'I'm still right upset over Amber.'

'Of course you are,' Halloran said. 'You were probably very close to her.'

'Not really,' said the girl. 'I only really knew 'er to say 'ello to but you don't expect someone you work with to . . . to go out like that.'

'No . . . nobody would,' said Halloran.

'How can I help you?' Pippa sniffed, her mouth still half full of Glacier Fruit.

'We'd like to speak to someone who worked closely with Amber, if we can,' said Kitt.

Pippa nodded. 'She worked in the archive offices with Meg Crampton,' she said, pointing to a door off to the right. 'Her office is through there. Down the corridor.'

'Thanks,' Kitt said. 'We'll find our way, and so sorry to have upset you.'

The girl tried to smile again and dried her eyes with a tissue.

Halloran took one last hard look at Pippa to decide if there was anything odd about her. Her posture had become very rigid after her outburst. She sat very still and quiet as though she didn't dare move whilst Halloran was watching her. Realizing he would probably learn no more about Pippa if his mere presence paralysed her, Halloran marched towards the door she had indicated and Kitt followed on just behind him. They found themselves in a corridor with doors all along it, none of which were marked.

'Probably storage space for the documents they keep here,' said Kitt. 'Keep walking.'

Halloran did as Kitt suggested and strode down the narrow corridor where the only sound was their footsteps on hard lino.

'By the way,' said Kitt. 'Evie and Banks are driving up later today, they want to go for tea at the Lion Inn at Blakey.'

'You didn't tell them we would, did you?'

'Yes, why? Is that a problem? We have to eat some time . . . or at least, I do and I don't want to eat at the Wold's End every night.'

'It's not the food, pet, it's the company. By inviting Banks we're putting her in a position where she might have to lie for us. Or Banks might tell Ricci that she's going to see me and let slip where I am. Ricci's not daft. She won't be anymore convinced by the idea that we're having a quiet week away in Castleton than Moira was. If she gets proof I'm taking the law into my own hands while I'm supposed to be on stress leave, she'll call me back to York and the odds are she'll have my badge for it.'

'Mal,' Kitt put a hand on his arm in an attempt to calm him, 'a little trust? I made it clear that our location shouldn't be disclosed to anyone else.'

'Oh,' said Halloran, running a hand through Kitt's long red hair. 'I'm sorry, pet. I should've known better. I'm not feeling quite myself. Being back in the village is doing some strange things to me.'

'You're forgiven,' Kitt said, just as the pair at last stumbled through an open door into an office space that was inhabited.

Halloran took a moment to survey the environment before interrupting the woman who was leafing through a file at a desk. A bookcase filled with heavy-looking volumes, many of which seemed to be about Anglo-Saxon history, ran along the back wall. There were two work stations, one of which Halloran presumed had belonged to Amber. His suspicions were confirmed when he noticed a series of framed degree certificates on the wall with Amber Downing's name printed on them. There was a bachelors, a masters and a PhD hanging there, still waiting to be taken down.

'Meg?' Halloran said to the woman. She turned, swishing her long black hair in the process. She had a thick fringe that covered the tops of her eyebrows and made her look more severe than Halloran had been expecting.

'Yes,' she said. 'That's me, can I help you?'

'I hope so,' said Halloran, deciding that after Pippa's outburst he would be a bit gentler this time round. 'I'm Detective Inspector Malcolm Halloran and this is my associate Kitt Hartley. We were hoping to ask you one or two follow-up questions . . . about Amber.'

'Please, come in,' said Meg, indicating one office chair and pulling up another.

Halloran took a seat, and Kitt followed his lead.

'We are sorry to bother you when you're trying to work,' said Kitt.

Meg shook her head. 'Come back as many times as you need to. Whoever did this to Amber, I want him caught. Although, I thought I heard that an arrest had been made this morning?'

'With cases like these, we have to ensure we've exhausted every possible line of enquiry, regardless of whether we've taken someone into custody,' said Halloran.

'You mean, you're not sure you've got the right person?' said Meg, her eyes widening. 'The killer might still be out there?'

'Probably not,' said Halloran. 'We're just in the process of eliminating any other suspects from our inquiry.'

'Who?'

'What?'

'Who are the other suspects?' said Meg. 'If I'm working alongside the people of this village surely I've got a right to know if one of them might be a murderer?'

'That's not really the way this works, I'm afraid,' said Halloran. 'Let's just say we're continuing our investigation to ensure some of the more vulnerable members of the community haven't been manipulated into playing any part in Amber's death. I'm afraid that's all I can tell you.'

'Oh . . . all right,' said Meg. 'I'm sorry but I'm still a bit on edge after what happened.'

'There's no need to apologize for that,' said Kitt. 'Anyone would be.'

'I know that Irendale has a bit of a dark history but it's never bothered me before. Everyone always seemed so friendly, I've always felt safe here. I suppose some part of me thought lightning couldn't strike twice. But I was wrong about that.' Meg's eyes filled with tears but she seemed to fight them back. 'Anyway, what can I help you with?'

'We know it must be painful for you to talk about Amber but, if you can bring yourself to, we would like some more information about how she behaved when you last saw her, and on the days prior,' said Halloran. 'You told DI Bailey the last time you saw Amber was before she left work on the Friday.'

'Aye, like I told DI Bailey there was nothing out of the ordinary that day – or at least not that I can remember. We did the usual chat work colleagues do when they're about to leave on a Friday: asking each other what plans they have for the weekend.'

'What did she say?' said Halloran.

Meg shrugged. 'Said she was going to have a quiet Friday night in with the TV. She made a joke about how much more glamorous my evening was going to be because I was off to the bright lights of Scarborough for the night. I don't go far myself much, to be honest, but I do like to catch something at the Stephen Joseph now and again.'

'Sounds lovely,' said Kitt. 'What did you see?'

'*Salad Days*. It was the best production of it I've ever seen. I stayed at the coast overnight so I could have a glass of wine or two at the theatre, and travelled back here for work early the next morning.'

'Do you usually work on Saturdays?' asked Halloran.

'No, but we have been lately because we've been trying to put in a bid for a grant that'll give us the funding we need to build a small museum on the side of the library. Amber specialized in Anglo-Saxon conflicts for her PhD, and over her time working here has acquired some dazzling artefacts on the subject that should be on public display, but we haven't got space. This bid was our chance to do something really special for locals and visitors to the area so me and Amber agreed to work a few Saturdays to get it finished.'

'But last Saturday Amber didn't come to work when she said she would,' Kitt said.

Meg sighed. 'When she was ten minutes late I didn't think much of it. But then an hour passed. I rang her, and obviously she didn't pick up. I tried a few more times and even went to her flat. When she didn't respond to the buzzer I got Pippa to call round the next-of-kin contact numbers we had for her but she wasn't at her parents' house either. Amber lived for her work. It really wasn't like her to just not show up. I've seen her come in with all manner of flu and viruses so I knew something had happened but I thought it would be some kind of accident, like she'd had a bad fall or maybe even a freak heart attack and wound up in hospital. I never expected . . .' Meg trailed off.

'We know this must be a distressing time for you,' said Halloran. 'But I wonder if you could think back to not just Amber's last day here, but her last week?'

'Week?' Meg repeated. 'It might not look like it from the outside but a lot can happen here in the space of a week. Anything in particular you want information on?'

'Was there a change in Amber's behaviour, for example? Did she seem anxious? Or on edge?' asked Halloran.

Meg looked between Halloran and Kitt for a moment, opened her mouth to say something but then closed it again as if unsure.

'Meg?' Kitt pressed. 'We really will struggle to find justice for Amber unless we have all the information.'

'Is there something we don't know about Amber that we should know?' asked Halloran, thinking about the money she withdrew and wondering if Meg might know why Amber needed fast cash.

'I don't know,' said Meg, scratching the side of her nose and thinking. 'There was something I didn't mention when I spoke to DI Bailey. I thought about it but it just seemed so silly and irrelevant – I didn't want to waste police time.'

'No detail, no matter how small, is irrelevant in a case like this one,' said Halloran.

'Well, all right, if you say so. The thing is, Amber's behaviour did change that week. She was a bit down, a bit on edge. But it was over the most stupid thing; honestly, some of the petty squabbles that go on in this village astound me.'

'What was it about?' Kitt asked, her nose crinkling.

'Scrabble,' said Meg.

'Scrabble,' Kitt repeated, before frowning and looking at Halloran.

He suppressed a sigh. For all he had just said about no detail being too small, he wasn't sure a Scrabble game was going to get them any closer to unveiling the true murderer than a copy of Seamus Heaney's translation of *Beowulf* would.

'Amber was a bit of a fiend for puzzles,' said Meg. 'Scrabble was one of her favourite games. She was a Scrabble champion and was even part of a local club.'

'I saw her trophy for it,' said Kitt, with a faint smile. 'But why would this in any way upset her? Did she lose a big match or something?'

'Sort of the opposite,' Meg explained. 'It were a couple of weeks ago now, she found out that she had been awarded a seat at the World Scrabble Championship.'

'Surely for someone like Amber that's the kind of news to lift you up, not make you anxious and distressed?' said Halloran.

'Aye, that's how it should have been,' said Meg. 'But she was awarded the seat over another member of her group, Sylvia Wise. Sylvia – from what I understand – has been playing the game longer than Meg but didn't have the same success rate at matches. This resulted in a massive argument. Apparently Sylvia went mad.'

'You're . . . suggesting that Sylvia might have killed Amber because she was jealous of the fact she was going to the World Scrabble Championship?' said Halloran. He'd seen people kill for all sorts of reasons but even he was having trouble squaring this one away.

'Not exactly,' said Meg. 'I'm sure Sylvia was frustrated at being overlooked for that kind of prestigious event, but if she had any hand in what happened to Amber – and mind you I have absolutely no evidence that she had – then I'd say it was more likely to be linked to the prize money – fifty thousand pounds in cash.'

'That's a lot of money for playing Scrabble,' said Kitt.

'The Wises need it more than most,' said Meg. 'They're farmers and have had some poor luck lately. Lost a lot of cattle to some disease or other. The whole village knows they're up to their eyeballs in debt. To Sylvia, that prize money would have meant saving her farm.'

'Did Amber talk about the argument she had with Sylvia? Describe what happened?' asked Halloran.

'She did. I can't remember everything she said about it now but I do remember that it got very nasty. Amber comes from a rich family and Sylvia was hurling all kinds of abuse at her, saying she was a rich bitch who didn't understand the struggles of real folk. She was so angry, and from the sound of things so desperate that the fight got physical. Sylvia pushed Amber against a wall and told her that she should have been going to the championship, not Amber.'

'Do you know exactly where and when this happened?' asked Halloran. 'Or if there were any witnesses?'

Meg shook her head. 'The only detail I'm sure of is that the argument happened on the Tuesday evening before she died. Amber didn't go into any detail about who else was there. She was more focused on the hateful things Sylvia had said to her, and the fact she'd pushed her around.'

'And you say that Amber acted strangely between then and the last time you saw her?' said Halloran.

Meg nodded. 'Amber wasn't right for the rest of the week. Quiet. Down. Seemed to be mulling over something in the back of her mind . . . I told her not to take it to heart. It's not like she could help what family she was born into, or was responsible for the amount of debt the Wises are in. But no matter what I said she never really properly bucked up. Look, it really might be nothing.'

'It was an altercation severe enough that it affected the victim's behaviour,' said Halloran. 'That's not nothing, even if the altercation was over something trivial. Although arguably fifty thousand pounds is not trivial, especially to a person who is in debt and desperate. Is there anything else you can think of that Amber did that week that seemed odd?'

'Now that I think about it, there was one other thing. She took off on the Wednesday afternoon. I mean, she went for her lunch break but was gone way longer than the usual hour. When she came back, she said that she hadn't been feeling well and had been to the corner shop to pick up some painkillers.'

'Sounds reasonable enough,' said Halloran.

'I thought so too, except when I went into the shop after work, I told Mrs Hargreaves who runs the place that Amber seemed to be feeling better after the tablets she'd sold her. But Mrs Hargreaves didn't know what I was talking about and said she hadn't had Amber in that afternoon.'

'Couldn't Mrs Hargreaves have been on a break or something when Amber came in?' said Kitt.

Meg shook her head. 'Mrs Hargreaves doesn't leave the shop floor between the hours of nine and six. Don't ask me how she does it. It's a village mystery. She must have a bladder like top-of-the-range Tupperware.'

Halloran tried not to smile at that rather graphic analogy and glanced at Kitt to see that she was also finding it hard to keep her composure.

'So, you think Amber lied about her whereabouts?' Halloran asked, keen to move the conversation forward.

'At the time I didn't think much of it. I thought maybe it was just that time of the month or something and she hadn't been feeling well and didn't want to talk about it with a workmate. But since I spoke to DI Bailey, the thought has nagged at me. I don't know why she would, or what she could have been doing, but yes, I think she might have been lying about her whereabouts . . . Oh God.'

'What's wrong?' asked Kitt.

'No, nothing, it's just in isolation, I didn't think much of these two things but maybe they were signs that something was wrong, and I missed them.' Meg's eyes glazed with tears and she looked down to her lap.

'The only person responsible for what happened to Amber is the person who killed her,' said Halloran, wishing he could heed his own wisdom. 'You can't blame yourself.'

Meg nodded but her face didn't brighten.

Before Halloran could ask anything else, an officious voice sounded out from the doorway and all three of them spun round in surprise. 'Can I ask, DI Halloran, exactly what your business is here?'

TWELVE

When Halloran turned towards the door, he saw a man he recognized as Sebastian Mountjoy. Mountjoy was dressed in a shirt that looked as though it had been designed by Jackson Pollock. He still wore the ridiculous toupee that was a slightly dirtier blonde than the rest of his hair. A pocket watch poked out of his blue corduroy waistcoat and he was wearing a bow tie in the same colour. Overall, he gave the impression of a man who had escaped from a different time. When Halloran had left for York he was chief curator at the library and archive and it looked as though he was very much still in post. He and Halloran had only properly crossed paths once when some kids had spray-painted an obscene word across the wall of the archive. As Halloran remembered, that obscene word was a fairly fitting description of Mountjoy himself.

'Mr Mountjoy,' Halloran said, rising from his chair and extending his hand. Mountjoy curled his lip at Halloran's gesture but reluctantly offered the loosest of shakes.

'It's Sir Sebastian these days, DI Halloran.'

'Congratulations,' Halloran said through his teeth.

'I hear you've been upsetting my staff.'

'Not intentionally, sir, I assure you,' Halloran said.

'Intentionally or not, you've had Pippa in near-hysterics from what she's been telling me.'

'We simply explained our business to her,' Halloran said.

'Which is?'

'We're following up on some leads for DI Bailey in relation to Amber Downing's death.'

'Well, I took the liberty of calling Eskdale station and they had no idea that you were even here.'

'What?' Meg said, looking understandably betrayed. 'You mean you're not working with DI Bailey?'

'I'm sorry you spoke to someone who is uninformed, Sir Sebastian, but DI Bailey is aware we're assisting on this case.' Halloran looked between Meg and Mountjoy, trying to keep them onside.

'Didn't you leave this constabulary for York some years ago?' Mountjoy eyed Halloran. It seemed he wouldn't be put off with the standard line. Though Mountjoy was indisputably being an officious arse, Halloran had to tread lightly. He wasn't supposed to be working this case and the last thing he needed was Mountjoy filing some kind of complaint about him harassing his staff. 'Do police officers from York usually get involved with matters so far from home?'

'If we have some expertise to offer, then yes, sometimes,'

said Halloran. 'But our intention was not to cause any disturbance or distress, I assure you.'

Mountjoy's eyes roamed from Halloran and fixed on Meg. She seemed to visibly shrink in her seat under the force of his glare. 'What have you told them about Amber?'

'N-not much at all,' Meg stammered. 'Just a few bits and pieces about her behaviour in the week before the murder.'

'Nothing that would bring this institution or Amber into disrepute, I assume? We don't need people telling the police tall tales.'

'No, nothing like that,' Meg said, her voice still meek.

'We have no desire to damage your reputation or Amber's,' Halloran said, feeling his body stiffen. 'We just want to get to the truth about her death and ensure justice is served.'

'From what I hear, an arrest has already been made,' said Mountjoy.

'We still have to follow every line of enquiry,' said Halloran.

'Well, in future, I suggest you follow that line of enquiry down at the station, Inspector, rather than traipsing into my place of work with your girlfriend and distracting my staff from the important work they should be focused on.'

'Fair enough,' Halloran said, his words clipped.

Determined to remain dignified in the face of Mountjoy's snideness, Halloran thanked Meg for her time and, as quickly as he could without looking like they were trying to make a break for it, he guided Kitt towards the office door.

'If I'd known that receptionist was going to dob us in I wouldn't have been offering up my Glacier Fruits so freely,' said Kitt once the pair had walked back out of the archive's main entrance. 'Does *Sir* Sebastian Mountjoy always behave like that?'

'I haven't spent a lot of time with him, but in my limited experience, yes.'

'How anyone gets through life like that, and rises to the ranks of a knighthood no less, I'll never know,' Kitt bristled. 'He seemed very defensive, didn't you think?'

'Yes, but he is a man who cares more about appearances than anything else, so it's no surprise, really. He won't want anything untoward coming out about a staff member that might reflect badly on the archive.'

'You don't think it could be more than that? Meg seemed like she was afraid of him.'

'She did,' said Halloran.

'And why would he naturally assume you were asking about things that would bring Amber or their organization into disrepute?'

'I'm not sure,' said Halloran. 'But you're right that it is a bit of a leap and it makes you wonder what he's hiding.'

'Maybe his part in Amber's death?'

'Maybe. But what would Mountjoy's motive be for killing Amber?'

'Maybe he's some kind of real-life Moriarty?'

'You think he is protecting all the criminals of England in

exchange for a commission of their profits?' Halloran said, in a lightly mocking manner.

'Well, maybe he doesn't have exactly the same set-up as Moriarty. But maybe he's up to something criminal. Amber found out about it and threatened to expose him.'

'And your evidence for this is . . .?'

'His employees seem to be afraid of him, for a start. And let's not forget he's what our mam would refer to as a "bad 'un".'

'Any hard evidence?'

'Other than his major attitude problem, no. That is . . . yet to be discovered,' said Kitt. 'But I wonder if that note on Amber's body comes into play here? It was written in Old English, after all. Maybe Amber was trying to point us in the direction of the archive, or more specifically Mountjoy.'

'I'm not sure—' Halloran began, but Kitt had already whipped her phone out of her pocket.

'I'll text Grace and ask her to look into Sir Sebastian Mountjoy while she's online. If there's any digital dirt to be dug up, Grace is the one who'll be able to find it.'

'Well, while she's chasing down that hot lead,' Halloran said, making sure his tone was dry enough to prompt a sharp look from Kitt, 'perhaps we should focus on the information Meg gave us.'

'Yes. All right. That makes sense. I think we already know what she was doing on Wednesday afternoon, don't we?'

'At a guess, making her last will and testament,' Halloran said with a nod.

'She had the argument with Sylvia Wise on the Tuesday and made her will on the Wednesday,' said Kitt. 'Could it be a coincidence?'

'It could be,' said Halloran, 'but there's really only one way of putting our minds to rest once and for all.'

THIRTEEN

The plan was simple: alert Bailey to the fact that Sylvia Wise was also a person of interest worth following up then drive out to the Wise farm and ascertain whether or not Sylvia had an alibi for last Friday night. Something about Dunwell's manner in the pub, perhaps the way in which he so readily offered up incriminating information about himself, meant that Halloran couldn't rule out that he was being set up. Or at the very least wasn't the brains of the operation. If Sylvia Wise had wanted Amber dead so she could take her place at the Scrabble Championship, maybe she had found a way of making sure Dunwell took the fall for her crime. Whilst he was on the phone to Bailey, he could also find out whether Goodchild had returned from his walk in the wilderness, and on their way back into town they could go and see Liam Long about that 'ungodly rattle' in the back of the car. With a bit of luck, he might even let something slip about his new inheritance.

Halloran and Kitt were walking around the village green back to the car, going through the key points they needed to relay to Bailey, when they passed the tea-room window. One moment Kitt seemed perfectly normal, calmly putting into order the information Meg had given them. A second later, however, she stopped in her tracks and stood poker straight, rooted to the spot.

'What is it?' Halloran asked her.

She didn't answer. Instead she frowned, took five paces backwards and glared into the tea room at whoever was sitting in the window seat they had occupied themselves the day before.

Halloran walked back himself and stared through the glass. There, sitting with a cup of tea in hand, was a familiar face: Ruby Barnett, a woman in her late eighties who frequented Kitt's library back in York. Ruby was convinced she had psychic abilities and had rung the station on several occasions with 'hot tips' about missing people. As far as he knew, not one of those hot tips had ever resulted in a case being closed.

'What is she doing here?' Halloran asked.

'Don't look at me. I didn't invite her,' said Kitt.

At this point, Ruby glanced out of the window and saw Kitt. She waved in what could only be described as a knowing manner and beckoned her inside.

'I'll have to go in,' said Kitt.

'If you do, you'll have to be discreet, Moira will be listening to every word you say, make no mistake.'

Kitt sighed. 'There's no chance of having a discreet conversation with Ruby. It's just not possible.' She looked back at the window and waved to Ruby that she should join them outside instead. Halloran wasn't convinced that would be any better. Passers-by in this village had a habit of hearing more than they should. By now their investigation was probably common knowledge, but Halloran liked to kid himself there might be one or two people who hadn't yet cottoned on.

Ruby obliged Kitt and came out of the tea room looking smarter than Halloran ever remembered her looking before. She had dyed her hair a deep purple – still diverting but more palatable than the Tango orange she usually favoured – and was dressed in a long floral summer dress. After the few occasions on which Halloran had engaged with this woman, he wouldn't have guessed she owned a garment that looked as conventional as this one.

''Ello, love,' said Ruby, leaning on her walking stick for support. 'Won't you come inside and have a cuppa tea with me? I've travelled up from York just to see you.'

'How did you know we were here?' Kitt asked.

'I saw it in the tea leaves,' said Ruby.

'Grace told you, didn't she?' said Kitt.

'She might 'ave been giving out a certain energy that directed my thoughts here,' said Ruby.

Kitt sighed, though Halloran could see a sparkle in her eyes that suggested she was at least somewhat amused by the fact that this particular library regular had stalked her all the way up to the moorland.

'I read in t' paper about the terrible thing that happened 'ere, but took particular notice when I learnt that poor lass had a rune carved into her hand. I'm an expert in the runes, you know, and once I sensed you were up here, I put two and two together and thought it was best I find you as quick as possible to offer my insight.'

'I don't think—' Halloran began, but then he saw the look on Kitt's face. Her eyebrows were raised beseechingly.

'You . . . want to hear what Ruby has to say about this?' said Halloran in some disbelief. Kitt had always been dismissive of Ruby's 'psychic' insights.

'I'm not saying it's going to prophesize anything,' said Kitt, crossing her arms. ('Shows what you know,' Ruby huffed.) 'But given recent events at the cottage, knowing more about the symbol might come in handy, you never know. At any rate, it can't hurt.'

'I want my head read for even entertaining this, but all right,' said Halloran pulling a notebook from his pocket. 'The rune on the victim's hand was this one.'

Ruby looked at the page. '*Jera*. Hmmm.'

'Initial research seems to point to it having something to do with the idea of reward,' said Kitt.

The old woman placed both hands on her walking stick and began to stare off into the distance. Halloran turned to see what it was on the village green that had caught

Ruby's attentions but there was nothing there. The green was empty, except for the war memorial, honouring the soldiers of World War One.

'Aye, it can be loosely interpreted that way, but it might be something more specific than that. Yes, it can mean something very pointed,' Ruby said, her eyes still wide and far away.

'How do you mean?' Halloran asked, slightly more interested after Kitt's reminder about what the vandal had done to the wall opposite the cottage. When Kerr had carved those runes into the victim's hands, he did it as a mark of respect to Woden, the Norse god. If the killer – or the vandal – had been under Kerr's instruction, the rune may well be of consequence.

'This rune is very much associated with the harvest,' Ruby explained further. 'A time for collecting a reward – as you say – for the toil of the farming year.'

'Reaping what you sow? Literally?' said Kitt.

'Aye,' said Ruby, 'which of course can be a wonderful thing, but it depends what you've sown and who is doing the reaping.'

'So . . . you think the rune the killer used was some kind of warning?' said Kitt.

At these words Ruby seemed to break from her trance and she looked between Kitt and Halloran before speaking.

'Well, I don't know much about the minds of murderers, like, but it's likely there's a lot of darkness trapped in there.

Sometimes people do use "you reap what you sow" as a sort of threat.'

'So the killer might have been sending some kind of message,' said Kitt. 'That Amber somehow deserved to die? That she was reaping what she'd sown?'

'That's what it seems like to me,' said Ruby. 'The murderer might think themselves justified in taking Amber's life for some reason.'

'Murderers usually do,' said Halloran.

'If you need to know more, I did bring me tarot pack along, just in case. I can set us out a spread easy enough, if you want to take a more in-depth look at the situation,' said Ruby.

'I don't think there's any need to go to that kind of trouble, Ruby,' Kitt said quickly. 'The information about the runes is probably all we need for now.'

'I agree,' said Halloran, not wishing to seem ungrateful for Ruby's kindness but also having no intention of having his tarot cards read. 'We must be getting on, but it was very good of you to come out and see us.'

'Well, truth be told I didn't just come to see you. Started seeing a chap up at Port Mulgrave. Met him online and he turned out to be pretty sane.'

'Oh, that's . . . nice, Ruby,' Kitt said, in a manner that made it clear she had never before contemplated the woman's dating situation. Or perhaps she was wondering whether the chap at Port Mulgrave would describe Ruby in the same terms as she had him.

'I hope you have a nice afternoon together,' said Halloran.

'You too,' said Ruby. 'Though I suspect you will.'

The woman gave a devilish smile then, as though she knew something Halloran and Kitt didn't. Not in the business of encouraging Ruby's 'psychic' readings any more than was absolutely necessary, the pair made an unspoken agreement to ignore the smile and continue back towards the car.

No sooner had they got into the Fiat than Kitt again became very still and very straight. She seemed to have slipped into a sort of trance, quite similar to the way Ruby had just a few moments ago.

'Mal,' she said, wide-eyed.

'What?'

'It was an instruction.'

'What was?'

'Listen.'

'I am.'

'No . . . the note. *Hwæt*! Amber knew she was going to die. You heard what Meg said about Amber, and what Liam said to Bailey, she was very much into puzzles. She left the note in her pocket as a clue, but it wasn't just a clue. It was an instruction. To listen.'

'Listen to what?'

'I . . . well, I don't know. Maybe some kind of recording on her computer?'

'Bailey's team will have gone through every file on her

computer, I think something like that would have come up by now.'

'But maybe they don't know what they're looking for. Maybe it's another clue but it's lost on them.'

'I can ask Bailey if they've come across a recording that is anything like the clue she left, but I'm fairly sure he would have told us about it. Like I said to you at the beginning, pet, if it was important the killer would have probably removed it.'

'Maybe the answer is back at her flat. Maybe we missed something. Can't we ask Bailey to let us back into that flat again? Just for a minute. Just to see?'

'I don't know, Kitt.'

'Please, please trust me on this. I've got a feeling.'

'A feeling? We're in Ruby's company for less than ten minutes and you're getting feelings.'

'And you've never followed a lead based on nothing but a hunch?'

Halloran looked at Kitt and could see by the seriousness of her expression that this meant a lot to her.

'OK, I'll ask. But I can't guarantee Bailey will let us in a second time.'

'Give over,' said Kitt. 'I'm sure you'll find some way to charm him.'

With a small smile on his face, Halloran pulled his phone out of his pocket and began to dial.

FOURTEEN

'Thanks for agreeing to this,' said Halloran. He was going to add that he didn't think it was really going to lead anywhere but knew Kitt wouldn't appreciate his sentiments. She was well aware of what he thought so there was no point restating it.

'No problem,' said Bailey. 'But before we go in, there's a couple of things you should know.'

'What's happened?' Halloran said.

'We think we know why Amber took that money out of the bank.'

'Why?' asked Kitt.

'We are still going through all the files on her computer, you understand. There's a lot of them and only a few of us so it took some time for this to come to light. But we've found files saved to a locked folder that suggest Amber bought something from somebody on the dark web.'

'What?' asked Halloran.

'A gun.'

'A gun . . .' Kitt repeated. 'I suppose that shouldn't be too much of a shock if she thought her life was in danger. Maybe she was trying to protect herself. But why didn't she go to the police rather than buy a gun from a criminal?'

'I don't know,' said Bailey.

'Maybe she didn't have evidence her life was in danger,' Halloran said. 'There was no forced entry so she was killed by someone she trusted. People like that don't need to send death threats through the post or via email. Maybe it was all verbal.'

'If it was, it would have been difficult for us to mount a case over whoever was harassing her,' said Bailey with a frown on his face.

'There's something else that doesn't add up,' said Kitt. 'You go to the lengths of making a will and buying a gun on the dark web, and then you let the person who has driven you to these lengths into your flat?'

'That's true,' said Halloran. 'It doesn't make any sense at all. I'm a bit surprised that an archivist even knows how to access the dark web to that degree, to be honest.'

'That's because in your head libraries and archives are still using rubber stamps and filing cabinets,' Kitt said with a bit of an edge to her voice. 'There have been huge leaps forward in digital archiving over the last decade. Archivists and librarians alike have moved with the times.'

'All right, I stand corrected on that one,' Halloran said. 'The big question is: where is the gun now?'

'We don't know that, either,' said Bailey. 'It wasn't in the flat. If she let the killer in despite all her reservations, she might've kept it to hand during their visit. My best theory is that either the pair struggled and the killer wrestled the gun off Amber, or the killer struck before Amber had a chance to even pull the gun out and the killer found it on her afterwards.'

'Either scenario suggests that the gun is now in the hands of the killer,' Halloran said, running a hand through his hair.

'All officers in the region 'ave been alerted,' said Bailey. 'They've all been warned to practise caution when stopping suspicious vehicles or individuals. Right now that's the best we can do. There's no tracking down the seller from the information we've got at the moment.'

Halloran nodded, and then looked over at Kitt. With a gun in play he would have to be extra-vigilant about her whereabouts at all times. As far as he knew she had no experience of being held at gunpoint and he didn't want that experience to start here.

'There's more on Liam too. We 'ad him down to the station for a quick interview and asked him about the will.'

'And?' said Kitt.

'He claims he didn't know about it. On one level, his story is plausible given Amber only made the will up a couple of days before. She might not have had a chance to tell him and maybe didn't confide everything in him about what was going on.'

'Equally, he might have been the one she was frightened of,' said Kitt. 'Perhaps there was some kind of abuse going on.'

'There were no marks on Amber's body except the ones on her hand, made by the killer,' said Bailey.

'It might not have been physical abuse,' said Kitt. 'It could have been emotional, verbal, hence why she didn't have any evidence of it.'

'Amber dunt seem the type to 'ave that happen,' said Bailey. 'Too smart not to see through that kind of manipulation, surely?'

'I'm afraid there is no such thing as a type when it comes to that,' said Kitt. 'For all we know Liam forced her into writing that will.'

'We didn't notice any signs that he might be like that when we interviewed him, but I do take your point. Folk like that can be right charming if they're hiding their true nature. But his alibi for the night of Amber's murder is rock solid, so if he was behind her death, he got someone else to do it.'

'Maybe Dunwell?'

'Maybe. But we've still not got any forensic evidence to tie him to the murder scene. I'll apply to hold him longer than the standard twenty-four hours given the severity of the case but if we don't find something in the next couple of days, I'll have to let him go.'

'Any suggestion that Kerr and Dunwell are connected?' Halloran asked.

'No. We have checked CCTV from Esk Valley prison. They don't have the biometric system in place to ID visitors yet and we wanted to be sure Dunwell wasn't visiting with a forged visitor order and identification. But it's definitely Goodchild who has been visiting Kerr. We have managed to get hold of Goodchild, though, and question him about his visits with Kerr.'

'What did he have to say for himself?' said Halloran.

'He has an alibi for the night of the murder. He was at home that night with 'is mother and her friend Bernice. They both confirm he was at home all night, either in his room or in the living room with them.'

'Did you question him about the visits with Kerr?' Halloran pushed. An alibi from your mum and her best friend was easy to arrange.

'He said they talked a lot about his mother, which I think matches what Kerr told you,' said Bailey.

'What about yesterday afternoon when the wall was vandalized outside the cottage? Where was he then?' asked Kitt.

'We don't know exactly,' Bailey admitted. 'He walked to a friend's house in Grosmont, which is of course the opposite direction to your cottage from Irendale. He stayed over last night and then walked back the next day. We've called his friend and they've confirmed he was staying with them. I can't say that he didn't somehow get a lift over in the Castleton direction at some point over the last twenty-four hours but from the evidence we have it's unlikely. We've swept the wall for DNA and prints. There were lots of partials with it being a wall on a main road but none of them matched Goodchild's.'

Halloran sighed. 'These alibis seem wishy-washy to me.'

'Look, we checked the traffic cameras on the roads near the cottage at around the time the vandalism happened. There was no sign of Goodchild walking along them or of any other vehicles registered to anyone associated with the case.'

'Who else could it be, if it's not Goodchild?'

'Liam might have sweet-talked his way through the interview but we are still looking into his finances and mobile records to see if anything suggests his involvement,' said Bailey. 'We're not discounting Goodchild either. We're going to be keeping an eye on him for any unusual behaviour. He's been told not to go off wandering in case we want to talk to him again, but right now we don't have anything concrete on him. He talks about Kerr as a friend who looked after him but he denied that they've ever talked about killing anybody, or even hurting anybody.'

Halloran nodded. 'I appreciate you keeping an eye on him. I understand we need evidence, of course, and right now we haven't got any.'

'Well,' said Kitt. 'The answer to unravelling this case could be sitting inside this flat, waiting for us to uncover it.'

Halloran and Bailey exchanged a dubious look but Bailey began unlocking the door anyway and the trio were soon once again faced with the upturned living room.

Kitt stepped into the centre of the room and looked around the now-familiar crime scene.

'What are we looking for, exactly?' said Bailey.

'I don't know,' said Kitt. 'Something that only fresh eyes can reveal. Something we missed the first time.'

Halloran tried to look at the room as if seeing it for the first time. Looking for any object that might link to the runes or the note found in Amber's pocket. A cushion sitting on the sofa caught his eye. It was patterned with scrawling handwriting. Halloran put on some plastic gloves and picked up the cushion. He squinted at the handwriting to see if it resembled the Old English word found on Amber's person but it was clear that the words were written in the alphabet he was familiar with. He put the cushion down and looked around the room again.

'What about that book on the shelf there?' said Kitt. Halloran resisted the urge to smile at the fact that Kitt's eyes had gravitated towards the bookshelf. Though noticing what was sitting on the bookshelf was what enabled him to put Kerr away the last time a murder like this happened in Irendale. Maybe history would repeat itself?

'*The Truth About Anglo Saxons*.' Kitt read the title. 'Maybe there's something hidden inside?'

Halloran walked over and took the book down off the shelf. Upturning the volume and holding onto the covers, he gave it a vigorous shake. Nothing fell out from between the pages.

Kitt's posture slumped.

'I'm not sure this is the best use of our time,' Bailey said, unable to hide a note of exasperation.

'I'm sorry, I didn't mean to be a nuisance,' said Kitt. 'I just can't shake the feeling that Amber was trying to tell us something with that note I . . .' Kitt trailed off and her eyes widened.

'What?' said Halloran.

'Can you hear that?'

'I don't hear anything,' said Halloran after a moment.

'Sssshhhhh, listen,' said Kitt, concentrating harder. A few moments passed. The trio stood in silence. Not a word. Not a move.

Following Kitt's lead, Halloran closed his eyes and tried to listen. There wasn't a sound . . . except. Except for a very faint ticking noise.

'I think I hear it,' said Halloran, with a frown.

'It's coming from over here,' said Kitt, stepping over to a small pile of Amber's belongings that had been knocked to the floor.

'Hang about,' said Bailey, pulling some plastic gloves out

of his pocket. He pushed aside some papers and an ornament of a lighthouse to find a small clock that had probably once been sitting on the mantelpiece.

'There, that clock,' said Kitt, with a note of triumph in her voice. 'It's the only noise in this room.'

'But what does a clock tell us?' said Halloran.

Kitt put her hands on her hips. 'Haven't you ever been involved in a treasure hunt, or, you know, anything fun?'

'Not had a lot of time for that over the years between investigations, I have to admit,' Halloran said, trying not to show his amusement over just how seriously Kitt was taking this 'fun' element of the case.

'The answers aren't just there on display. They're hidden. Does that clock open at the back or anything?'

'No,' Bailey said, looking at it. But then he turned it upside down. 'Oh, there is a catch underneath, though, hang on.' A few moments later he cracked a smile as he opened the intricate latch on a small door in the bottom of the clock.

Peering inside, he reached two gloved fingers into the mechanism and pulled out a piece of paper, rolled into a tiny scroll, tied with what looked like a short length of cotton thread.

'See,' said Kitt, 'I told you.'

'We don't know what it says yet, pet,' said Halloran, knowing he'd never hear the end of it if the name of the killer was written on this piece of paper.

Slowly, Bailey unravelled the tiny scroll and looked hard at it.

'What does it say?' Kitt asked.

'I . . . er . . . I don't know.'

'What?' Kitt said, disappointment sounding out in her voice.

Bailey turned the paper so she could take a look for herself.

'*Brimes faroðe*,' she said.

'What the bloody hell does that mean?' said Halloran.

'I know this,' said Kitt. 'It's a line from the first part of *Beowulf*, just like the first note.'

'So you can translate it?' Bailey said, a hopeful shine in his eyes.

'Yes, just give me a minute,' said Kitt. She tapped a few times on her phone. 'Ah, yes, here it is. It translates as . . . "the sea surf".'

'So, not the name of the killer then?' Halloran said, trying not to make it sound too much like an 'I told you so'.

'No,' Kitt said with a defensive note in her voice. 'But look, this isn't here by accident. Amber is trying to lead us to someone . . . or maybe to something.'

'This just gets creepier,' said Bailey. 'The will suggests she feared for her life, that I can 'andle. People know when they're in deep water and that. But 'ow could she leave a clue for us in this room without advanced warning that this is the very place she would die?'

'You're right,' said Halloran. 'Unless they plan their own murder – which seems unlikely to say the least – nobody can know which room they're going to die in. What if this isn't a clue from Amber? What if it's a ruse by her killer to distract us from solving the real murder?'

'Sylvia Wise is probably as fond of puzzles as Amber was by the sound of things,' said Bailey.

'I like my story better,' said Kitt. 'But I can't deny it's a possibility. Especially if Sylvia is the real killer and has just set Dunwell up . . . but maybe the clue itself will give us a sense of whether Amber is more likely to have hidden it than her killer.'

'But what does "the sea surf" even mean? What are we supposed to do with that?' asked Halloran.

'Well, we're not far from the sea surf here. At a guess, it means either the answer to the puzzle, or the next clue, is hidden somewhere along the coast.'

'Oh, well, that narrows it down,' said Halloran.

'It would be somewhere close,' said Kitt.

'But the clues are in Amber's handwriting,' said Kitt.

'Doesn't mean she wrote them as clues,' said Halloran. 'Maybe, given her job, she had cause to copy out the opening to *Beowulf* and the killer saw an opportunity ot lead us down the country path.'

'What makes you say that?' asked Halloran.

'Except for Wednesday afternoon's short disappearance, Amber's movements in the week before she was killed are accounted for. Did any transactions pop up in coastal towns at all when you were looking at her financials?' said Kitt.

'Hmmm,' said Bailey. 'Yes, there was one transaction at a pub in Staithes on Wednesday evening. We called the pub and ask about her movements there. The staff said she just came, sat and 'ad a drink and a bar snack and then left. They said she wasn't acting strangely or anything.'

'Staithes,' said Kitt, tapping her phone a few times again. 'According to Google, that's the nearest beach to Irendale.'

'That sounds about right,' said Halloran. 'But are we really going to search the whole of Staithes when this could be a wild goose chase?'

'The whole of Staithes comprises of a small street down to a tiny bay and an equally minute residential area. But anyway, we're not really searching the whole of Staithes,' said Kitt. 'The message is specific.'

'The sea surf,' said Halloran.

'It will be somewhere in the cove. You can walk it from end to end in less than ten minutes. I can't think that searching it is going to take longer than a couple of hours at the most. We just need to get there at low tide in good light to have a look. Grab your sunhat, Mal, we're going beachcombing.'

FIFTEEN

After the discovery of Amber's new note, Kitt and Halloran's plans for the rest of the day had to change. Bailey, who was not particularly keen to sell a treasure hunt slash distracting scheme cooked up by a murderer to his superintendent, took the note back to the station as evidence and agreed to question Sylvia Wise about the argument she'd allegedly had with the deceased. Meanwhile, Kitt and Halloran were to follow up on the idea that there was another piece of the puzzle hidden somewhere in the small seaside bay at Staithes. Consequently, Evie and Charley had agreed to meet Halloran and Kitt there instead of up at Blakey Ridge.

Looking over the small fishing port bathed in afternoon sunlight, Halloran had to admit that there were worse places a murder investigation could lead you. The village itself was sheltered between two distinctive coastal cliffs: Cowbar Nab and Penny Nab. Having walked down from the moor top and along the cobbles of the village's only street, which was lined with souvenir shops, ice-cream vendors and the odd pub, they were now greeted with the delightful curve of the bay. Even though it was not quite summer holiday season, several families, friendship groups and the odd lone visitor with the latest bestseller in hand were making the most of the June sunshine. The unmistakable lines of Penny Nab loomed ahead. Every time he looked at them Halloran thought of the flither girls he had learnt about in school. For generations they had scaled the treacherous rocks and waded around the cliff base in search of limpets their fishermen husbands could use as bait. Their relentless hunt wore in the coastal paths the tourists walked now between here and Filey.

After they had walked the length of the shoreline a couple of times and had nothing to show for it, Halloran and Banks moved their search to the small sea wall that bordered the beach and restarted their treasure hunt there.

'I'm still not clear exactly what we are we looking for,' Charley said in her strong, Glaswegian accent.

'To be honest, neither am I,' Halloran said.

'Aye, it's a strange one all right. Never heard of a victim deliberately leaving clues behind before – or a killer for that matter. But Kitt seems to be doing pretty well with all this, considering the context,' she said, looking over to the rocks where Evie and Kitt were searching. Evie had taken the whole treasure hunt aspect rather seriously. She was wearing vintage safari shorts, heavy duty walking boots and a pair of binoculars that Halloran wasn't convinced were going to be of use in this kind of quest. She and Kitt were systematically lifting small stones in their search along a rocky outcrop at the end of the bay.

'She's putting a brave face on it but I think she's taken the whole thing to heart almost as much as I have. She believes solving this case is the best chance of us having a future together.'

'She's probably right,' said Banks.

Halloran raised an eyebrow at his partner.

'I don't mean to overstep, sir. But I know myself what old demons can do to a person if you don't find some way of laying them to rest.'

'Oh, how's that, Banks?' said Halloran. His sergeant had never been one to share much about her history. She carried something she had never talked about, this much he knew from the many times she had deftly changed the subject on him, but despite his own disclosures she had never confided in him.

'That would be telling,' she said, with a small, bitter smile. 'But trust me, it's a good thing to put the past behind you.'

'And you think solving this case will somehow help me do that?'

'I don't know. But you've come back here of your own free will.'

'I suppose I did, though now that I'm here I admit it

doesn't really feel that way. More like I'm being held hostage until I uncover the truth.'

'Maybe in a way you are being held hostage, by yourself. Maybe you came back here because you needed to face something before you could move on properly.'

'Aye, maybe,' said Halloran with a shrug.

'Well, I guess that's the end of that TED talk,' Banks said, patting Halloran on the back.

Halloran chuckled. 'I want to move on. I really do. Until all this, I thought I had. But I see now that it was just surface. Deep down it's a different story.'

'Well,' Banks said with a smile. 'If anyone can help you change the ending to your story, I think it'd be a librarian.'

Halloran smiled. 'I live in hope.'

'By jingo!' Evie's exclamation was loud enough to echo around the bay and get the attention of Banks and Halloran. Both of them gave vague smiles. Though they were used to the way the vintage-loving Evie used words that hadn't been spoken by anyone since their grandmothers' time, this little tic never failed to amuse.

'Mal!' Kitt called. Evie whispered something to her which in turn caused Kitt to give her a playful shove. 'Come, quick!'

Halloran and Banks exchanged a quick look of curiosity and then marched across the sands to the rocky outcrop by which Evie and Kitt were standing.

'Found something, pet?' Halloran asked as he approached.

'I'd say so!' Evie replied before Kitt had a chance.

'Here,' Kitt said, pointing at a small nook in the rocks. Pulling an evidence bag and some plastic gloves from his trouser pocket, Halloran put on the gloves and reached into the tight space. What he retrieved surprised him: a small trinket box covered with sea shells. The kind of item they sold in all the tourist shops in seaside villages just like this one.

Slowly, Halloran opened the box and inside he found another piece of paper, rolled into a tiny scroll, just like the last one. A low sea breeze almost whipped it away but he caught it just in time.

'Careful, sir, don't want to be losing that,' said Banks.

'Yes, thank you, Banks, after fifteen years on the force I think I'm capable of holding onto a piece of evidence,' said Halloran.

Banks raised her hands in mock submission.

Placing the box in an evidence bag, Halloran then began to unroll the paper and sighed. 'I can't read this any better than Bailey could the last one.'

'Here, let me have a go,' said Kitt, craning her neck to look. '*Weorðmynd*. Huh. I must admit, I had hoped there would just be a name we recognized written on there. Or a clear letter explaining who wanted to kill Amber and why. Looks like it's probably another word from *Beowulf*. Let me check.' She brought her phone out of her pocket and started tapping away.

'Have you got signal down here?' said Evie, instinctively

checking her own phone and holding it up in the air to try and catch some signal herself.

'Don't be daft,' said Kitt. 'I downloaded a pdf of *Beowulf* to my phone days ago.'

'Oh, well, of course you did,' Evie said, looking over to Halloran and Banks with a cheeky smile.

'Ah, here it is,' said Kitt. '*Weorðmynd*. Translates as "an honour of war".'

'Like a medal or something?' said Evie.

'Maybe . . .' said Kitt.

'What about a war memorial?' said Banks.

'The war memorial in Irendale!' Kitt and Halloran said at once. They both looked briefly triumphant but then Kitt's face fell.

'Oh . . . does this mean we're going to have to go back to Irendale before we get any tea?'

SIXTEEN

'Are you trying to make me dizzy?' said Kitt, as Halloran made what must have been at least his twentieth lap of the car since they had got back to Irendale. They had beaten Evie and Banks back to the village green and hadn't wanted to wait in the suffocating heat of the car. The only problem was, Halloran hadn't been able to stand still and spent the entire time pacing.

'Sorry.'

Kitt held out her hands and pulled him into a hug. 'Come here, you daft thing.'

He wrapped his arms around her and breathed out a short sigh of relief. The odd pensioner might be staring from behind their lace curtains and tutting in distaste but a few prying eyes wasn't enough of a concern to tear himself away from his one source of comfort in what had turned out to be a much more involved case than he had expected.

He had convinced himself the first clue Amber left behind

couldn't have been anything worth pursuing. But now they had a second and for all he knew the third would be the one to solve this case . . . assuming this wasn't an elaborate ruse by the killer. If he'd had his way, their search of the war memorial would have already begun to answer that question once and for all but Evie had made them promise to wait, suspecting correctly that her vintage car wouldn't fare as well on the steep banks of the moorland as his Fiat had. Hanging on to what little patience he had left, he tried with all his might to focus on the lavender in Kitt's perfume. It was a calming scent but he wouldn't feel completely at ease until Irendale was a dot in the rear-view mirror.

Halloran was so engrossed in Kitt and his thoughts that he didn't notice the woman approach him from behind. She moved quickly and without a sound and the second Halloran was in reach she jabbed him hard in the back with her umbrella.

'Oof.' Halloran whipped round to see who was mounting the assault on him. He turned to see a grey-haired woman wearing a pair of green wellies that were covered to the shins in mud and worse.

'Words you can make out of the letters in "allegedly",' she said, with no introduction or explanation. 'Legally, eagled, gelled, yelled, gladly, alley, delay and that's just a few of them. How do I know this? Because I am the best Scrabble player this side of the Pennines and I don't need to kill my competitors to rise to the top.'

'Mrs Wise—' Halloran said, putting together the pieces of the puzzle. But the woman was uninterested in hearing from Halloran right now.

'*Allegedly*, you told DI Bailey that I might have cause to kill Amber Downing.'

'We were told you had an argument with her,' said Halloran, straightening his posture so he looked a bit taller to his assailant.

'We may have exchanged some unpleasantries, but that's just part of knocking around a village. Everyone gets under everyone's feet.'

'Well, be that as it may, the police have to look into it when someone gets under a murder victim's feet a few days before she is killed.'

'For your information, I were up at the farm with the vet trying to save one of our cows when Amber died. We didn't manage it. We lost the cow. So thank you for making a bad week worse.'

'That was never my intention, Mrs Wise, I'm sorry that—'

Again, the woman cut him off. 'You want to think twice before you go around accusing people. It's not like I'm not the only one who 'ad an argument with Amber the week before she died.'

'What do you mean by that?' said Halloran.

'Oh, now you want information. Well I told it all to DI Bailey because he's actually a police officer around here.

From what me 'usband tells me you upped and left a good five years ago.'

Halloran stared at the woman. He wanted to know who Amber had had an argument with but it was easier to just get the information out of Bailey than it was to try and coax it out of Sylvia Wise.

'I did leave, Mrs Wise,' said Halloran. 'And you needn't worry, I won't be here for much longer.'

With nothing but a dissatisfied huff, Sylvia Wise continued walking up the village green to wherever she had been on her way to before they'd crossed paths.

'Clearly the long arm of the law doesn't faze Sylvia Wise,' Kitt said, watching after the woman and shaking her head. 'Are you OK? You're looking a bit pale.'

'I'm all right,' Halloran said. 'This is all just much more of a jumble than I was expecting it to be.'

'We'll unravel it, I promise,' said Kitt. 'I've just heard word from Grace. She's looked into Sebastian Mountjoy and hasn't been able to find a single smirch on his good name. And if Grace hasn't come up with anything he really must be squeaky clean.'

'We didn't have any hard evidence on him anyway,' said Halloran.

'I'm still not dismissing him from my suspect list,' said Kitt. 'If you ask me he's a bit too virtuous.'

'I'm not sure that's really cause for suspicion,' Halloran said, with a small smile.

'It is from where I'm standing,' said Kitt.

A few moments later Evie's old Morris Minor pulled up to the village green. Halloran rooted around in his pockets, checking for gloves and evidence bags – unnecessarily, and for the umpteenth time since they arrived.

The pair stayed seated in their vehicle for what seemed like an eternity. At last they climbed out of the car and without a word Halloran started off in the direction of the war memorial at the other end of the green, leaving the others to catch him up.

Like many of its kind the monument consisted of a tall stone obelisk erected to commemorate those lost in the First World War. The names of fallen soldiers had been carved into the stone and a wreath of plastic poppies lay at its base.

'Now that I look at it again, I'm not convinced there's anywhere to hide anything on this memorial,' Halloran said as they approached.

'Looks can be deceiving,' said Kitt, quickening her step. 'It's not supposed to be obvious, remember. Otherwise the killer would have sussed it out. Amber has been careful to make sure the clues take some finding.'

'In all the old adventure movies, there's usually one stone that's a bit loose. You pull it out and hey presto! There's your treasure,' said Evie, who out of everyone had been the most excitable about the 'treasure hunt'.

'We've got to be a bit careful, you lot, this is a war memorial,' said Banks. 'We can't just take it apart piece by piece.

If some neighbourhood watch member sees what we're doing, knowing our luck they'll report us for damage to public property.'

'We can't start digging up the flowerbeds either,' said Halloran, indicating the landscaped arrangements nearby. 'I don't think you appreciate just how seriously flowerbeds are taken in a place like Irendale.'

'We'll be careful,' said Kitt. 'The aim isn't destruction of property, it's finding justice for Amber.'

With this agreement in place, the group separated, each focusing on a part of the memorial that might hide some clue. Banks gently lifted the wreath of poppies, and examined it front and back to no avail. She moved onto the notes tied to small bunches of flowers to see if Amber had written one of them. Halloran put on some gloves and ran his fingers through the soil in one of the flowerbeds, being very careful not to damage the flowers and feeling for anything hard and solid, like the box they had found the last note in. When nothing presented itself, he patted all of the earth back into place and then moved onto the next flowerbed.

Meanwhile, Kitt and Evie were circling the base of the memorial, pressing and pulling on the base stones. When none of them budged even a little bit, Kitt sighed, put her hands on her hips and started reading the engravings instead.

'Maybe Amber didn't leave something physical to be found this time,' said Kitt. 'Maybe the answer is in these engravings.'

'Well, none of the notes on the flowers are in Old English or say anything that seems out of place,' said Banks. 'There really isn't anywhere else to look except the engravings.'

'None of the engravings are in Old English either,' Kitt conceded, 'but that doesn't necessarily mean that Amber wasn't trying to point us at something written here.'

'You really think one of the engravings could be the next clue?' said Halloran.

'I'm not sure. It's mostly a list of names,' said Kitt. 'But at the bottom it reads "These heroes fell for King and Country, forsaking all that they held dear so future children of this county could hold their loved ones near."'

A thoughtful silence descended on the group.

After a couple of minutes, Kitt shook her head. 'I've a feeling this isn't going to be a mystery we solve today.' She started taking photographs of the names inscribed on the memorial. 'I'll send these to Grace and see if she can do some research, in case they have some kind of connection with Amber or something like that.'

'Not to worry that we didn't find anything here. It was a bit of a long shot, pet,' said Halloran, trying to convince himself this was a wild goose chase after all and not the key to solving the whole case – a key that they seemingly hadn't found. 'Maybe Bailey has had more luck with whatever it was Sylvia Wise told him. And we still haven't talked to Liam Long yet, so don't lose—'

'Oi! What're you doing?' came a man's call from across

the green. Halloran cringed. He knew he shouldn't have tampered with the flowerbeds. When he turned, however, he realized the call was not directed at him or anyone else in his group. It had come from an old man lighting a cigarette outside the Wold's End and he was shouting at a figure dressed in black, balaclava included. The figure was running away from the village green – more specifically from Halloran's car. He deduced this from the fact the driver's side door was wide open and the window had been smashed.

'Oh my God,' said Kitt. 'The evidence we collected at Staithes. You left it in the glovebox, didn't you?'

'Yes,' Halloran growled, and with that he ran full pelt towards his car. The black figure vanished around the far corner of the green, into the residential back streets of the village. He upped his pace, but by the time he rounded the same corner the figure in black had already turned another one. He kept running anyway, straight down a long road with many others shooting off it. After a few minutes his lungs began to burn with the effort of sprinting full pelt in the heat but he ignored the pain. Instead he focused his attention on finding the assailant. He looked left and right down each side road but the figure in black was nowhere to be seen. After a couple more minutes he stopped and put his hands on his knees, panting. His heart was thundering but over the sound of its pounding Halloran realized he could hear something else behind him. Footsteps. Someone else running.

He whipped round but it was just Banks following after him. He started walking back towards her, shaking his head.

'He's in the wind,' he said.

'Come on,' she said. 'Kitt and Evie are back at the car checking out the damage.'

When Halloran and Banks got back to the green, Kitt and Evie were standing side by side, leaning against the car and talking to each other in subdued tones.

'Did they take the evidence?' Halloran asked.

Kitt nodded. 'I asked the man who raised the alarm, and he didn't see much more than we did, so we've got no clues as to the thief's identity. Whoever it was, they broke in through the window and emptied the glove compartment. I think the only thing they took was the box from Staithes, and the note that was in it. Did you have anything else important in there?'

Halloran shook his head. 'That was the only thing worth taking, bloody hell,' he said, kicking a nearby stone into the grass.

'I think it's safe to assume that our thief and our killer are the same person, or are at least in cahoots,' said Kitt. 'There's nobody else it could be. I can't think of anyone else who would think the information in that box was valuable.'

'At least you got a look at the note before it was taken,' said Banks. 'You have the same information they have.'

'That's true,' said Kitt, brightening a little. 'The box and the paper themselves weren't that important.'

'I suppose,' said Halloran. 'It's just, this is the first piece of evidence I've ever lost.'

'You didn't lose it,' said Evie. 'That scoundrel stole it from you.'

'Banks is right, love,' said Kitt. 'It's not the thing itself but the information that matters. The most important thing is we figure out the next clue before they do.'

'Well, if anyone can do that, I'm sure it's you,' said Halloran.

'Too right,' said Kitt, then indicated the smashed car window. 'And at least now we have a legitimate reason to go and visit Liam at the garage. It'll be shut by now but we can swing by there first thing tomorrow.'

Halloran forced himself to smile at the group that surrounded him. Even in his despair at losing their hard-won evidence, he couldn't ignore the fact that they were doing all they could to soothe him.

'Come on,' said Evie. 'We can ask at the pub for something to cover the car window. They might have some tarpaulin lying around somewhere. Then I'll drive us up to Blakey Ridge as planned. I think getting out of Irendale for a bit would be a good idea.'

'You're right,' said Halloran. 'That thief knew just what to take and when to strike. I would say someone in this village is watching us. And I'm not talking the usual curtain-twitching. Whoever it was must have been following us very closely.'

'Did you notice anyone looking suspicious back at the cove?' said Kitt.

'No, but I wasn't expecting to be followed. As far as I was aware, we were the only people who knew about the second clue,' Halloran explained, inwardly cursing himself for letting his guard down.

'To know you had something worth taking, they must at least have followed us to Staithes,' said Banks. 'But I didn't notice anyone either. And I'm younger and sharper than Halloran.'

'Oi!'

'Just telling it how it is, sir,' Banks said with a small smile that he couldn't help but mirror.

'Maybe they weren't following us so closely,' said Kitt, lifting Evie's binoculars in demonstration. 'Maybe they just had a good vantage point.'

'Well, however they did it, they're on the run right now,' said Halloran. 'After doing something so bold as breaking into a police officer's car and stealing evidence, they'll likely be lying low.'

'So we'll go up to Blakey, get a bit of distance and think about what to do next?' said Banks.

'There's a spare room at the cottage,' said Kitt. 'You could stay over and drive back to York early tomorrow morning if it's a fit with your work commitments?'

'Aye, that'll work for me,' said Banks, looking at Evie for

her approval. 'We'll drop you back off in Irendale on the way so you can get your car to the garage.'

With that all settled, Halloran nodded and stalked towards the Wold's End in search of something to cover his car. Rain didn't seem likely after a week of hot weather but given the luck he was having right now, he wasn't going to risk another misfortune.

SEVENTEEN

Despite the group's low spirits it was far too pleasant an evening to be cooped up inside a pub and so Halloran, Kitt, Evie and Banks retired to the beer garden at the Lion Inn. As this sixteenth-century freehouse stood at the highest point of the North York Moors National Park, they all looked out over an expanse of purple heather and a sky oranging in the grip of the looming dusk. The uninterrupted panoramic views of Farndale and Rosedale might, Halloran reasoned, just about take their minds off all that had transpired in Irendale an hour ago.

'I really hope the killer doesn't crack that last clue before we do,' said Kitt.

'I know, pet, I know,' said Halloran. 'We'll do our best, but given the war memorial was the most likely place to find the next clue, and there was nothing there, we have to prepare ourselves for the fact that we've followed the trail as far as it goes.'

'Halloran's right,' said Banks.

'Eyup, I don't hear those words often from you, Banks.'

Banks gave Halloran a grudging smile. 'The thing is, Amber might have been smart enough to know her life was in danger, but it doesn't mean she got time to put everything in place before she died. For all we know, she planned to put something at that memorial but never got that far.'

'Dash it all,' said Evie with a sigh, 'I hadn't thought of that. I don't want to think of it really, that she came so close to leading us to the killer but was snuffed out before she managed it.'

'I'm not discounting the possibility, but I'd prefer to think we're just not reading the clue right,' said Kitt.

'You mean, that it might not be a reference to the war memorial?' said Evie.

'Or maybe that's the last clue. Maybe that's supposed to be enough to lead us to the murderer but if it is I don't know who it's supposed to point to. Grace is looking into the list of names from the memorial back in York, at any rate, and will get back to me if she turns anything up.'

'Maybe someone in the village has a military history?' said Evie. 'Maybe they're the killer.'

'In all likelihood, the case is already at least part-solved. Bailey probably has one of the culprits in custody and might be able to get him to give up whoever it was that broke into my car this afternoon,' said Halloran.

'If the answer is as simple as Max Dunwell, someone most of the village knew had been making unwelcome advances towards her, then why this elaborate puzzle?' said Kitt.

'It could be a private game Amber was working on for her own amusement, for all we know,' said Halloran, trying to convince himself as much as Kitt. 'So far, the only thing that suggests it's important to this case is the fact that one of the clues was stolen and the killer – or accomplice – might only have stolen that box in case it led to anything incriminating. They might be in the dark about what these clues really mean as much as we are.'

'I suppose that's the only good thing about the box being stolen,' said Kitt. 'It suggests that the clues were laid out by Amber and not the killer after all. It wouldn't make any sense to steal it otherwise.'

'Even so, we've hit a brick wall.'

'So that's it? We give up on this line of enquiry after we've come so far with it?' Kitt asked.

Halloran put his hand on Kitt's arm and gave it a little squeeze in an attempt to soften the blow that this might be the end of her puzzle-solving quest but as he did so, his attentions drifted from her face to a figure ambling up the roadside to the pub. There was something recognizable about the way the man walked. A sort of half-limp. At first he wasn't sure – if in a moment of exasperation over reaching another dead end, he was just seeing what he wanted to see – but as the figure grew closer, there was no mistaking the dark unkempt hair that hung to the man's shoulders and the slight bend in his posture that made him look older than his twenty-three years.

'Goodchild,' Halloran heard himself growl.

'What? Where?' Kitt asked, turning her head and fixing her stare on the man approaching the gate to the beer garden.

Evie and Banks, who had overheard their fair share of conversation about Goodchild since they arrived earlier in the afternoon, turned to see the man Halloran still suspected was in the thrall of his ex-wife's killer. Could it be coincidence that he was arriving just a short time after they had? Or was it Goodchild who had been following them around? Perhaps he was the one who had stolen from them this afternoon? No, with a limp like that, Goodchild could never outrun Halloran the way the suspect had earlier. But that didn't mean he hadn't been following them and informing someone who was faster on their feet. Either way, Halloran wasn't about to let Kurt Goodchild slip through his fingers on a technicality. 'I think it's time I spoke to him for myself.'

'I'll go with you,' said Banks, a concerned look crossing her face.

'No,' said Halloran. 'I need him alone.'

'Sorry, sir,' said Banks. 'I'm under strict orders from Ricci.'

'Ricci?' Halloran said, his focus switching away from Goodchild. 'What do you mean? She knows you're here?'

'Sir,' said Banks. 'Ricci didn't rise up the ranks as quick as she did by being slow on the uptake. She hoped that you'd take the stress leave seriously but had a small inkling you'd take matters into your own hands, especially given your connections in the community. She understands the case is personal to you and isn't unsympathetic but she has to maintain plausible deniability. She's sat back at the nick in York praying every spare second that common sense will keep its hold on you enough that you don't do anything too drastic. I'm supposed to keep half an eye on you to make sure you don't do anything that's going to cost you your badge.'

Halloran looked over at Kitt who had been the one to arrange dinner with Evie and Banks. 'Did you know about this?'

'Mal . . .' There was a wounded note in her voice that pulled at something inside him. 'No. I'm not in the business of going behind your back.'

'I'm . . . I'm sorry, pet,' he said, sighing. 'I'll be back shortly. Just wait here.'

'I assume you're talking to everyone except me,' said Banks.

'Fine.' Halloran nodded. 'Come along but let me lead.'

'How's that different to any other day?' said Banks, standing up and following Halloran over to where Goodchild was still hobbling towards the pub entrance.

'Kurt,' Halloran called out as they approached. Goodchild kept moving and didn't slow his pace. In three swift strides

Halloran had closed the gap between them and manoeuvred himself so he was standing between Goodchild and the door of the pub. 'Kurt, didn't you hear me call your name?'

Goodchild stared at Halloran for a moment from behind a curtain of unbrushed hair and then shook his head.

'Do you remember me? I lived here in Irendale a few years back. I worked with . . .' Halloran paused and had to work hard to get the name past his teeth. 'DI Kerr.'

'Are you friends with 'im, like?' Goodchild asked and Halloran could only hope the turmoil playing out inside him at having to admit his association with the man who killed Kamala didn't show on his face.

'I was, when I lived here, yes,' Halloran managed. 'This is Detective Sergeant Banks.'

He indicated his partner and Goodchild looked her up and down. 'Are you a nice lady, then?'

'I do my best to be,' Banks said.

'We were wondering if you could help us, Kurt,' Halloran said. 'Do you know Amber Downing?'

Goodchild frowned. 'She was the smart lady. A nice lady. A smart lady. A nice lady.'

'Yes,' Halloran interjected, interrupting the rhythm Goodchild was lulling himself into. 'She was, but she died and we're trying to find out why.'

'Police already talked to me about it. I couldn't 'elp 'em.'

'Did you know Amber well?'

Kurt shook his head.

'Do you know anything about her murder?'

Again Kurt shook his head.

'What about DI Kerr? You visited him, didn't you?'

'I did,' said Goodchild. 'He's my friend.'

Halloran tried not to grimace but utterly failed. 'Did he say anything to you about Amber? Think hard. It might help us catch the person who killed Amber.'

Goodchild shook his head.

Losing patience, Halloran took a step closer. 'Where were you this afternoon?'

'Can't tell you that,' said Goodchild.

'Why not?' asked Halloran.

'It's my secret,' Goodchild said.

'Secrets can be very dangerous, Kurt. I'm not sure now's the time to be keeping them,' said Halloran, his fuse shortening by the second.

'Everyone's got secrets and this one's mine.'

'That's not good enough. You better answer the question,' said Halloran, jabbing Goodchild in his shoulder in an attempt to wake him up to the seriousness of the situation.

'Sir . . .' Halloran heard Banks say with a note of warning in her voice. He took half a step backwards to show he'd heard, but no more.

Goodchild's eyes widened at the unexpected contact. 'I go about me business, and it's nobody else's business but mine.'

Halloran took in a deep breath and alongside the smell

of hops drifting from the pub, there was an unmistakable hint of jasmine and peach.

Quick as a whip, Halloran grabbed the collar on Goodchild's coat and pulled the man's face close to his. 'Kerr is using you, Kurt. I don't know how, but he is.'

'Lemme go, lemme go,' Goodchild started to shout, much louder than Halloran would have liked. Loud enough to make the other people sitting in the beer garden look over, Kitt and Evie included.

Banks put a hand on Halloran's shoulder and gripped tight enough that her nails dug into his skin. He glared at her but took a couple of steps away from Goodchild anyway, trying to recover himself.

'Kurt,' Banks said. 'I know Kerr is your friend, but if he's said anything about Amber, we need you to tell us.'

'He didn't, I just said,' Goodchild said, anger flaring in his voice. He pointed a finger at Banks. 'You, you shouldn't be here if you're a nice lady. Bad things happen to nice, smart ladies round 'ere. You should go away and be safe. Otherwise you'll end up like the smart lady.'

'Who makes the bad things happen?' Halloran demanded.

Goodchild eyed Halloran and shook his head. 'I don't know. The smart lady died. Lots of ladies die around here.' Goodchild put a hand on Banks's shoulder. 'It's not a good place for smart ladies.'

'All right, thanks, Kurt, never mind us, eh?' said Banks. 'Go and enjoy a pint and we'll say no more about it.'

Kurt nodded and ambled into the pub.

Once he was out of earshot Halloran turned on Banks. 'Why'd you let him go?'

'Because you were getting so much quality information out of him? Sir, none of this is admissible anyway, he's not under caution. I hate to say it, but I don't think he knows anything. He's not agile enough to be the person who escaped us this afternoon, and to be honest, after the theft, I don't think Jeremy Kerr has anything to do with this murder. The culprit or culprits are clearly people who are roaming free, not serving a life sentence up at Esk Valley prison.'

'When it comes to Kerr, thinking isn't good enough. Take it from someone who has some experience in dealing with him. I need to know for sure, without any doubt, that he hasn't orchestrated this.'

'That's not going to happen by talking to Goodchild,' said Banks.

'If he's so innocent, why wouldn't he tell us where he was this afternoon?'

'Because, sir, he didn't feel comfortable talking to you. People like Goodchild need to feel safe. You know that. What you need is some hard evidence of Kerr's involvement. Letters he's sent, communications, anything that really ties him to—'

'I know how investigations work, thank you, Banks.'

'Maybe it's time to start acting like it, then. We've all got a past, sir, and if she were here I doubt Kamala would thank you for using her as an excuse for this kind of behaviour.'

The words were unexpected and cut deep. Banks had been nothing but respectful of him ever since he came to work at York station just over four years ago. In the time they'd been on the job together, he'd told her snippets of what had happened back here in Irendale. Even if he hadn't, gossip was rife amongst officers and she probably knew a lot more than what he'd told her. So on the odd occasion when he'd bent the rules to follow hunches, she'd supported him, knowing the rationale; understanding the background. For her to say something like this to him, he must really be overstepping the mark, and in his heart he knew she was right.

Unable to bring himself to say anything outright, he offered Banks a stiff nod. She patted him on the back and walked him over to the table where Kitt and Evie were waiting. As Halloran saw the concerned look on Kitt's face he began to wonder what the hell he was doing here, chasing old ghosts across the moor top when Amber Downing's death, tragic though it was, seemed to have nothing to do with the loss he had suffered five years ago. Bailey had been accommodating enough and everyone, Ricci included, had given him about as much rope as they could but it was time to face facts: he didn't have any business here. He wasn't following protocol so nothing he was doing could ultimately do the case any good. Perhaps the worst truth was that clinging onto unfinished business in his old life was preventing him from properly starting a new one.

Kitt wouldn't like it, that was an understatement, but the second they were alone together in the cottage he'd explain himself and suggest going back home first thing in the morning. It was really Bailey's case and their little side-show was probably only going to hinder him. Sure, they had tipped Bailey off to one credible suspect in Sylvia Wise but he'd already confirmed she had an alibi for the night Amber was murdered so that hadn't amounted to anything. Whilst trying to build a case against Max Dunwell and Liam Long, the last thing Bailey needed was Halloran insisting Kerr had some connection to the case when he had no concrete evidence. That's without even mentioning the treasure hunt that had petered out after clue two.

Between all that and losing a piece of evidence, Halloran wagered Bailey could do without their 'help'. Perhaps CCTV cameras from the village green had caught the theft on camera and could help Bailey identify Dunwell's accomplice, but it wasn't like one of Bailey's team couldn't look into that of their own accord. In short, Bailey probably already had everything he needed to solve the case without him and Kitt continuing their distracting *Beowulf*-inspired puzzle.

It was time to get out of this mess while they still could.

EIGHTEEN

The living room back at the let was deathly quiet. Evie and Banks had long since retired to their room and Kitt was taking a pre-bedtime shower. This left Halloran standing alone, staring along the chorus line of faces hanging above the fireplace, wondering if Max Dunwell's really was the face of a killer.

He sighed and reached over to Liam Long's photograph, tugging it down, and as he did so mentally relinquishing the responsibility of deciding if he had his part to play too.

He'd gone too far with Goodchild. If Banks hadn't been there who knew how far he would have pushed it? That was one question he never wanted to find the answer to.

One by one, he continued to unstick the photographs from their place on the mantel, then crumpled them all and threw them into the wastepaper basket. He paused when he got to Amber's photograph and tried to avoid her searching eyes. The sound of running water in the bathroom stopped and the silence in the cottage was suddenly oppressive. It was not in Halloran's nature to give up on a case. Once he had committed himself to finding justice for a person, he always saw it through. He scoffed at himself. Justice? Is that what he'd managed to convince himself the obsessive hunt for Amber's killer was about? After what happened earlier, after the look he'd seen on Kitt's face when Goodchild had his outburst, he couldn't hide behind that idea any longer. He couldn't even claim he had been working towards further justice for Kamala. Vengeance had been a far more dominant motivator and at that thought an emptiness throbbed in his chest. How had he got so lost?

He looked again into Amber's eyes and a thousand questions swarmed in his mind. What message had she been trying to send with those notes? Had she even been trying to send a message at all? Why was she killed and what happened to the gun she purchased from some unknown criminal on the dark web? He closed his eyes, trying with all his might to silence these thoughts. No good could come from asking them and, frankly, they weren't even his questions to ask.

Opening his eyes, he reached out to pull Amber's photograph down from the mantel but as he did so a sudden crash of what sounded like breaking glass sounded out. It came from the bathroom. Quickly, he strode towards the bathroom door.

'Kitt?'

He waited a moment for some other sound. Nothing. This time, he knocked and raised his voice. 'Kitt? Are you OK in there?'

No response.

'Kitt!' Halloran shouted louder, a hot panic starting to grip him. He beat his fists against the door. He rattled the doorknob. But the door was locked and not budging.

Scraping his fingers through his hair, he paused and pressed his ear to the door. That was when he heard it: a tiny whimper and some small dull thuds from the other side. It was the sound of a struggle, and it sent a chill through his whole body.

'Mal!' Kitt then called, her voice part scream, but then the sound was muffled again and the whimpering returned.

'Kitt!' he called back. 'Hang on, I'm coming!'

Not wasting another moment Halloran took a few steps backwards, raised his leg and kicked at the door, at its weakest point just below the handle, over and over.

In his mind's eye, he saw in graphic detail the scene on the other side of the door. After their confrontation back at Blakey, Kurt Goodchild had followed them back to the cottage. He'd watched the building closely for an hour or two, lying in wait until he saw a light on in the bathroom window. The glass was frosted but with the light on he would have been able to look at the dappled outline and know from the size and shape that the person on the other side of the glass was a woman. The bastard would have taken the time to watch her shower, the suggestion of bare flesh and running water enough to work him up, knowing what he was about to do to her. Then, after, when she was relaxed and dreamy from the spell of hot water following a long hard day, that was when he'd made his attack.

All the while this vision played out in his mind, Kitt's cry echoed in Halloran's ears. He wouldn't lose her like he'd lost Kamala. He had to get to her, now. He gave the door one final kick and the wood made a splintering sound. The door gave and with one hard shove of his shoulders, Halloran burst through.

The first thing he noticed was the black-gloved hands around Kitt's throat. The second thing was the fact that the assailant wasn't actually inside the room, but was leaning in through the open ground-floor window. The pane wasn't broken as he would have expected after the smash, but the potted plant that had been sitting on the sill was now in pieces, soil strewn across the once spotless tiles. The attacker was wearing a balaclava, just like the thief, making it impossible to identify him. Kitt's eyes were wide and streaming with tears. She'd managed to put her nightdress on before the attacker made his move so she was at least clothed but her face was red raw from the effort of trying to breathe.

'Get the hell away from her!' Halloran bellowed. The attacker released his grip as though Halloran's voice had given him some kind of electric shock and then he vanished from sight. Kitt stumbled towards him, hunched and coughing.

Halloran glared at the window and started back towards the door.

'No!' Kitt called after him.

He turned to look at her.

'Please,' she whimpered. 'Don't leave me just now.' He stared at her, torn between comforting the woman he loved and going after the assailant he presumed to be Goodchild.

'Mal,' she whispered, and that was enough to make up his mind. He moved back towards her, wrapped his arms around her and held her head against his chest, not quite believing what he had just witnessed.

'What's going on?' said Banks, appearing at the door in a tank top and shorts, Evie just behind her.

'Someone's here,' said Halloran. 'Possibly Goodchild. Possibly the thief from this afternoon. He leant in through the window and tried to strangle Kitt.'

'Bloody hell,' said Banks, already starting in the direction of the front door. 'I'll call it in and check outside.'

'God, Kitt, are you all right?' said Evie, her eyes tearing at her friend's obvious distress.

Kitt managed a nod.

'Evie, can you look after Kitt for a minute? I can't let Banks go out there on her own,' said Halloran. 'Whoever did this might be armed.'

Evie joined Kitt and put an arm round her. At the mention of Banks's safety, Kitt didn't insist he stay a second time.

Stalking out of the bathroom and towards the front door, which Banks had left open, Halloran looked outside. She wasn't there, but the headlights on Evie's car were turned on and the driver's-side door was open. Halloran looked down the road in one direction and then turned, looking down the road in the other. Looking for any sign of light or life.

Out of the darkness, a hand grabbed his arm from behind. Halloran jumped and in his shock yelled out at the top of his voice. He whipped round, raising his fists.

'Sir,' Banks said. 'It's only me.'

'Bloody hell.'

Banks smirked. 'Sorry, sir, I didn't mean to scare you.'

'You didn't scare me.'

'Of course not, that only sounded like a scream of panic. It was really a war cry.'

'Where did you get off to?' Halloran said, keen to change the subject.

'I've checked the perimeter of the cottage. I turned the car lights on so I'd be able to see better if I wound up chasing anyone out onto the road. But there's no one there, sir. At least, not that I can see. It's pitch black out here. If they're even fifty yards from the cottage we probably wouldn't see them from here.'

Halloran cursed under his breath. He looked both ways

one last time but Banks was right. The only light was some way in the distance, cast by a couple of cars travelling a road along the moor top. Everything else was quiet and dark.

'Did you call it into Bailey?'

'Not yet, I'll do that now.'

'Thanks. Maybe Kitt can remember something telling now she's had a few minutes to collect herself. Bailey will probably want to have the bathroom swept for DNA and prints. Can you let him know that we'll seal it off for him?'

'Will do.'

Halloran turned back into the cottage and headed back to the bathroom. Kitt and Evie weren't there. For just a split second panic rose in him once more, but then he heard Evie's voice from their bedroom.

He knocked and Evie called him in.

Kitt sat in the chair by the dressing table whilst Evie was keeping her company, sitting cross-legged on the bed.

'Is Charley OK?' Evie asked.

'She's fine,' Halloran reassured her. 'The suspect was nowhere to be found. She's calling the police station now.'

His eyes fixed on Kitt then. Though she may have important information that could bring her attacker – and likely Amber's killer to justice – his first priority was her well-being. Evie checked once more that Kitt was doing better before making her excuses to leave the room.

Kitt rose from the chair and Halloran pulled her into a hug. She was gripping him tighter than she ever had before.

'I'm sorry,' he said, stroking her hair. He pushed her away just a touch to take a closer look at her neck. He could already see a purple shadow where a bruise was sure to follow. Halloran winced. There was no justice in Kitt suffering like this; all she'd tried to do was help.

'I think we should take you to Scarborough hospital and get you checked out,' he said.

Kitt shook her head. 'I'm all right,' she croaked, pausing for a moment. 'I mean, I will be, it was just a shock.'

'For both of us. I'd never forgive myself if anything happened to you,' Halloran said.

'Based on your behaviour the last few days, I believe you on that.'

'I'm so, so sorry,' he said, his voice breaking at the thought of what he'd almost lost.

'It's not your fault,' she whispered – which seemed to be less painful for her than talking. She pulled back for a moment to stroke his beard. 'Kamala wasn't your fault and if anything happened to me that wouldn't be your fault either. I came here of my own free will, remember?' Slowly, she leant towards his arm. More specifically, she leant towards the tattoo of Kamala's name which was just visible below the sleeve of the T-shirt he was wearing. Those who had seen it probably thought he got the tattoo as a mark of enduring devotion to his deceased wife. In truth, the tattoo was his punishment; his constant reminder that in his line of work trust wasn't a luxury he could afford.

Without another word, Kitt pressed her lips against the ink, and kissed along his ex-wife's name.

This gesture of acceptance and forgiveness meant more to him than he could ever express in words. All he could think to do in return was stroke her damp hair and hold her close again in the hope of soothing her after her ordeal.

A skittering sound in the passage broke the moment.

'Banks?' Halloran called out.

Banks pushed the door open, and Evie was at her side.

'You've called in to Bailey?' said Halloran.

'Aye, he's phoned it through to dispatch so they can look at traffic cameras and see if there are any cars in the area that look as though they might have come from this direction. Not much traffic on moorland roads at this time of night so, if there are, they should be easy to spot.'

'Kitt, what happened exactly?' said Evie.

'It was so stupid really,' said Kitt, massaging her throat in a way that made it clear it was still difficult to speak. 'I opened the window to let the steam out after my shower, changed into my nightclothes, and when I went to close the window again, they, those hands, reached through out of nowhere and grabbed me.'

'Cripes!' said Evie. 'Now I'm bound to have nightmares.'

'You and me both,' said Kitt.

'I know you're probably in shock,' said Halloran, unable to wait any longer before finding out some concrete details, 'but did the attacker give anything away about their identity? Anything at all?'

Kitt reached for a cup of water on the dressing table that Evie must have fetched her and took a couple of sips before speaking again. 'They were wearing a mask, so I didn't see their face. In the struggle I couldn't even make out their eye colour. Whoever it was, though, I don't think they were very strong. I was able to break free enough to call out to you. They got a hold on me more out of surprise and panic than brute strength – at least, that's how it felt. They . . . they did say something to me, though.'

'What did they say?' said Halloran. 'Did you recognize their voice? Was it a man or a woman?'

Kitt shook her head. 'I couldn't tell you for certain because they didn't speak properly. They sort of hissed the words.'

'What words?' asked Banks.

Kitt looked at Halloran sidelong. 'I can't be sure. But it was either "Kurt wants you dead or" . . . "Kerr wants you dead".'

NINETEEN

It was mid-morning the next day when Halloran and Bailey checked in with the officer on duty at Esk Valley prison. Bailey's team had turned up at the crack of dawn to make a sweep of the bathroom at the cottage, concentrating on the window area. They had also taken swabs from just outside the window in the hopes of obtaining some DNA evidence. Whilst waiting for those results to materialize, Kitt had been invited down to the station to make an official statement about the events of the night before and Bailey had applied to talk with Kerr in an official capacity. The officer had called everyone of influence he knew to explain the seriousness of the case and get the request pushed through quickly, and news that Kerr had agreed to see them arrived soon after.

The pair were directed to an interrogation room where, they were told, Kerr was waiting for them. Halloran walked in time with Bailey along the polished floor of the corridor, trying to prepare himself for facing down Kerr a second time. Truth be told, the emotional yo-yoing of this case was taking its toll. Last night, before the attack on Kitt, he'd convinced himself that Kerr couldn't possibly be involved and he was best leaving this case to Bailey and his team. This morning, he was facing one of two possibilities: either that the killer was trying to make them believe Kerr was involved, or that from behind bars Kerr had orchestrated a personalized attack on both him and Kitt. All the suspicions and borderline paranoid thoughts that he'd been poised to forget had come bubbling back to the surface. After everything he'd promised himself about not letting Kerr play him again, he'd still managed it. If Kerr really was behind this, all that talk about the killings not being personal didn't hold much weight given the events of the night before.

'I know this case is personal to you, and you'll be hoping for real results when we talk to Kerr, but you know this is a long shot, don't you, sir?' Bailey said, slowing his pace a touch. 'Despite what Kitt's attacker said, as yet we've still got no hard evidence that Kerr is in any way involved. Like we discussed back at the cottage, it could just be a way of throwing us off the real trail.'

'I know that. I'm not discounting that idea, just so you know. But can you actually give me another viable suspect at present? Sylvia Wise had an alibi, you've got nothing forensic on Dunwell and we'd all be a little bit surprised if he'd managed to mastermind something like this on his own.'

Bailey nodded. 'Dunwell will be being released around now. I couldn't justify keeping him any longer without any forensic evidence and didn't 'ave enough to charge him. The evidence is slowly stacking against Liam though.'

'How so?'

'Sylvia Wise reckons she overheard Amber talking to one of the other members of her Scrabble club. Talking about a fight she'd 'ad with Liam. He was away when she was murdered but from our interviews we know he 'ad a door key. He could have slipped it to the murderer.'

'So why isn't he in custody?'

'Same problem as Dunwell. We don't have any physical evidence at all. We've been through all of his financial and phone records with a fine-tooth comb and nothing 'as stood out.'

'It's worth your time to keep looking into Liam. Maybe Amber's parents had more reason than snobbery alone to take a dislike to him? But after everything that's gone on, I can't take any chances when it comes to Kerr and Goodchild. If you break down the timeline, it's not such a long shot. We see Kurt Goodchild up at Blakey Ridge an hour after someone steals evidence from us and less than three hours later Kitt is attacked at the let. You know the rest. The cause of death and the mutilation of the body. The visits from Kurt Goodchild. Taking all that into account, don't you think there's a fair chance he's got some connection with this case? It's circumstantial, I'll grant you. But you know just as well as I do that circumstantial evidence is often an indicator that there's something deeper happening under the surface.'

Bailey was quiet for a moment before he spoke again. 'I think we just 'ave to be careful about seeing the patterns we want to see rather than what's there.'

Halloran stopped walking. 'We? You mean me, don't you?'

Bailey sighed. 'I'm not trying to be disrespectful, sir. It's just . . .'

'What?'

'I'm not sure I should say, sir.'

'I don't think we should be going into an interrogation with the likes of Kerr with something unsaid between us. He'll take any chance to divide us, you know that. Best we settle whatever you've got to say now, out here.'

'It's just, I can see a change in you, since you left Irendale, sir. And it wasn't the change I was expecting.'

'Go on,' Halloran said.

'Please understand that this comes from a place of concern, sir. We were all sad to let you go from Eskdale. But I thought getting out of the area after what happened would help you move on. But some of the things you've said and done since you got here – particularly what passed between you and Goodchild yesterday evening – 'ave made me wonder whether you ever put what happened to Kamala behind you.'

'It's not as easy as just moving house,' said Halloran.

'It would be wrong of me to say I understand, sir. But I can imagine. Thing is, like you say, when we go in there Kerr is going to try every trick he can to get to both of us. He's got nothing better to do in 'ere. And if any complaints are brought about our conduct, I'll be held responsible. So I need to know that when we're in that room, you're going to be able to handle yourself.'

Halloran stared at DI Bailey for a long moment but then nodded. 'I'll push him as far as I'm allowed to, and no further.'

'Given how sly Kerr can be, sir, it might not be you pushing him.'

Halloran sighed. 'I know what he's like. I'll be on my guard.'

Bailey offered a faint smile and then started walking again along the corridor until they reached the interview room where Kerr waited for them.

'Good cop or bad cop?' Bailey asked quietly.

Halloran stared at him. 'I think you already know the answer.'

Halloran pushed open the door to see Kerr slouching behind a desk in his prison uniform. The two officers guarding him nodded at Halloran and Bailey, excusing themselves from the room.

'Hello, Malc,' Kerr said with an overconfident leer. 'So lovely to see you again.'

TWENTY

Halloran didn't respond to Kerr's greeting but instead walked across to the other side of the table from him and watched as Bailey closed the door.

'And DC Bailey, too, into the bargain,' Kerr continued. 'I didn't think the likes of me were important enough to be visited by two busy police officers.'

Bailey sat down in a chair opposite Kerr. Halloran remained standing. 'It's DI Bailey now,' he said.

'Ee, congratulations, son,' said Kerr. 'I hope Halloran at least treated you to a pint at the Wold's End when you got yer promotion.'

Without a word, or any indication he'd even heard what Kerr had said, Halloran turned on the recording equipment sitting on the desk. 'Interview with prisoner number AA91287GG. Present in the room is Detective Inspector Damian Bailey and Detective Inspector Malcolm Halloran.

Date of interview: Wednesday, seventeenth of June 2020. Time, 11.04.'

Kerr eyed Halloran and Bailey in turn. 'Putting our conversation on the record this time, are you, Malc? Must be serious.'

'Sir, we've got a couple of very simple questions we need to ask you and depending on the answers we shouldn't keep you too long,' said Bailey.

'It's not like I 'aven't got time on me hands. Good old Malc saw to that,' said Kerr. 'Ask away.'

'When was the last time you spoke to Kurt Goodchild?' said Bailey.

Halloran watched Kerr closely. The man frowned at the question.

'Funny you should ask. I picked up a voicemail from 'im through the system this morning that sounded a bit panicked. So I give 'im a ring from one of the phones 'ere.'

'What was the message regarding?' said Halloran.

Kerr looked at him askance. 'Well, you should know, Malc.'

'If I knew,' Halloran said, 'then I wouldn't have asked the question.'

'Well, I don't know if you want me saying owt about this in front of DI Bailey but Kurt got in touch with me because you'd rattled him. Told me you'd pushed him around. Asked him questions he didn't know how to answer.'

Inwardly Halloran cringed, but he kept his face perfectly

still. He'd brought this on himself, of course. He'd rattled Goodchild enough that he'd gone straight to Kerr about it and now he knew all about his moment of weakness. His second in the last week, after the outburst in Ricci's office. The only good fortune was that Kerr couldn't use it to drive a wedge between him and Bailey. Halloran had had to come clean about his altercation with Goodchild back at the cottage that morning. Still, hearing his actions described by Kerr brought on a searing shame. No matter what he suspected Goodchild of, Halloran knew there was no justification for the way he had handled that particular situation.

'I'm sorry to hear he felt that way,' Halloran said.

'Aye, the lad were reight shaken,' Kerr said. 'So, of course he turned to someone he trusted.'

'So you discussed Kurt Goodchild's interactions with DI Halloran earlier in the evening at length?' said Bailey.

'Aye, lad,' said Kerr. 'Well, as much as Kurt can do "at length". His mind tends to wander a lot, you know. Probably down to some of the drugs 'is doctor's got 'im on, by the sound of things.'

'The drugs affect Goodchild's behaviour?' Halloran asked.

'I in't a doctor but from our chats he seems to find it 'ard to stay focused on one topic. Sometimes he says it's 'ard for him to remember things.'

'Did you talk about anything else?' asked Bailey.

'Not particularly, just tried to calm the lad down given

how het up 'e was. But if you wanted to, you could listen to the conversation yerselves. I'm sure it was recorded.'

'Oh, we will be listening to that recording,' Halloran said. 'But first of all we want to know what you've got to say about your communications with Goodchild.'

'From what I 'ear, Malc, my communications with 'im 'ave been a lot more civil than yours 'ave.'

Halloran folded his arms across his chest and meandered his way around the desk.

'Did Kurt tell you where he was earlier in the day? Around five o'clock?'

'Why, what 'appened at five o'clock, like?' Kerr licked his lips. 'Was there another murder?'

'Were you expecting there to be one?' said Halloran.

Kerr smiled. 'No, just that last time you were 'ere that's what you came about. I know you try very 'ard to make sure nobody dies on your watch, Malc, but we both know you haven't got the best track record.'

Halloran met Kerr's cold, mean stare and worked hard to ignore the itching in his fists.

'DI Halloran asked you a question, sir,' Bailey pushed. 'Do you know where Kurt was at that time?'

'No idea. He was too busy talking about what 'ad passed between 'im and DI Halloran to talk about the rest of his day.' Kerr's eyes riveted on Halloran. ''E did mention, though, that after you talked, 'e'd seen you snuggling up to some red-haired beauty. She sounds like a real catch, Malc. Congratulations.'

Halloran glared at Kerr. So he knew about Kitt. If he was informed by Goodchild, he only would have found out about her after Kitt had been attacked, assuming his story about picking up Kurt's message that morning was true. But maybe that was just a cover and he'd known about Kitt all along. Inmates did have limited, supervised access to the internet and there had been some light press around Kitt assisting him on a couple of murder cases in the last year. It wouldn't have taken much for him to suspect that their relationship might be more than just professional. And if he did know about Kitt before this morning, there was a chance he'd orchestrated the attack on her. 'And what did you say to Goodchild,' Halloran said, 'when he described this red-haired beauty?'

'Not much of anything,' Kerr said with a shrug. 'It's not really my business who you're 'aving it away with these days, Malc. I just tried to calm 'im down and told 'im that although you take things a bit personally you were only trying to do your job.'

It was taking all of Halloran's willpower to ignore Kerr's digs but he had to hold it together, at least in front of Bailey, if he wanted to see this interrogation through.

'Goodchild said his whereabouts yesterday afternoon are his secret – do you know what he means by that?'

'I do, actually,' said Kerr.

Finally. An admission that he and Goodchild were hiding something.

'What did he mean by it, sir?' asked Bailey.

''e's a funny one, our Kurt,' Kerr said with a huffy little laugh. ''e found this little old shack on the edge of one of the moorland farms. I've only ever 'eard him describe it but from what I can tell it's about a mile or so from Blakey Ridge in the direction of Rosedale Abbey. He goes there sometimes to sit and read, sometimes to camp. 'e calls it 'is secret place.'

'What's in there?' said Halloran.

'Like I said, I've never been, but to the best of me knowledge there's just a bit of rusting farm equipment in there. It sounds as though it 'asn't been used in years.'

'If it's so innocent, why is it a secret?' said Halloran.

'Because he doesn't want anyone else using his secret place. 'e only told me about it because 'e's a bit of a kid at heart and can't 'elp himself. And 'e knows I won't be using it any time soon.'

'And there's no way he could be using the shack as a base for doing things he doesn't want anyone else knowing about?' said Bailey.

'Kurt is a nice lad. But 'e's not a good liar. If he was up to something he shouldn't be, I'd know about it.'

I bet you would, Halloran thought.

'Well, sir, that's been very helpful,' said Bailey and he stood, readying to leave. 'We'll check on Kurt's secret place and just make sure 'e's not getting himself into any trouble we should know about. Especially after what you've said about the effect the drugs he takes can 'ave on his memory.'

'Probably a good idea,' Kerr said, with a grin. 'I'd be surprised if you found anything but then no matter 'ow well you know a person you really never can tell what they're capable of. At any rate, I'm always 'appy to help out old friends.'

Keen not to look at Kerr's face any longer than he absolutely had to, Halloran turned to follow Bailey out of the door.

'I tell you what, though, Malc. Kurt mentioning your new missus did get me thinking that maybe I did you a bit of a favour five years ago, gettin' Kamala out of the way for you.'

Halloran's whole body stiffened. He turned back to face Kerr, daring him with his eyes to say another word on that particular subject. Unfortunately for both of them, he accepted the challenge.

'After all, you know what they say about redheads.'

Kerr barely had time to blink before Halloran's hands were on him, grabbing him by the collar and slamming him against the nearest wall.

'Don't you dare talk about her!' Halloran shook Kerr hard.

'Now, who do you mean when you say that, Malc? Your new redhead or Kamala?' Kerr's voice was gleeful. Halloran didn't care that he was playing right into his hands; he couldn't let Kerr's comments stand.

'Say another word and I promise you'll regret it,' he said, reaching for Kerr's throat.

'That's enough, enough!' Bailey bellowed, pulling Halloran away while Kerr's breathy cackle rattled in his ears.

TWENTY-ONE

'It's the one on the end of the row,' Halloran said to Kitt as they passed the house he and Kamala used to live in on their way to Irendale Motors later that afternoon. He glanced over to gauge her reaction. After making her statement at the police station she had visited one of the village gift shops and bought a chiffon scarf to hide the bruising on her neck. Soon after, she'd decamped to the tea room for a soothing cup of tea. It would take time but she would heal. He'd make sure of it.

'Seventy-two, Rosedale View,' Kitt said, reading the door number as they drove by. 'I can see why you chose it. I imagine the view out in the back garden would be grand.'

'It was idyllic,' Halloran said, glancing at the stone cottage where he had once envisioned his whole life unfolding. 'That's partly why everything that happened here came as such a shock.'

'I hate the fact that we hadn't met then,' said Kitt. 'That I couldn't help you through what must have been an unthinkably difficult time.'

'Knowing you then would have probably only complicated things,' he said. 'I wasn't in a space where I was looking for anyone new.'

'I know that, daft thing,' said Kitt. 'This may come as a shock to you but I do have some self-control when the situation calls for it. I just wish I could have been a friend to you, when you needed one.'

Halloran flashed her a smile and she reached over to run her hand through his hair. Self-control was something he had lost since this whole nightmare began. Maybe he hadn't really been in control since Kamala died; certainly he found it ever harder to follow protocol when the stakes were personal. Regardless of where this all began, he needed to regain his composure as a matter of urgency. After what happened back at the prison, Bailey had made it clear he wanted Halloran back on the road to York as quickly as possible. He had apologized for losing it but the officer had understandably been uninterested in apologies over that level of unprofessionalism. In the fallout from his reckless behaviour, he found himself questioning, not for the first time, whether he was fit to continue in this line of work. Perhaps he was kidding himself to think he could go on as a DI after Kerr's betrayal and Kamala's death had changed him for ever in ways he hadn't fully understood until he returned to the moorland. If that was the case, the outcome of any meeting with Ricci on his return might be irrelevant. If he was a liability to his colleagues or to the public he would have no choice but to resign.

'I'm really sorry we ended up driving past this place in the end,' Kitt said, breaking Halloran out of his thoughts.

'It's all right,' he said. 'There was no point going three miles round the houses down back lanes when this is the quickest route to the garage. Though, of course, if the theft had never happened, we could have both been spared. Just another reason why we'd be better off leaving the village as soon as we can. The longer we stay here the more danger we're exposed to.'

Kitt nodded.

Not wishing to get into another heated discussion over leaving the moors sooner rather than later, Halloran put his full attention back on the road ahead. He rubbed his eyes, trying to ignore how much they were stinging from the lack of sleep. Neither he nor Kitt had had much rest the night before, and by the look of them this morning, Banks and Evie had suffered the same fate. They would be back in York by now, well out of this mess, and very soon he and Kitt would be too. He glanced up in his rear-view mirror to take one last look at the cottage he and Kamala used to live in and decided that behind him was the best place for it. Picking at old wounds had only opened new ones.

A couple of quiet minutes passed before Halloran pulled the car into Irendale Motors. In truth, if he'd had a car in working order, he would have driven Kitt back to York and safety last night but as it was he was reluctant to leave his vandalized vehicle parked in the village square for longer than necessary. It was fit for the short journey between the village and the garage, but no further. At least the breeze fluttering in through the missing window was welcome on such a warm day.

Though he'd tried to convince Kitt it was the best course of action, she wouldn't hear of going back to York with Evie and Banks that morning; probably worried that left to his own devices Halloran would go off on some reckless solo investigation. He couldn't really blame her for suspecting. The garage would likely give him a courtesy car so he could drive Kitt back to York and he'd have to come back to Irendale to collect his vehicle in a few days. Despite Bailey's warnings, and his own desire to put this whole episode behind him, if an official arrest still hadn't been made, he didn't know for sure if he'd be able to resist making a few more off-the-record enquiries. That, it seemed, would prove to be the true test of whether he'd managed to regain some control and had learned to leave well enough alone. Right now, though, he was focused on getting his car fixed and getting Kitt home. If the police's current prime suspect happened to let something slip in the course of conversation, well, he couldn't help that.

Halloran turned off the ignition and climbed out of the car, breathing in the dizzying cocktail of petrol, overheated rubber and strong solvents. Kitt followed and after a few moments Liam Long came out onto the forecourt to greet them. Halloran recognized him from the day they'd arrived in the village when he had been one of the curious onlookers, and, of course, from the photo that had been pinned to the mantelpiece at the let over the last few days.

'All right?' said Liam, rubbing some oil off his hands onto his overalls.

'Liam, isn't it?' said Halloran.

'Aye,' Liam said, eyeing Halloran a bit more keenly. 'Have we met, like?'

'No,' said Halloran. 'My car was broken into yesterday. Driver's-side window completely smashed in and DI Bailey said you were the man who could fix it for me.'

Slowly, Liam looked at the car and then back at Halloran. 'Oh aye. I could take a look at it if you want me to. I'm sorry to hear about the break-in. That's really rare round here. Mind you, there are some opportunists who play on tourists, like.'

'That's pretty much what happened to us, I think,' said Halloran. 'They emptied our glovebox looking for something to take, but of course there was nothing worth their while in there.'

'Course not,' said Liam, smiling. 'Only an idiot would leave valuables in their glovebox these days.'

'Er, yes,' Halloran said, catching Kitt's smile at Liam's accidental insult. Or was it? Bailey had said it himself, the evidence was slowly mounting against Liam. Could he have broken into their car yesterday? Could he be the mysterious man in black that attacked Kitt last night?

'I can have it fixed for you in a couple of days,' Liam said, nodding back to the car.

'Thing is, we sort of need to drive to York today,' said Halloran. 'Any chance you've got a courtesy car lying around?'

'Oh aye,' said Liam. 'We'll get you sorted out. Come in t' office.'

They followed Liam through the garage and into a small office space at the back. The room was an absolute mess of papers and car parts. Oil was smeared across the walls in various places and the only decoration was a predictably raunchy calendar. June depicted a long-legged brunette straddling a Harley Davidson motorcycle, wearing nothing more than a bikini and a pair of red heels.

Halloran glanced over at Kitt to see that she had noted his interest in the calendar. She raised her eyebrows in an mock-unimpressed manner. While Liam was faffing around with some papers in a drawer he leaned over, brushed the hair away from her face and murmured in her ear: 'Don't worry, pet, I was only thinking how she doesn't hold a candle to you.'

Kitt shook her head and gave him a playful shove.

'Just need your driving licence then,' said Liam, holding a clipboard.

Halloran handed his ID to Liam who started writing but then stopped. 'Oh, hang about, this is the wrong form.'

Halloran suppressed a sigh. He wasn't surprised Liam couldn't find the right form in this mess. It was a wonder he could find anything, in fact.

'Sorry, I'm shattered. Late night last night,' said Liam, rummaging around in a drawer behind him and pulling out another form. 'Still haven't properly woken up yet. I won't be able to do these early starts for ever. Here's to early retirement, eh?'

Late night? Alongside his little dig about the gloveboxes earlier, these words pricked at Halloran's instincts.

'Been burning the candle at both ends, have you?' said Kitt, perhaps thinking the same thing he was.

'Not quite,' said Liam, his whole face dropping. 'I . . . had some bad news recently. I haven't really been able to sleep since.'

Halloran looked at the ground. Of course. He hadn't slept a wink for weeks after Kamala died. If Liam was in fact innocent, why should he have supposed it was any different for him? Sure, they hadn't been dating long. But he hadn't been there when his girlfriend was strangled to death and that thought must prey on him. He must know that if he'd been here last weekend rather than on a stag do in Amsterdam, Amber might still be alive.

As he thought about this, another possibility rose in Halloran's mind: given his generous inheritance, there was a chance that Liam did have something to do with Amber's death, and the guilt was keeping him awake.

'I'm so sorry,' said Kitt. 'I should know better than to make flippant remarks like that.'

'You weren't to know,' said Liam, starting to fill out the form again. 'Although if you've been in the village a few days you probably heard about the woman who died?'

This comment didn't add up either. Liam knew they had been in the village a few days. He saw them arrive. Was he now pretending he wasn't sure when they had got there? Or, in his grief, had he just forgotten he'd even looked their way?

'There has been talk about it,' said Kitt. 'People are trying to make sense of something so tragic.'

'She was me girlfriend,' Liam said, not looking up from the form.

'I'm sorry for your loss,' Halloran said – the words he heard a thousand times over when a similar thing happened to him. He knew what little comfort they were but right now that was all he had to offer.

'As am I,' said Kitt. 'That's a horrible thing to happen to anyone. But I hear the police are working hard on the case.'

'They took a bloke into custody, aye. I know the guy. He was always buzzing around Amber. But whether it really was him I don't know.'

'What makes you say that?' said Halloran.

'It's not the first time something like this has happened in Irendale. When I moved here a few years back one of me customers told me about a case they'd had that was almost identical and it was a police officer who'd done it,' said Liam. 'For all I know one of them's at it again and making sure Max Dunwell takes the fall. You can't trust anyone now, you know? Not even t' police.'

Halloran's shoulders clenched. Bailey had assured Halloran that he would look into all that Kerr had told them and find Kurt Goodchild's secret hideout, but Bailey wasn't particularly open to the idea that either Kurt or Kerr had anything to do with the current case and Halloran couldn't be sure he would push hard enough to get to the truth. Liam might be trying to deflect suspicion, of course, but either way he was right. You couldn't trust anyone. Kerr, or a police officer loyal to him, could still be behind this somehow.

'Well, we've obviously been in contact with DI Bailey over the break-in to the car,' Kitt said. 'He seems very good at what he does.'

'You're probably right,' Liam said, tearing a strip off the bottom of the form and handing it to Halloran along with a set of keys. 'I'm not in the best frame of mind and likely looking on the negative. Now, here's the keys to your courtesy car. It's a Nissan Micra, all in working order and should get you through the next few days no trouble. Just need the keys to your car so we can lock it up once we're done with it.'

'Thanks,' Halloran said, handing the keys to Liam.

The mechanic escorted them back out to the forecourt then and pointed them in the direction of their courtesy car.

Once inside, and once Liam had disappeared back into the garage, Halloran looked at Kitt. 'What did you think of his behaviour?'

'I'm not sure,' said Kitt. 'He does seem genuinely down about Amber's death. But that comment about the glovebox was interesting.'

'Agreed. Not to mention that remark about the late night and that crack about early retirement,' said Halloran. 'There was something not quite right about him.'

'It could just be grief.'

'Could be. I wish I could've pushed to find out where he was last night or get him to let something slip about the will, but there didn't seem to be an easy way to introduce it into the conversation without giving away that I suspected him.'

'I know the will seems incriminating but from what Bailey initially said nothing suspicious came up in his financial or phone records. And he has an alibi.'

'But there's also the lack of forced entry to consider. Liam might say he knew nothing about the will but if he's lying and saw a chance to profit big, he might have slipped someone the key to Amber's flat and hired them to do his dirty work. That's Bailey's current line of thought anyway. It's plausible that if he got paid in cash for some of the jobs at the garage he might be able to save enough to pay for that kind of job without anyone . . .'

Halloran paused and squinted at the car that was parked in front of theirs in the forecourt.

'What's the matter?' Kitt asked.

'That car in front,' Halloran said, 'near the number plate.'

Kitt frowned in the direction Halloran indicated and then her eyes widened.

Halloran whipped his phone out of his pocket and started dialling.

'Bailey?'

'Halloran, I assume this is important?'

'It is, I wouldn't have called you otherwise, but I thought you should know we've discovered some paint on a vehicle that matches the paint on the wall opposite the cottage.'

'I thought I asked you to leave this to us now?'

'Oh, we are, we were just at the garage picking up a courtesy car to ride home in and that's when we saw it.'

A sigh echoed down the receiver. 'You sure it's the same paint?'

'I'm certain. It's exactly the same colour. The vehicle in question is sitting in the forecourt at Liam Long's garage.'

'Bloody hell, if he's got some of that paint stashed with his fingerprints all over it that might be the physical evidence we need.'

'My thoughts exactly.'

'Well, whatever you do, don't approach the car. If Long's in on this somehow we want the element of surprise on our side. Can you get a clear photograph of the paint mark without drawing any attention to yourselves?'

'Yes, the car is parked right in front of ours so I've got a clear shot.'

'Great. Send the photo over to me and I'll run the plates, check that the car belongs to Liam and he's not working on it for someone in the village.'

'All right, I'll do that now.'

'And Halloran?'

'Yes?'

'After that, it's probably best you make your way straight home.'

'Yes . . . all right. I understand,' said Halloran, hanging up the phone.

Without a word he aimed his phone at the paint mark, zoomed in and snapped a few shots. They wouldn't be perfect, taken through the windscreen, but they were clear enough for the paint to be unmistakable. If the car did belong to Liam, and he tried to remove the evidence, his auto stamp app which logged the precise date and time a photo was taken would prove what he and Kitt had discovered.

'Mal, start the car,' said Kitt, an urgent note in her voice.

Halloran looked up to see Liam staring at them from the garage doorway. He started walking in their direction, possibly to ask if there was a problem with the car; possibly to ask why he was taking photographs of the car in front.

'Just smile as though everything's OK,' Halloran said,

turning the key in the ignition and manoeuvring the car around.

Halloran give Liam a little wave as he eased off the forecourt, not wanting Liam to think he was any rush. Liam's face was unreadable but he raised his hand in response to Halloran's gesture as they set off up the road. In his mirrors, Halloran could see Liam watching after them and couldn't help but worry that he had just accidentally tipped off the man responsible for Amber's death.

TWENTY-TWO

Halloran glanced over at Kitt in the passenger seat of the car as he pulled up at the T-junction. The sign to the left pointed back to Irendale while the sign to the right pointed to York. Halloran indicated right and tried to ignore the tears he could see forming in Kitt's eyes as they turned the corner onto the road home. They had spent most of last night and some of this morning talking about leaving the cottage and returning to York. She had been understanding about it, particularly after she had been attacked, but over the past few hours, despite his attempts to cheer and comfort her, her smile had not been as full, her wit not as quick and the light in her eyes had appeared somehow dimmed. Clearly, she was sad to leave without resolving the question of who murdered Amber Downing to her satisfaction. Despite the danger she'd encountered, she was getting a taste for this kind of work. An empty ache pulsed in his chest. He never should have let her get embroiled in this mess, his mess, in the first place. Halloran knew better than anyone the dark places that path led, so even though her spirits were low now, it was a price he was willing to pay to ensure she wasn't put in any further danger.

The message tone on Halloran's phone pinged.

'Check what that says for me, will you, pet?' said Halloran.

Kitt snatched Halloran's phone off the dashboard and tapped the screen a couple of times. 'It's from Bailey. The car with the red paint is registered to Liam. They're going to take him in for questioning. If an arrest is made he'll let you know.'

A moment's silence passed between them as they digested this information.

'Do you think we should go back?' she asked.

'No. I had some goodwill on my side when we arrived at the top of the week but that's not the case anymore. He can't afford to keep me around, getting in the way. This is Bailey's case now.'

'But what if they miss something you wouldn't?'

'They won't, pet. They've had the same training I've had.'

'But they haven't got your experience,' Kitt countered.

'Experience isn't always an advantage,' Halloran said, trying to keep the bitterness out of his tone. 'They'll go further back into Liam's financial and phone records and if there's anything to be found, they'll find it.'

'I hope you're right. Mal?'

Glancing at Kitt again, he saw she was looking out of the window, seemingly mesmerized by the blur of rugged rock and heather.

'Yes, pet?'

'How are things going to be when we get back?'

'How do you mean?'

'I mean,' Kitt's voice was close to breaking, 'I saw how you went at Goodchild yesterday and from the sound of it things got pretty heated between you and Kerr this morning.'

'I take protecting the people I love very seriously,' he said, as he turned another sharp bend in the road.

'I know that, and I understand your protective nature, but . . .'

'But, what?'

'Is this going to eat away at you? Wondering if somehow Kerr got away with murder again? If he was involved with Max, or Liam or Kurt or someone else in some way we haven't been able to get to the bottom of?'

'No,' Halloran replied, trying to sound confident even though his answer was based more on hope than anything else.

Kitt sighed. Her eyes lowered to her hands resting in her lap. She didn't believe him.

'Look, I thought coming up here, confronting Kerr, trying to get the truth myself would do some good. That's what heroes do in all the storybooks you're so fond of.'

'Books do generally insist that the truth sets you free,'

Kitt said, with a smile. Halloran suspected she wouldn't be able to resist perking up if books were mentioned.

'But the truth is, for the most part being back here has been close to agonizing and although I can't promise this is the end of the matter, I'm not sorry to be leaving. I suppose when all's said and done I'm not much of a hero.'

Kitt put a hand on Halloran's knee and stroked her way up to his thigh. 'You are to me. Coming up here was brave. Confronting things you'd sooner forget is no easy thing. I just wish you had let me in a bit more so I could help you through the agonizing bits. Bravery doesn't mean pretending everything is OK all the time.'

'Force of habit. I don't mean to. I know you feel shut out when I do.'

'Not just force of habit, love, force of patriarchal norms. You're taught vulnerability is weakness. It's sickening.'

'Don't remember signing up for Women's Studies 101,' Halloran couldn't help but tease.

'Oooh, will you give over,' Kitt said, giving his arm a playful tap. 'Wouldn't do anyone I know any harm if he did sign up for it.'

Halloran chuckled but then straightened his face again. 'The truth is, I don't trust myself up there. As you've probably guessed, I'm not in complete control.'

'That can be dangerous,' said Kitt.

'This whole trip has been dangerous, especially for you, and . . .'

'And what?'

'My mind was playing tricks on me.'

'What kind of tricks?' Kitt's voice was gentle, tender.

'Now and again, when I got angry, I thought I could smell Kamala's perfume.'

Kitt was quiet for a few moments, long enough to make him wonder if he had wounded her with his honesty. When she did at last speak, what she had to say surprised him.

'Mal, what you went through with Kamala was a trauma. There's no other accurate word for it and because of that you've got to expect some fallout when you come back to a place associated with that trauma.'

'Yes, but, smelling your ex-wife's perfume is pretty much a hallucination. Aren't you worried that I'm going mad? I know I am.'

Kitt gave his words a dismissive wave. 'Keep company with Grace and Ruby long enough and you become quite acclimatized to madness. What you experienced is perfectly natural and understandable. If it continues when we get back to York, just tell me and I'll do everything I can to help.'

Halloran let out a breath he wasn't aware he'd been holding and shook his head at Kitt.

'What?' she asked.

'Nothing, you're just an extraordinary woman.'

Kitt smiled and looked back at the view outside the

window. 'You're not the first to say it. But you might be the first to mean it as a compliment.'

'I doubt that,' said Halloran.

Kitt's phone buzzed.

'Hello, Grace, everything OK?' said Kitt. 'Oh . . . yes. Sorry. I meant to tell you, we're not looking into those names on the war memorial any more. I hope you didn't spend too long . . . Up till three a.m.? Oh dear, I *am* sorry. Things got a bit out of hand up here last night. Yes, I'll explain it all when I get back to York. All right, bye.'

'Forget to tell Grace we'd called off the investigation?'

'Yeah. She didn't sound too pleased about it. Six hours of research had turned up nothing for her. A bit of a waste of time. I should have got in touch with her sooner.'

'There are extenuating circumstances; you were attacked. I'm sure she'll forgive you.'

'Eventually, but she'll probably hold it over me for her own amusement for a good few months first.'

'There are worse things,' said Halloran, slowing for some sheep that were blithely congregating in the middle of a sharp bend in the road.

'Come on,' Halloran said, touching the horn a couple of times to disperse the flock. As he sped up again the car passed a heritage sign for a Saxon battle site. Not three seconds later, Kitt grabbed Halloran's arm so abruptly he jumped and swerved the car.

'Easy,' he said, correcting the steering wheel.

'Mal, turn the car around.'

'What? Why?' Halloran checked there was no one behind them and then brought the car to a stop. 'Did you forget something back at the let?'

'No, no, no.' Kitt shook her head quite furiously. 'I know what it means. The honour of war. We've got to go back to Irendale. We were looking in the wrong place. I know where the next clue is, or maybe even the answer to the whole puzzle. The identity of the killer.'

'Where?'

Kitt opened her mouth to speak but then closed it again, giving Halloran a suspicious glare. 'I'm not going to say where, I just want you to turn the car around.'

'Why won't you tell me?' Halloran asked, his tone somewhere between amusement and mild annoyance.

'Because if I tell you, you'll just say it's nothing and you won't turn the car around and then we'll never know.'

'But if you don't tell me, curiosity will get the better of me and I'll be forced to turn the car around?'

'Something like that,' Kitt said with a small smile.

'I really don't want to go back, pet. Not for something that may or may not pan out,' Halloran said, wondering what Bailey would do if they happened to cross paths with him.

'Mal, do you trust me?'

'What?'

'Do you trust me?'

He thought for a moment. In the seven months that he and Kitt had been together he'd been more honest and forthright about his thoughts, his wants and his needs than he had with any other partner before her. Even Kamala.

'Yes, I trust you.'

'Then turn the bloody car around.'

He reversed the car and made the U-turn back to Irendale, silently formulating theories about what Kitt's hunch might be and what might happen next if it paid off.

TWENTY-THREE

Halloran didn't exactly know why he was surprised when Kitt led him back to the library at Irendale. He should have known that that was the first place a librarian would head for answers. On entering the building, however, instead of heading left towards the book stacks, she veered right towards the archive.

'Just popping back to clear up a few more things with Meg,' Kitt told Pippa.

She gave an uncertain nod and watched as they pushed back through the door and into the corridor leading to the office.

'You think Amber left the next clue at her place of work?' Halloran said, still trying to work out exactly what Kitt's hunch was all about.

'In a manner of speaking,' Kitt said, knocking on the open office door to announce their presence to Meg. The archivist was sitting much as she had been last time: at her desk poring over some papers.

'Oh, it's you,' said Meg, jumping a little at Kitt's knock. 'Everything all right?'

'Is Mountjoy anywhere about?' Kitt said.

'No, he's on annual leave, think he said he was taking his wife to Whitby for the day,' said Meg. 'Why? Did you need to speak to him?'

'No,' Kitt said. 'But I'm afraid we're on the beg for help again. I wondered if you'd mind us taking a look around Amber's workspace?'

Meg frowned and looked over at the desk that used to be Amber's. 'Oooh, I don't know about that. Inspector Bailey's team have already done a sweep of it so it's just personal effects and Amber's family are coming through to collect them in a few days. They might not like people rummaging through them before they've had a chance. Besides that, Mountjoy specifically told me that I wasn't to say anything else to you. He said I could only talk to DI Bailey.'

'We wouldn't ask if it wasn't very important,' said Halloran.

'And I promise there'll be no rummaging. I just want to take that certificate down off the wall for a few minutes and inspect it.' Kitt indicated Amber's PhD qualification hanging in its gilt frame.

'Why?'

'I know this sounds strange but I won't really know why until I take a closer look at it.'

'You won't damage it?' said Meg, still a little uncertain.

'We'll be very careful,' said Kitt.

'All right,' said Meg. 'Sorry. I just – I'm just a bit nervous about seeing Amber's parents. Don't really know what I'm going to say to them and I just want everything to be right when they get here. Given you're still looking into this, I take it Max Dunwell wasn't the right man after all?'

'This certificate might answer that question once and for all,' said Kitt. 'It will only take a moment.'

Meg nodded then and gestured towards the wall.

Halloran handed Kitt a pair of latex gloves which she put on as she approached the wall. Reaching up, she removed the frame from its hook and looked hard at it. Halloran moved in for a closer look and on reading the text on the certificate he at once understood the connection Kitt had made. The certificate stated, as Meg had relayed, that Amber's specialism was in Anglo-Saxon conflicts – in other words, the certificate was an 'honour' related to 'war' . . .

Kitt lay the frame face down on Amber's desk and began unlatching the pins at the reverse. She removed the backing and looked carefully at what was behind it before letting out a little gasp.

'What is it?' he asked.

'It's a document,' said Kitt. 'Written in Old English.'

'Oh my God,' said Meg, her mouth hanging open. 'How on earth did you know this was here?'

'Amber led us to it,' said Kitt. 'She left little clues for us to follow.'

'That sounds like our Amber,' Meg said.

'Do you know what the document is?' Halloran asked.

The archivist shook her head. 'Hmmm, I don't think so. Can you lift it up to the light so I can get a better look?'

Kitt obliged, lifting the document which was written on parchment. 'Look at the illumination,' she said, pointing at a letter that vaguely resembled a capital T but had been illustrated with all sorts of loops and spirals.

'Looks sort of Celtic,' said Halloran.

'Well, Celtic is very influential in the history of language,' said Kitt, clearly in her element now. 'Though in the case of Old Brythonic, as far as I know, nobody can read it.'

'Thanks for the history lesson,' Halloran teased, though it was somewhat humbling to think that the document in front of him was written over a thousand years ago.

Meg pushed her face closer to the document, studying it. 'I've not seen this before,' she said.

'Why would Amber hide it?' asked Kitt.

'I don't know,' said Meg. 'I can think of a couple of possibilities but I'm not sure I want to pull too hard at this thread.'

'Why not?' asked Halloran.

'Well, one of them is innocent enough. It could be a

document that she bought fair and square, one that she kept behind her PhD certificate for sentimental value. Could have been a really important document in her research or something like that. But to be honest, that doesn't ring true at all. Amber was a big advocate of open data – you know, making historical and cultural documents accessible for everyone to enjoy. I can't really see her thinking it's a good idea to keep something hidden in a frame like this.'

'What's the other possibility?' asked Halloran.

'It's possible that Amber took this document and wanted to keep it to herself.'

'Took? You mean stole?' said Halloran.

'Well, yeah, but I've known her for a couple of years now and I really don't think she'd do that. It does happen, occasionally, in the archive business. Most people get into the job with the best of intentions – they want to preserve treasures for future generations to enjoy – so for the most part, stealing something for personal gain doesn't much enter into their heads.'

'But . . .' said Halloran.

'But, eventually, an archivist or a curator might stumble over something they love so much they want to keep it, and some of them have been known to take such things home with them. Technically, Amber didn't do that. It's still in the archive, just not filed as it should be. So, it's not so bad. I suppose we just don't know what her long-term plans were for it.'

'I can think of a third possibility,' said Kitt. 'Amber's flat had been turned over. The killer had been looking for something.'

'You . . . think they were looking for this?' said Meg. 'Not jewellery or money?'

'As far as we know, nothing of that sort was taken, even though Amber had a bit of it lying around,' said Halloran. 'Maybe this document is valuable in some way. Is that possible?'

'It could be,' said Meg, though she didn't sound sure. 'I mean, there are some documents that are valuable. But it would have to be something of great historical or cultural significance . . . Oh no!'

'What?' said Halloran.

'Oh no, oh no, oh no,' Meg continued, shaking her head and chewing on a fingernail.

'What's wrong?' Kitt pushed.

'Mountjoy,' said Meg. 'It might be nothing, surely he wouldn't . . .'

'What? Surely he wouldn't what?' said Halloran.

'The Monday after Amber died, Mountjoy came in here first thing. He conducted a thorough search of Amber's desk. I thought it was a bit much, but we know better than to challenge his behaviour. He has fired people for the flimsiest reasons in the past and he makes it clear on a regular basis we're all replaceable. I did find a way of casually asking him about it though and he just said that he wanted to make sure that Amber's parents didn't take away anything that belonged to the archive.'

'But now you think maybe he was looking for this?' said Halloran.

'I don't know. Though I still thought he was acting funny, when he explained himself it seemed fair enough to me. He's obsessed with keeping equipment and assets in check so it didn't seem out of character. But what if . . .?'

'What if this document is of some huge historical significance and Mountjoy wanted either the money or the prestige of being the one to bring it to the attention of the world,' said Kitt.

'If it was found at the archive he oversees wouldn't he get the prestige anyway?' said Halloran.

'Probably,' said Kitt. 'But maybe he wanted to profiteer from the document privately somehow.'

'And so Amber hid it from him so he couldn't profit from it,' said Halloran. 'Can you read it? Maybe there's a clue in the text as to whether or not it's worth something. Whether it would really be worth someone going to that amount of trouble for.'

'Mmm . . . bits and pieces,' said Meg, looking closely at the document again. 'But nothing stands out as unusual or special. There are some references to land but that's all I can make out. I'm afraid Amber was the Anglo-Saxon specialist. I studied prehistoric culture, so I don't think I can be much help on that score.'

'What about your colleagues, then? Is there anyone else here who could help us decipher the document?' asked Kitt.

Meg squinted. 'Your best bet is probably to take it over to the Airedale Museum.'

'What?' Kitt said. Her voice had a shrill note to it, though Halloran couldn't guess why. 'Isn't there another way? I mean, that's a bit of a drive from here. There must be someone between here and there that can give us a sense of what the document is.'

'I'm sorry, not that I know of,' said Meg, frowning. 'If you hang around a little bit I can take a few photos of the document and email it to some colleagues who might be able to help. We might get lucky and save you a trip but I can't promise anything. It depends who's in office. Who's picking up the phone this afternoon. This is an in-depth translation. It's quite a specific skill.'

'Why don't we just go to the Airedale if it's our best bet, pet?' Bailey had made it quite clear the pair weren't welcome in Irendale so pursuing a lead elsewhere seemed like a good compromise. Especially if this document did turn out to be the thing the killer was looking for. Bailey would perhaps forgive some of Halloran's previous misdemeanours if he had some concrete evidence to bring to the table.

But Kitt was hesitating over something. There was a red flush building around her neck. She was doing her best to act casual even though something was clearly bothering her. 'I just think it's a long way to go,' she said.

'Can't we email the photos to whoever you know in Airedale?' said Halloran. 'Save going all the way out there? If we're going to confront someone as powerful as Mountjoy, it would be good to be armed with all the information.'

'Ordinarily you could just email some photographs but the Anglo-Saxon specialist there isn't the most generous academic known to mankind,' said Meg. 'He'll probably take quite a bit of persuasion if you want help. Going in person with a police officer in tow would probably be enough to sway him, though.'

'All right, how about this? Try your luck with your contacts first while we report this finding to DI Bailey. If by the time we get back you haven't had any luck, we'll go out to the Airedale Museum and talk to this specialist. What did you say their name was?'

'Theodore Dent,' Meg said.

'Theodore . . .' Halloran repeated and then, realizing why he knew that name, he stared at Kitt. Theo. An ex-boyfriend from ten years ago, a man who by Kitt's own confession had broken her heart and caused her years of pain. He was their only immediate hope of getting this document translated?

'Er,' Halloran said, looking back at Meg. 'You sure there isn't anyone else we could go to about this?'

TWENTY-FOUR

'Sir, I thought we had an understanding,' said DI Bailey, slumping down on a chair in his office at Eskdale Police Station. He sighed and looked between Halloran and Kitt.

'We did, lad,' said Halloran. 'I don't want to be here anymore than you want me here, but on the way back to York, Kitt had an epiphany of sorts, and well . . .' Halloran produced an evidence bag containing the strange document they had uncovered and handed it to Bailey.

The inspector looked at the document for a moment and then back at Halloran. 'What the hell's this?'

'We think it's what the killer turned Amber's flat upside down for.'

'You think?'

'We won't know for sure, until we get a full translation.'

'Where did you find it?'

'Hidden behind a university certificate in Amber's office. Apparently the nearest academic able to do a translation,

Theodore Dent, works over at the Airedale Museum and we'll need to see him in person.'

'You leaving Irendale for Pontefract seems like a good idea to me,' said Bailey.

'Look, I know I've made some mistakes, but this is where Amber's clues have led us. There's a chance this document is valuable and that its contents are what she was killed for.'

'A chance. Do you know how difficult it's been to explain to my superintendent some of the things that have gone down while I've been working this case?'

'I can imagine your superiors being less than thrilled about a couple of things, yes,' said Halloran, thinking back to times when he had tried to persuade his superiors to go down a particular investigative track and failed to inspire their support.

'Even if I wanted to, and I'm not saying I do, I can't go chasing over to Pontefract right now. We found Goodchild's hideout and it was just as Kerr said, there was nothing in there except rusting farm equipment, so now we've got to turn all our focus on Liam, especially after the paint you found on his car.'

'You don't have to go over to Pontefract with us, we could just go and check it out and report back to you,' said Halloran.

'And if something goes wrong? Who ends up copping for it? It's my investigation, so it'll be me. Maybe if you'd proven yourself a little bit more reliable we could have worked together on this but I haven't got much time for wild theories about ancient documents and clues right now.'

Halloran lowered his eyes. It was true that they had caused Bailey more than enough trouble and put his investigation at risk. After what happened at the prison and after various other dead ends he and Kitt had led Bailey to, it was highly likely he'd had an official dressing-down about the state of this case. Still, Halloran couldn't just leave it. They had stumbled across something real here. Something the victim had seen fit to hide and leave a trail to. It wasn't something to be ignored.

'We can't get into much trouble just by driving over to a museum and getting an academic to look at a document. We won't even take the real thing with us so there'll be no chance of it going missing if it is important. We'll just take a few photographs and show them to our contact in Pontefract. If we've nothing to report back, you don't lose anything. If it turns out the document is important to the case, like we agreed before, you can take all the credit.'

Bailey shrugged. 'If you want to follow it and find out where it leads, I'm not going to stop you, so long as you stay out of the village and let me lead my own investigation here.'

'I see,' said Halloran.

'Look, it's not that I'm unsympathetic. But you know as well as I do that the first few days of any murder investigation are crucial and while you've been here it's felt a little bit like we've been led round in circles.'

'You're right,' Halloran said. 'We have been led. Someone in the village has led us to believe that Amber's murder had something to do with Kerr's serial murders five years ago. Out of all of us, I've been the easiest led, and I'm sorry for that. But now it seems it was all about this document.'

'Well, we can't know that for sure,' said Bailey.

'No, but I can't think Amber was hiding this document just for the hell of it. The question is, who would have an interest in a historical document?'

'And I suppose you have someone in mind?' said Bailey.

'Sir Sebastian,' said Kitt.

'Ohhh, are you cracked? You can't go after Mountjoy,' said Bailey, 'you haven't got a shred of evidence. His lawyers will crucify you.'

'No one said anything about going after him,' said Halloran, hoping Kitt would go along with the story he was about to sell. If Bailey had lost faith in him the best thing was to play things down and hope that the officer would get to the point where he'd do anything to get him out of his hair. 'But he is a curator and will have some interest in this document. He might even know something about it. Like who else might be after it. The document was found in his archive, after all. You agreed that he runs a very tight ship. If it's that tight, he'll know about everything that goes on there.'

'So, you just want to ask him a few questions about this document?'

'Yes, just find out if he recognizes it. See if it's worth going out to Pontefract for or whether we should just go home and leave you to it. When all is said and done he's an expert, and if it's not worth bothering about he might save us some trouble. I've no intention of ruffling Mountjoy's feathers. If anything, I'll underline how helping us find the person who murdered one of his employees will reflect very well on him.'

'I suppose, if you're polite and by the book, I can't stop you asking him some questions but given recent experience, you can't claim any association with us. We've already had Mountjoy on the phone once in the past few days and he's not the kind of bloke you want to make an enemy out of.'

'Fair enough,' said Halloran. 'I really hope that paint we discovered on Liam's car helps, and goes some way to making up for the trouble I've caused.'

Bailey nodded. 'The car is registered to Liam but his story is that it's a brand new mark that could only have been made on the car either last night or this morning. Said he would've noticed it if it 'ad been there yesterday.'

'And you believe him?'

'We won't need to,' said Bailey. 'He's got cameras on the forecourt and we've got an officer down there now retrieving last night's footage. If what he says is right, we should 'ave the damage recorded on camera. If he's lying to us, we'll know very soon.'

'If you've caught the culprit on camera, that would be a

major break,' said Kitt, excitement rising in her voice. 'You could have video footage of the murderer trying to cover their tracks.'

Bailey, who seemingly had no grievance with Kitt, looked at her and smiled. 'That's the hope, Ms Hartley. But I'm afraid you'll have to excuse me now. I really do have to get on with this case. As you say, we could be close to a breakthrough.'

'Before we go, perhaps you could do us one last favour and triangulate Mountjoy's phone for us,' said Halloran.

Bailey shook his head. 'I can't be doing that, sir. I told you, if you go and question Mountjoy you're doing it alone. We've not got any concrete reason to contact him right now.'

'But you only know about the paint on Liam Long's car, and Max Dunwell, because of us,' said Halloran. 'Couldn't you do this one favour for us in return?'

'After the way you carried on with Kerr and the reports of how you were with Goodchild, I'm afraid you're out of favours with me.'

Halloran nodded and went to stand. Kitt, however, remained seated.

'If Halloran is out of favours, then do it as a favour to me,' said Kitt.

'I can't do that—'

'Please,' Kitt said. 'The longer we spend up here the more difficult it is for both of us. I don't think I need to explain to you why that is. We can't leave until this is resolved. Mountjoy might be the key to understanding this document and its relation to Amber's death. His colleague said he was in Whitby but it could take us ages to find him on foot – it's very easy to miss someone down those winding back streets. Won't you do us this one kindness and at least give us a sense of the area he's in?'

TWENTY-FIVE

Halloran turned the courtesy car down a side track off the main road out of Kildale. The track was overgrown with summer foliage. White cotton grass waved in the low breeze while alder and oak trees created a secluded canopy above, making it the perfect hideaway for anyone who was up to something they shouldn't be.

'Are you sure it's worth looking down here?' Kitt said as the car went over a bump big enough to jolt both of them out of their seats.

'There isn't much to Kildale. If Mountjoy is still here, this is the last place I can think we might find him,' said Halloran. He hadn't been surprised when the triangulation had placed Mountjoy a good twenty-five miles away from where he said he'd be in Whitby but he'd played it down in front of Bailey, suggesting that maybe he'd taken his wife for a picnic in Kildale before going on to the coast. Deep down, however, Halloran suspected that Mountjoy had some reason for deliberately misleading his work colleagues about where he was going that afternoon. Coupled with the fact that he'd searched Amber's desk at the first opportunity, this deception only lent more weight to the idea that Mountjoy was up to something, and that it had to do with the document Amber had led them to.

'I thought you wanted to know what the document said before we approached Mountjoy, anyway?' said Kitt. 'Or were you just playing down how much you suspected Mountjoy in front of Meg?'

'There's a bit of that,' said Halloran. 'Knowing my luck she'd have started gossiping about it with Pippa and someone who wanted to get into Mountjoy's good books would have called him and given him a head's up. But no, it's not totally that. I decided on a Plan B.'

'Which is?'

'Tantalize Mountjoy with the document and see if we can goad him into doing something stupid that lets us know he's after it.'

'Sounds . . . risky.'

'It is a bit,' said Halloran, 'but it's a risk that I think is worth taking.'

The path curved to the right, and as it did so a red Porsche slid into view, parked at the side of the track, part-camouflaged by the greenery.

'Bingo,' said Halloran, looking at the number plate that read S3B 4 J0Y.

'A personalized number plate,' Kitt said. 'Now I know he's a suspicious character.'

Smiling, Halloran pulled over to the other side of the track and watched the car for a moment. There was movement inside, coming from the back seat. Occasionally, bare flesh flashed in the rear window and from the way the car was rocking there were no prizes for guessing what might be going on inside.

'I'll bet you a thousand pounds that's not his wife in there with him,' said Kitt.

'There's no way I'm taking that bet,' Halloran said, opening the car door.

'Where are you going?' Kitt said, a note of alarm in her voice.

'To question Mountjoy.'

'Now?'

'Yes.'

'Shouldn't you wait until . . . after? We probably won't have to wait very long . . .'

Halloran shook his head and chuckled. 'So I can wait until he's contented and full of himself? No thanks. If I intervene now the odds are he'll be so shocked at being caught in a compromising position he'll be much more cooperative.'

Sighing and shaking her head, Kitt unbuckled her seatbelt and followed him. As they approached, it was possible to hear a woman giggling.

Halloran tapped hard on the tinted window, averting his

eyes as much as possible. He wanted the tactical advantage of catching Sir Sebastian Mountjoy in the act, but he didn't need to see it. There were some things in this world that once seen could not be unseen.

The woman inside the car shrieked. There was some more shuffling around, the creaking of leather seats, and then the window opened a crack. Sir Sebastian's beady dark eyes peered out.

'DI Halloran, what are you doing here?' Though Halloran couldn't see Mountjoy's whole face he could tell he had said those words through gritted teeth.

'I *was* out for a lovely stroll across the moorland with my girlfriend,' said Halloran. 'But your cavorting has put an end to that. I must admit I'm surprised to see you here. Word at the village is that you'd taken your wife to Whitby for the day.'

Mountjoy's eyes narrowed. 'Why don't you mind your own business?'

'You do know outraging public decency carries a hefty fine?' Halloran pushed.

'Money, I've got,' came Sir Mountjoy's reply.

'That's true,' said Kitt. 'But no amount of money can rebuild a reputation once it's ruined and the local papers would have a field day with this kind of behaviour.'

'Can't you both just keep your mouths shut?' Mountjoy snapped, an edge creeping into his voice.

'I'm sorry sir. I can't neglect my duty. This will have to

be reported. Good day to you.' Halloran turned as though about to walk away.

'Wait, wait, wait!' said Mountjoy. Enough shuffling ensued that Halloran could tell Sir Sebastian was putting his trousers back on. Halloran tried not to dwell on the fact he'd just been having a conversation with a trouser-less Mountjoy but a moment later the car door swung open. Mountjoy was still buckling his belt and even the sight of that was enough to turn Halloran's stomach.

The young blonde woman sitting in the back of the car opened the window on her side and lit a cigarette.

'Now, look here,' said Mountjoy. 'I don't know why you're trying to cause trouble for me but I'm not the kind of person you want to be on the wrong side of.'

'I'm not in the business of making enemies, I'm merely doing my duty, sir,' said Halloran, wondering if Amber had managed to get on the wrong side of Mountjoy and whether that was why she was no longer alive.

'Then there must be some arrangement we can come to,' said Mountjoy, his voice taking on a sly quality. 'It will do no good if this afternoon becomes common knowledge; all it will do is upset my wife and I'm sure you wouldn't want that.'

Halloran tried to suppress a grimace. That kind of attitude was so typical of the likes of Mountjoy. He was the one responsible for any grief his wife suffered but he'd rather deflect that onto the people who caught him out.

'I would take no pleasure in upsetting your wife, sir,' said Halloran.

'Mal, maybe Sir Sebastian can help you with that question you had,' said Kitt with a knowing smile. 'Hardened criminals make deals with the police all the time. Surely someone as upstanding as Sir Sebastian could be given a pardon for a minor indiscretion if he provided a bit of information for you.'

Mountjoy licked his fingers and ran them over his toupee in an attempt to straighten out the mess he'd made of it in the back seat. 'Your good lady talks a lot of sense, DI Halloran. Though her affiliation with you does make me question her tastes, she at least recognizes good breeding when she sees it.'

Halloran didn't dare look at Kitt. If he did one or both of them would probably laugh at how officious Mountjoy was and right now they had to play their parts straight.

'Now that Kitt mentions it, there is something regarding Amber's case that we've been puzzling over and over. I think you might be able to help us with it. In fact, I don't know why we didn't think to ask you sooner, given your intellect and historical specialism.'

Mountjoy eyed Halloran and for a moment he thought he'd laid it on a bit thick but then Mountjoy burst into a broad smile. 'I am rather unsurpassed when it comes to my intellect. What's the puzzle? If it guarantees your discretion over this afternoon, I'll be more than happy to help.'

'We've uncovered a document that we think Amber was trying to hide away, but we can't figure out why.'

'What? What kind of document?' Mountjoy said, his whole posture straightening. 'Uncovered where?'

'It's written in Old English,' said Kitt.

'Oh,' said Mountjoy, his shoulders sagging in what looked like relief. 'So it's something from the archive?'

'We're not sure,' said Kitt. 'Because it's related to the case, it's currently sitting in the evidence room at Eskdale station, but we did take some photographs of it. Here.' The librarian offered her phone to Mountjoy and he scrolled through the images.

'Does it look familiar?' said Halloran, watching Mountjoy's reactions with care.

Mountjoy shook his head. 'It's not one I'm familiar with. Where did you say you found it?'

'It was hanging in a frame above Amber's desk, tucked behind her PhD certificate,' said Kitt.

'Was it now?' said Mountjoy, a frown settling across his brow. 'Are you telling me Amber stole this document from the archive?'

'We don't know,' said Halloran. 'We can't discount it as a possibility, but until we know what the document actually is it's perhaps not wise to point the finger at a dead woman.'

'Can you translate it?' said Kitt.

'Me? Oh, heavens no. I hired Amber as the Anglo-Saxon specialist. I'm very good with my Latin but Old English is not something I can translate with any degree of accuracy, I'm afraid.'

'Do you know anyone else in the region who might be able to decipher it for us then?' asked Kitt. 'Meg says the nearest person who can help us works at the Airedale Museum.'

'Yes, yes, yes. That sounds right to me,' said Mountjoy.

'I see,' said Halloran with a sigh. If Meg didn't come up with someone else to translate this document, a drive to the Airedale Museum would be inevitable.

'If that's all your questions, Inspector, perhaps I should return to my companion?' said Mountjoy.

'I did have one more question, actually. Call it a bonus favour since you weren't able to shed any light on the document we uncovered.'

'What do you want?' Mountjoy said, his face at once hardening.

'We have it on good authority that right after Amber's murder you searched her desk. Can you explain that?'

'She's an employee, I've got every right to search her desk.' Mountjoy was beginning to bluster. 'She could have had anything of import in those drawers. Things that belonged to the archive and had to stay at the archive.'

'The thing about having been a police inspector for as long as I have,' said Halloran, looking Mountjoy's reddening face up and down, 'is that you can tell with absolute certainty when a person is lying to you. And right now, Sir Sebastian, you are not being truthful with me.'

'It is the truth,' said Mountjoy.

'All right, have it your way. Looks like I'll have to file that report after all,' Halloran said, turning to walk away.

'All right. All right. All right,' Mountjoy said.

Halloran turned back to face him and waited.

The man was pulling so hard at his toupee Halloran wondered if he was about to accidentally rip it off.

'I was looking to see if Amber had anything in her personal effects that concerned me.'

'Like what?' Halloran said.

'Like a note or a diary entry or anything like that.'

'Why would there be anything about you in Amber's diary?' said Kitt.

'You didn't threaten Amber, did you?' said Halloran.

'Threaten? What kind of man do you take me for? No, I did not threaten the girl. But we did share a secret of sorts. We were . . . intimate with each other, just the once, around the time she was hired.'

Halloran frowned. 'Around the time she was hired or just before she was hired?'

'I'm sure I don't know what you—'

'I'll be clearer. Did you hire Amber on the condition that she had sex with you?'

'That's a sordid way to put it,' said Mountjoy. 'I could see from the moment she walked into my office that she was in awe of my experience and intellect, I merely took her up on an offer she was too shy to make. A man can't be blamed for that, can he?'

Halloran curled his lip at Mountjoy. There was a lot he wanted to say in answer to that but if he went off at Mountjoy and caused trouble for Bailey it might well be the end of his career. He had to at least try to keep his cool. 'And you thought Amber might have left something incriminating in her desk?'

'Well, I never expected her to die like that,' said Mountjoy. 'I didn't know what kind of things she kept in that desk. I had to be sure my wife wouldn't find out. That nothing would come to light about it.'

'Perhaps it would be easier to protect your wife if you weren't constantly going behind her back,' said Halloran.

'There's no need to be rude, Inspector, I've answered all of your questions.'

'Yes,' said Halloran, 'I suppose you have. I will have to report your involvement with Amber to DI Bailey but as long as that's as far as your relationship went, your wife will never know.'

Mountjoy sighed in relief. 'Thank you. Now, if you don't mind, I was in the middle of something rather important.'

Without an ounce of compunction, Mountjoy opened the car door once again and slid in beside his mistress. Not wishing to witness any more than they already had of Mountjoy's indiscretions, Kitt and Halloran turned their back on the vehicle and walked towards their own.

'Can you really tell one hundred per cent of the time when a person is lying to you?' Kitt asked as they got back into the car.

'Why? Are you planning some grand deception?' Halloran said, half-smiling at her.

'No,' Kitt chuckled. 'But it might make planning a surprise birthday party for you more problematic than I anticipated.'

'Of course I can't always tell,' said Halloran. 'I mean, I can most of the time but there's always someone who gets one over on you.'

'Good job Mountjoy didn't suss out your bluff,' said Kitt. 'You believe him then?'

'I think so, for now at least. It seems plausible that it was his manipulation of Amber he was trying to cover up all this time rather than his role in Amber's murder. But either way we'll know soon enough. If he is after that document he knows it's at Eskdale Police Station now and if he makes any kind of play to get his hands on it, we'll know he is more involved in this than he's letting on.'

Kitt shivered. 'I sort of hope Mountjoy isn't the murderer. Imagine that face being the last face you ever see.'

'Doesn't bear thinking about,' said Halloran.

Kitt's mobile chimed.

'Oh – that's a text message from Meg. She hasn't managed to find anyone to translate the document,' Kitt said, her eyes widening as they looked into Halloran's.

'All right,' said Halloran, trying to remind himself that the case was more important than anything else just now. 'I hate to say this but I think it might be time to ring Theo.'

TWENTY-SIX

The Airedale Museum was an eighteenth-century Georgian sandstone building on the outskirts of Pontefract. With its tall pillars, ornate windows and Latin engravings, to Halloran's mind it was an intimidating building to look at and he didn't expect it to feel any less intimidating on the inside.

'How did you know Theo worked here, again?' Halloran asked Kitt as they approached the stone steps up to the entrance. He was doing all he could to keep his tone casual, but knowing how good Kitt was at reading him, he was prepared for her to see straight through that. 'Have you been in touch with him since I saw him at the library that night?'

'No,' said Kitt. 'Just before he turned up at the library that time I caught an accidental glimpse of his Facebook profile and saw he worked here.'

Halloran wondered how someone got an 'accidental glimpse' of someone's Facebook page but decided not to push the subject. He trusted Kitt to do right by him and hopefully she trusted him too.

As soon as they entered the museum he clapped eyes on the man he had hoped neither he nor Kitt would ever see again. He had only fleetingly seen Theo when he'd visited Kitt at the library about seven months before. She'd been in a right old state after Theo had left, and from what she said he'd tried to beg her back. Even though he had failed, Halloran's jaw tightened at the prospect of putting Kitt in his path once again.

Halloran eyed Theo as they approached. He was standing by the main reception desk as he and Kitt had agreed. He was the kind of bloke one could easily imagine Kitt going for. Thick glasses. Black Converse. A dark grey blazer that would no doubt have elbow patches sewn into them in a few years' time. He had the bookish look going for him and with a specialism in Anglo-Saxon history, there was no question he was educated in a way that Halloran simply wasn't. Inwardly, he cursed himself for not finding another way to get a translation on this text. He should have gone back to the archive and pushed Meg harder to find someone else in her contacts, or asked her for the next closest specialist in this field. He wanted to solve this case, of course, but now that Kitt and Theo were actually in the same room again he realized he'd sooner have driven to Land's End than put his intellectual girlfriend within twenty feet of this guy.

Kitt had called through to the Airedale Museum from the car after they had left Kildale. Halloran had secretly hoped Theo wouldn't be in the office that day. But of course, there had been no such luck. Theo was in the office and, despite what Meg had said about him not being a generous academic, he had seemed very enthusiastic indeed, from what he could hear of his and Kitt's conversation. Halloran wagered that for the chance of seeing Kitt again he would have agreed to anything she asked of him.

'Hello, Theo,' Kitt said, offering him a polite nod. 'I don't think you've properly met Inspector Halloran.'

Theo's brown eyes riveted on the inspector. He looked him up and down and then extended a hand which Halloran ensured he shook a little too firmly.

'Good to meet you,' Theo said, before turning his full attentions back to Kitt. 'I'll admit, you've got me intrigued with this one.'

Kitt didn't smile at Theo's attempt to rebuild the bridge between them. 'I need you to be serious about this, Theo. A lot is riding on us being able to understand what the document is.'

'Come on up to my office,' Theo said. 'I'll be able to hook your phone up to my PC and look at the photos on there. It'll be easier to read on a bigger screen.'

Kitt gestured for Theo to lead the way and he turned to a grand curved staircase just behind him. Two flights later, they turned into an office covered in floor-to-ceiling bookshelves. Halloran noticed an unmistakable light in her eyes as they entered.

'What a wonderful space. These books look well organized,' she said approvingly.

Halloran, who hadn't expected to have to compete with an ex-boyfriend over the size of his bookshelves any time soon, made a mental note to order some for his spare room the moment they returned to York. He didn't have a lot of books to fill them with but had an idea that Kitt would be more than happy to help him with that.

'It's because I've been working here since the beginning of time,' said Theo with a light chuckle. 'When you settle in somewhere it makes sense to get the space how you want it.'

'I agree with you there,' said Kitt as Theo walked over to his computer. Kitt handed over the phone. It only took a moment or two for Theo to hook it up to the USB port and scroll through the files. 'There are . . . some nice shots of you two on here.'

Halloran smiled, knowing his beard would camouflage much of the smugness. It wouldn't do Theo any harm to see seven months' worth of photos they'd snapped on various outings and dinners.

'I don't need you looking through the whole back catalogue of photographs, thank you,' said Kitt, grabbing the mouse off him. 'Here. These are the shots of the documents.'

Theo smirked at Kitt taking over the mouse and playfully snatched it back. Kitt merely rolled her eyes in response and stepped away from the computer, giving him some space to read. Halloran imagined that if they didn't need Theo's help right now, he'd be getting a much sterner response than an eye roll.

Theo was quiet for a few minutes. his eyes scanning the images and, with a bit of luck, deciphering the text. He read slowly at first but then a minute later his eyes were flitting back and forth across the screen at a furious rate and a frown deepened across his brow. 'Oh . . . my . . . God. Kitt. Where did you find this?'

'What? What is it?' asked Kitt.

Theo tore his eyes away from the screen and looked up at her. Then he was standing, pacing, holding a hand over his mouth, then looking back at the screen again.

'Theo, come on, stop messing about – out with it,' said Kitt.

'I'm sorry, I just can't quite believe it.'

'What?' Halloran pushed, losing patience. Not that he had had any with this particular individual to begin with.

'Clovesho,' Theo said, looking only at Kitt.

'Clovesho?' Halloran repeated, trying to establish Theo's attention.

'What about it?' said Kitt. 'Is it mentioned in the document?'

'Not just mentioned,' said Theo. 'This document points to a map that leads straight to where the councils took place . . . Do you know what this means?'

Halloran raised his hand. 'Er, I don't.'

'This is one of the most important historic discoveries of the last few hundred years. This document – that map, they're priceless,' said Theo.

'Oh my God,' Kitt said, laughing and jumping up and down on the spot. Theo joined in her laughter and grabbed hold of her hands in what appeared to be elation.

'What is Clovesho?' Halloran asked.

'I'm surprised you haven't heard of it,' Theo said with a thin smile on his face.

'Don't be daft, Theo, there's no reason why he would,' said Kitt, releasing her hands from Theo's and turning to Halloran. 'The Councils of Clovesho are legendary. They were essentially meetings that took place between Anglo-Saxon nobles.'

'Kings, bishops, you name it – if they were important then they came along to these meetings,' Theo explained.

'I am surprised I didn't notice that word in the document, though,' said Kitt, almost pouting. 'I was poring over those pictures on the way here but I didn't recognize the word Clovesho.'

'It's because you're only familiar with its most common spelling. In the document it's spelt as Clofeshoch.'

'What's so special about these councils? Why is the document so important?' Halloran asked.

'The exact location of the gatherings has never been confirmed. We just haven't had the evidence. Some scholars believe that the councils were held somewhere in the Midlands but obviously that's a broad area. The exact location of the councils has been one of the biggest mysteries in Anglo-Saxon history and this document solves the mystery. Given the fact that all of the attendees were rich nobles, there's a strong chance that there is a treasure hoard just sitting there waiting to be discovered. Gold, historical artefacts, the lot,' said Theo.

TWENTY-SEVEN

Halloran took in a deep sigh, trying to digest what Theo had just told him.

'So let me get this straight,' said Halloran. 'This document leads to a map and the map points to where these special meetings of Clovesho took place?'

'Exactly.'

'And so this document is valuable because of its historic relevance?'

'Yes, there's that. But the site of the meetings is likely to be an archaeological goldmine. Possibly quite literally. I mean, if we get a team of archaeologists down to the site, wherever it is, who knows what they'll find there?' Theo said.

'So when you said this document was priceless, we are genuinely talking millions here?' asked Kitt.

'Oh, without a doubt. There will be museums and private collectors who would pay an outrageous amount of money to get their hands on it.'

'Sylvia Wise's fifty grand Scrabble jackpot sort of pales in comparison,' said Halloran.

'Not half,' said Kitt, still smiling from the jubilation of what they had discovered.

'Who?' said Theo.

'I think we've got our true motive for the murder now,' said Halloran quickly, not about to let Theo in on their joke.

'But we still don't know why Amber didn't declare this discovery to the world rather than waiting for someone to kill her over it,' said Kitt.

'It is strange,' said Halloran. 'If she had gone public with it the killer couldn't have killed her for it. It would be public knowledge that she had found it and therefore couldn't be sold on for profit by anyone else.'

'All right, let's break this down,' Kitt mused. 'Somehow, Amber comes across this document in her research. Being a specialist in the field, she knows immediately the significance of what she's uncovered.'

'Before telling the world, however, she shares the news with someone close to her. Someone she trusts to share in the excitement,' said Halloran.

'But instead of being excited about the discovery of the document, that person starts talking about profiteering from it, which Meg told us was totally against Amber's moral standpoint when it comes to historical artefacts,' said Kitt.

'Then, for some reason that we're yet to understand, she

doesn't announce the discovery, which would stop the killer profiting from it. Instead, she decides to hide the document so that this person can't profit from something she believes belongs to everyone,' said Halloran.

'Furious, the killer starts threatening her,' said Kitt. 'The threats get so serious, she starts to fear for her life. But there's no evidence of the threats, they're all verbal, and she knows it's the killer's word against hers.'

'So she tries to find ways of protecting herself. She buys a gun on the dark web,' said Halloran.

'A gun? Bloody hell,' said Theo, 'you might have mentioned that before you dragged me into this.'

'Oh, stop fussing,' said Kitt. 'You're not in any danger in the ivory towers of the Airedale Museum.'

'In case she dies, she leaves some clues to the whereabouts of the document in the hope that whoever works her case will solve the puzzle and uncover it,' Halloran continued, doing all he could to ignore Theo's outburst. He swallowed hard then, digesting what this meant about the other theories he'd had. 'If this is the case, the similarities to the murders Kerr committed were staged to throw us off the scent. There's no way Kerr could know about that document, and it's unlikely Kurt did.'

'Which means the guitar strings that link Max Dunwell to the murder might also be a smokescreen, although it would probably still mean it had to be someone in the village. Someone who knew Amber; someone who also knew Max Dunwell murdered Oasis songs every Friday night,' said Kitt.

'Given the paint we discovered earlier, it could be Liam,' said Halloran. 'He had an intimate relationship with Amber. She might have told him about the discovery she made and how much the document was worth.'

'He did pass some comment this morning,' said Kitt. 'About not wanting to do his job for ever. What if he thought that document was the key to his early retirement?'

'We know he had a key to Amber's flat and there was no forced entry,' Halloran said with a nod.

'He may have got an accomplice to murder Amber but what if Liam's the thief? And the person who attacked me last night?'

'You were attacked?' Theo said. 'By who?'

'If we knew that for sure, they'd be in a police cell,' said Kitt.

Theo glared at Halloran. He didn't say anything but it was obvious what he was wondering: how could Halloran let something like this happen to Kitt on his watch? Pretty rich from the man who abandoned Kitt for over a decade before bothering to get back in touch.

'Liam knew about the murders Kerr committed,' said Kitt. 'He saw us when we arrived and must have guessed what brought us to town. He could have easily followed us in a range of different vehicles because he's got so many sitting on the forecourt at his garage. If he did attack me last night, he would have known just what to say to make us think Amber's murder was somehow linked with the murders that happened here five years ago.'

'This is all true,' said Halloran. 'But there is something that doesn't add up with this theory. If Liam was the killer, and Amber suspected he was going to kill her at any moment, why didn't she ask for the key back or change the locks on him? Why spend over a thousand pounds on a gun and not just spend a fraction of that on changing the locks?'

'I see your point,' said Kitt. 'Even if she asked Liam to hand it back and he wouldn't give it up, any sane person would change the locks before buying a gun on the dark web.'

'It seems Amber either let in a person who was going to kill her, in the hope of defending herself with the gun, or gave the killer their own key. Neither of which make much sense, if you ask me.'

'Obviously I'm only following half of this and may be speaking out of turn, but there are actually a couple of possibilities that solve one or both of the questions you can't answer,' Theo said, while he could get a word in edgeways.

Halloran glared at him, but Theo had the advantage of fresh eyes. Though it killed him to admit it, there was a chance he'd seen something they hadn't.

'Go on,' said Halloran.

'Well, the first thing to consider is that she was scared to go public about the document for some reason. If I'd discovered this document I would be shouting it from the rooftops at the earliest opportunity. There must have been something stopping her from doing that because this is seriously huge. Maybe Amber's not as innocent in all this as we'd like to think. Maybe she didn't come across the document in a completely honest fashion, for example.'

'How do you mean?' said Kitt. 'You think Amber stole the document from someone else rather than discovered it?'

'Possibly. If it wasn't really her discovery then she would know the person who had discovered it first would come after her if she went public.'

'But wouldn't that person just go to the police about the theft?' said Kitt.

'If it's such a valuable document, I think they would,' said Halloran. 'But perhaps that depends on what they had to hide. She took part in a fleeting affair with Mountjoy, though how willing a participant she was in that I don't know. She might have stolen the document from him to spite him after he took advantage. Another question to consider is, if she was willing to go to bed with Mountjoy to forward her career, what else might she do?'

'Wait. Amber had an affair with Sebastian Mountjoy?' said Theo.

'It's *Sir* Sebastian now,' Halloran corrected. 'Do you know him?'

'Aye, I've crossed paths with him a couple of times. We're in a similar field of study and we attend a lot of the same annual conferences. I try to avoid him because to be honest he hasn't got a clue what he's talking about, save a bit of Latin he learnt at school, but it's not always possible.'

'Well, I can understand the urge to avoid him,' said Halloran. 'Maybe he has some part in this that we don't understand. Perhaps he was just pretending not to recognize the document when we showed him the pictures.'

'Despite his bravado, I highly doubt Mountjoy had any clue what he was looking at,' said Theo. 'Unless Amber told him what the document was.'

'Or maybe he came across it on his own, uncovered what it was, told Amber about it and that's when she tried to steal it from him as payback for manipulating her? Robbing him of the chance to go down in history.'

'The staff at the Irendale archive are really on edge around Mountjoy so I suppose it's possible that he has an even darker side than we've already seen,' said Kitt. 'Amber stealing something like that off him would certainly be motive. Perhaps we can't put murder past him. Though there's also a chance that Amber took her discovery to him and, like Meg said happens sometimes, this was the one thing Mountjoy couldn't resist. He tried to convince Amber that they should sell it for personal profit instead of give it freely to the community. When she refused to go along with this, Mountjoy then arranged to have Amber killed.'

'There you go again, assuming that because Amber's dead she's the innocent party,' said Theo.

'You have another theory?' said Kitt, bristling.

'You should know this one, Kitt, it's the oldest crime story there is. Two people agree to steal something together but one of them gets greedy and kills the other one for it.'

'So you think Mountjoy and Amber agreed to steal the document for themselves and then Mountjoy killed her so he could be the sole beneficiary of all the fortune and prestige?' Halloran said, thinking.

'It would solve the mystery of why she didn't just announce the discovery. And explains why she let the killer in to her flat – she was working with him,' said Theo.

'But it creates two problems: why did she buy the gun and why did she leave the puzzle that led us to the document in the first place?'

'True,' Theo conceded. 'I don't think any theory is going to provide the answers to all of the questions you've got hanging over this case.'

'Only the truth can do that. Come on,' said Halloran. 'We need to get back to Bailey with this asap. Mountjoy's got some more explaining to do. I should have known that slimy little toerag wasn't telling the truth.'

'You laid it on pretty thick. I'm surprised he had the gall to lie to you, but maybe he's just got away with whatever he wants to for so long he doesn't believe there'll be any consequences,' said Kitt, before turning back to Theo. 'I'm so grateful for your help but Mal's right. Now we know how important this document is we've got to get back and get to the bottom of who killed Amber for it.'

Theo smiled a smile that was far too winning for Halloran's liking. 'Are you kidding? There's no need to thank me. I got to be one of the first people in the world to look at this document. And trust me, the whole world is going to want to know about it. More than that, though, it means a lot that you came to me about this.'

'Well, truth be told, you were just the nearest Anglo-Saxon specialist to us but it was useful to be able to call in a favour.'

Theo frowned. 'You were up in Irendale, weren't you?'

'Yes,' said Halloran. 'Why?'

'Nothing, it's just there are definitely other specialists in Anglo-Saxon history between here and Irendale, better respected than me too,' said Theo. 'I thought you came to me because of my link with Kitt.'

'Not really . . . Meg Crampton at the Irendale archive told us you were the closest specialist,' said Kitt.

'Who?' Theo asked, shaking his head.

'She worked with Amber at the archive,' said Kitt. 'You've never crossed paths with her?'

'I don't think so.'

'Oh, just, she gave the impression you might have met a couple of times,' Kitt said, with an awkward smile. It was clear she didn't want to reveal exactly what Meg had said about him, though Halloran didn't think it could do him any harm to know what his reputation was amongst his peers.

'I'm usually really good with names and faces,' said Theo. 'I've said hello to Amber at the odd conference here and there but I've never heard of Meg Crampton.'

'Mal . . .' Kitt said, turning to the inspector wide-eyed.

'She has an alibi, said Halloran. 'She said she was in Scarborough the night Amber was murdered.'

'Oh yes, that's right,' said Kitt. 'But something is going on here. She's sent us out all this way for no reason. What if she's in on this with Mountjoy somehow? Perhaps he told her to send us out here. He said that she was right about Theo being the nearest person we could work with.'

'So either Mountjoy is even more clueless about the finer workings of his job than I thought, or he is in on it. said Theo, his voice pensive. 'Did you show Meg this document?'

'She was there when we discovered it,' said Kitt. 'We tried to get her to read it but she could only make out bits and pieces.'

'Are you sure?' said Theo.

'What are you getting at?' said Halloran.

'This document is huge all on its own,' said Theo, 'but the real prize is the map it points to. Whoever uncovers that map will be able to definitively declare the location of the Clovesho councils to the world. Their name will go down in history. If she lied to you, if she could read it, she might have gone after the map for herself.'

'And sent us off on a wild goose chase so she could get her hands on it before anyone else?' said Kitt.

'Exactly,' said Theo.

'And if she's willing to manipulate us like that,' said Halloran, 'she might have manipulated someone else, too, allowing herself the perfect alibi in Scarborough while somebody in the village did her dirty work and killed Amber.'

'Dunwell?' said Kitt.

'Maybe, or maybe she offered Mountjoy a good time and a lot of money if he came along for the ride,' said Halloran, before turning to Theo. 'Where exactly does the document say that map is?'

'Thornborough Henges.'

'A prehistoric settlement,' said Kitt. 'That's Meg's specialism. What if she was lying about how much Old English she really understood? If she can translate it, I'd bet my first editions that she recognized what we were looking at straight away. But . . . surely there've been some digs there in the past? Wouldn't they have uncovered the map?'

'There have been some,' said Theo. 'But you're looking for one scrap of paper and it's actually quite a wide area. If there are trees or anything like that in the way it can make it difficult to get good coverage. Something could easily have been missed.'

'Well, I don't know if Meg's working with Mountjoy or Dunwell, or anyone in fact, but either way she's definitely put one over on us.'

'If we're right, she never sent the photos of the document on her phone to anyone else. She took them so she could find the map first,' said Halloran. He looked at his watch. 'Thornborough is about an hour from here. She would have had to get there from Irendale, and she might have even taken the time to pack up her belongings if she was looking to make a run for it with the map. There's a chance we might just catch her in the act if we go now.'

'I'm coming with you,' said Theo.

'Oh, no, you're not,' said Halloran. 'This is police business.'

'Not purely police business, though, is it? I mean, it's a document of huge historical significance and who knows what will happen when you get to the henges? Having a specialist on hand to fill in the blanks for you probably wouldn't hurt.'

Halloran took a step towards Theo and was about to tell him where to stick it when Kitt caught hold of his arm.

'Mal . . .' she said. 'Let's keep things civil, shall we? There are big things at stake here. We don't know whether we'll need Theo's help again. To decipher the map, for example.'

Halloran looked at Kitt and offered a nod of acquiescence. He really didn't want Theo along but right now, catching the killer was more important than anything else.

'All right, I assume you have your own transport?' said Halloran. It was one thing to let Theo tag along but he was not going to have him sitting in the back seat of the car for an hour baiting him about all the books he'd read that Halloran hadn't.

'Yeah, I've got my car.'

'All right, I'll call Bailey and let him know about all this. God knows what he'll think of it but we can only relay what we've found. Once we're at the scene, though, both of you will have to do exactly as I say.'

Kitt nodded and began walking towards the door. When Halloran was sure she was out of earshot, he turned to Theo and issued one final warning. 'Don't take this as a mark of ingratitude for the help you've given us but I don't like the way you treated Kitt. She may be willing to put it behind her and let bygones be bygones but it doesn't mean I am. Watch your step with her.'

Smirking, Theo breezed past him towards the door.

TWENTY-EIGHT

'Mal, you're going to have to slow down a bit,' said Kitt. Halloran glanced over to see Kitt was clinging to the inside handle on the passenger door. 'At this rate we're not going to make it to Thornborough Henges in one piece.'

'We can't waste any time. If Meg leaves before we get there, tracking her down might prove difficult. From what we've uncovered there's a good chance she's the murderer, or at least is in league with who is.'

A peculiar look crossed Kitt's face. Annoyance? Incredulity? 'That's your story, is it?'

'What do you mean?'

'I mean, Theo is a specialist in history, he knows his way to Thornborough Henges. You're not going to lose him by putting your foot down. Besides it's not like this Micra can outpace another car, especially with the two of us in it.' Halloran noticed Kitt coupled this statement with a smile and something about it made his shoulders relax. He hadn't even realized he'd been tensing them until that moment. But in the forty minutes since they'd left the Airedale Museum he had, of course, done everything he could to lose Theo in the teatime traffic. Still that pesky little Ford Fiesta taunted him at every turn.

'I'm sure I don't know what you're talking about,' Halloran said, returning her smile.

'You've no need to feel threatened, you know.'

'I don't feel threatened.'

There was that look again. Kitt chuckled. 'Not much.'

'Well, how would you feel if I came face to face with an ex?'

'I think that question has already been answered this week, don't you?'

Halloran opened his mouth to speak but then thought better of it. Kitt had been utterly understanding about the fact he had wanted to get involved with a case connected to his ex-wife. But that was different, wasn't it?

'No, no, no, you're not getting me like that,' said Halloran. 'Theo is a living, breathing ex. With ideas and motives.'

'And Kamala's the *Rebecca* to my unnamed narrator.'

'What?' said Halloran.

'It's . . . Oh, never mind. The point is, if you ran into a living, breathing ex, would I have any need to feel threatened?'

'Of course not.'

'Well then, there you go. Just calm yourself so we can focus on the real matter in hand, will you?'

'Yes, ma'am,' Halloran said, easing his foot off the accelerator a touch. But only a touch.

'Now, let's think,' said Kitt, again focusing her mind on the investigation. 'Let's say for just a minute that Meg is the killer. That means she would have known about the document, and probably seen it for herself before Amber died.'

'If she is the killer, she must have done. That document is too important, it has to be what the killer was looking for.'

'But then, if she's seen the document and read the document, why didn't she just go and find the map for herself rather than killing Amber for it?'

Halloran thought for a moment. That was a pertinent question. 'Maybe she didn't get a good enough look at it? Or maybe Amber told her about it but didn't show it to her at all.'

'So she knew Amber had this priceless document but hadn't seen it? That seems odd given they worked together. Surely a discovery of that magnitude would be something you'd share with a work colleague? And, if that's the case, why would she need to kill Amber for it?'

'That argument's all fine if you assume Amber trusted Meg,' said Halloran. 'If she didn't, from her point of view she'd be handing over a priceless document to someone who might steal it for themselves. That might be a risk she wasn't willing to take.'

'So Amber didn't trust Meg and hid the document. Maybe Meg had something over her and threatened her and that's why she made the will and the puzzle, rather than going public. She wanted us to know she knew she was going to die and hoped that would lead us to look for the true meaning of the word she'd left in her pocket.'

'Except Bailey said that the envelope had already been opened,' said Halloran. 'So Meg must have seen that word. Must have guessed from the fact it was written in Old English that it had something to do with the document. So why leave it there when it's a piece of evidence that could lead back to you?'

'I'm not sure,' said Kitt. 'Oh, but remember what Banks said when the evidence was stolen from the car? It's not the thing itself but the content that matters.'

'So Meg made a note of the word and started working on unravelling the puzzle but left it there in case the police were able to figure it out before she did? So she planned on somehow following the police or stealing the clues as the police found them?'

Kitt reached a hand under the chiffon scarf she was wearing and gently stroked the red marks on her throat left behind by the attack the night before. 'Not so outlandish a thought given all that's befallen us over the last twenty-four hours. If we're right about this, it's a fair bet that she was the one following us. That she was the one who stole the next clue from the car, and the person who attacked me.'

'This all seems very out of character for an archivist

– would she even have the physical strength to attack you the way she did? And why do it anyway?' said Halloran, rubbing his beard.

'I agree, it's not the kind of behaviour we'd normally expect from someone in that line of work but remember, I said the attacker didn't feel very strong, so it could have been her. As for why she did it, well, the answer is in what she hissed at me when she had her hands round my neck.'

'"Kerr wants you dead",' said Halloran. 'She was trying to throw us off the track. Or scare us off the case now that she had the next clue in the series. She maybe thought she could figure it out for herself from that point forward.'

'All along, the person behind all this has tried to make it look like Kerr was somehow involved with Amber's death. But those were serial murders and this time there has mercifully only been one body. Not just that, you noted a difference in the MO – the fact that the guitar strings belonged to the killer, rather than the victim. So actually all along there have been some differences that hint at a copycat rather than a repeat by the same culprit. If Kerr had orchestrated this, he probably would have been meticulous in his instructions – surely that would be part of the fun for a psychopath like him, seeing his bidding being carried out with such precision. So such significant differences in the MO doesn't add up.'

Halloran sat quietly for a moment, thinking. If this was truly what had been going on all along then he had been blinded by his own agenda. But had he really just seen what he wanted to see? No. He had had some help on that score.

'Perhaps because they knew I was in town and would know about any differences in MO the killer went to some lengths to convince us Kerr was involved. Painting the rune on the wall near the cottage to make me suspect we'd been targeted personally, and of course the attack in which we were told Kerr was the one who wanted you dead.'

'Besides anything else, the document points to the only logical motive for this crime and there's only two people that we know of who could have really understood the value of what we've uncovered.'

'Meg and Mountjoy,' said Halloran. 'Meg may have been in Scarborough that night, but we don't know where Mountjoy was. Probably killing Amber and relying on his respectability to save him from suspicion.'

'In my experience people like Mountjoy never do their own dirty work. It's more likely he hired someone to do the deed.'

Out of nowhere, Kitt started chuckling then.

'Not really sure there's anything funny about that. Is it a private joke or something you can share with the whole group?'

'Sorry, it's just, if this is all true, think about how hard it must have been for Meg to keep her cool this afternoon when we uncovered the very thing she'd been searching for, sitting in the same office she'd been working in for the last week. It's almost like Amber deliberately put it there to taunt Meg when it was uncovered, like she wanted the last laugh even from beyond the grave.'

'Let's hope that's right, eh?' said Halloran, who also couldn't help but smile at that idea, and the fact Meg hadn't got what she wanted out of all of this. Amber might be dead but ultimately she'd got the better of her killer, or killers. Because of the trail she left behind, justice would soon be served.

Halloran's thoughts were interrupted by the buzzing of his phone.

'Put it on speaker phone, will you, pet?'

Kitt fished the phone out of Halloran's pocket and put the call on speaker.

'Sir, are you at Thornborough yet?' came Bailey's voice down the line.

'Another few minutes away, why?'

'Liam's CCTV footage from his forecourt tells a bit of a tale. Sure enough, in the early hours of this morning, around three o'clock, someone sneaked into the forecourt and sprayed that car with the paint.'

'Let me guess, they were dressed head to toe in black?' said Halloran.

'You guessed it. There's no way of identifying who it is but from their description, it's the same person who stole the evidence from you and attacked Kitt. From the looks of things, yesterday was a very busy day for them.'

'If they're not identifiable, couldn't the figure in black still be Liam?'

'Not likely by their dimensions,' said Bailey. 'Liam is tall and broad, this person is short and thin. If I had to guess, I'd say it was a woman. Putting this together with what you told us about the priceless nature of that document, I'd say the most likely suspect is Meg.'

Halloran was surprised that Bailey had come around to this way of thinking so quickly, but tried not to let it show. 'Has anyone been to the archives to see if Meg is still there?'

'Yes, that's another reason why I suspect her. According to Pippa she dashed out of the archive just a few minutes after you left claiming she felt really ill. Nobody's seen her since. We knocked on her door at home and nobody's answering.'

'That is suspicious, I agree. Until we get there, though, we won't know if Mountjoy and Meg are in on this together,' said Halloran.

'We tracked Mountjoy's phone, it is showing as being out in the Whitby area. We tried to do the same for Meg but for some reason we can't track the phone registered to her, which again just adds to the suspiciousness of her disappearance.'

'Have you dispatched some officers out to Mountjoy?'

'Yeah, they should be with him any time now. But there's more. Something pretty major that suggests Meg's played a bigger part in all this than he has.'

'What is it?' said Halloran.

'We looked into Meg's alibi. She checked in at the hotel she was staying at in Scarborough around six o'clock but the receptionist said she was out all night and didn't come back until about one in the morning.'

'She said she was going to Scarborough for a night at the theatre.'

'Yes, we've checked her financials and she did buy tickets to see *Salad Days* at the Stephen Joseph but nobody at the theatre recognizes her photograph. Of course, they see a lot of people but we can't find any CCTV footage from the surrounding area that places her at the theatre that night, and there are quite a few cameras on that stretch.'

'So, you don't think she went to the show?'

'I can't prove it, yet. But after you told us about how valuable that document is I knew we'd be remiss if we didn't do a little digging, no matter what the superintendent has to say about it. And then we uncover all this. We're leaving for Thornborough now to back you up. Based on what you've told me, there's a good chance that she never went to the theatre that night, that she came back to Irendale, tried to get Amber to tell her where the document was and when she wouldn't she killed her.'

'What about Dunwell?'

'We've shown him the document. He says he's never seen it and has never spoken to Meg. I've got DC Enders making the rounds at local guitar shops with Meg's photograph to see if she's made a cash purchase in the last week or so.

Given what you and Kitt have uncovered, it seems much more likely that she's behind this whole mess than Dunwell or Mountjoy, but bear in mind that we're basing our understanding of his location on his phone data. He might have lent it to his wife or planted it on her as a decoy. There's still a chance when you get there he might be helping Meg recover this map.'

'All right, thanks for letting us know. I'll keep that in mind. We're nearly at Thornborough now.'

'Tread carefully, Mal,' said Bailey. 'Right now, we really don't know what either Meg or Mountjoy are capable of.'

TWENTY-NINE

Halloran pulled up on the roadside just outside Thornborough and watched in his rear-view mirror as Theo did the same.

Kitt slung her satchel over her shoulder and slid out of the car. Halloran followed her lead and the trio regrouped at a gate that led into a large field. The henges themselves lay beyond in the middle distance and consisted of three circular mounds that had always reminded Halloran more of crop circles than anything else. Historians believed their formation was linked to the stars in Orion but that was as far as their alien link went. Although, given the strange turn this case had taken with clues, ancient maps and historical treasures, Halloran wouldn't have been that surprised to see a spaceship hovering over them. The site had a somewhat grand atmosphere about it. Perhaps this was in part created by the knowledge that thousands of years ago distant ancestors had stood where Halloran did now and left their own indelible mark on history, or maybe Halloran's senses were heightened because he knew he would likely soon be facing down another murderer.

'We'll have to walk it from here,' said Halloran.

'From what I can find out online, there's a bit of a walk between them. The northern henge is sheltered by a small wood and it's about five hundred metres to the central henge from there.'

'Wouldn't this be a lot quicker if we split up?' said Theo.

'Quicker yes, safer no,' said Halloran, though he wouldn't have minded having to spend less time with Theo.

'Is this really the time to play it safe?' Theo countered. 'Remember, the document only told us where the map was.'

'I remember,' Halloran said through gritted teeth.

'So if Meg and Mountjoy get away with the map now, we don't have any idea where they're headed. Their vehicle isn't anywhere in sight either. So we don't know what they're driving or how to track them.'

'I'm aware of all this,' said Halloran, losing patience.

'So, isn't it worth taking the small risk of splitting up at this point for the chance of stopping them now rather than having to launch a full-blown manhunt after the fact? I take it Kitt will be going with you anyway.'

'Yes, I would be, if I was given any say in the matter,' Kitt said, her voice dry enough to convey she didn't appreciate being excluded from the conversation.

'So there you go: I can look after myself and it's not like

I'm going to do anything stupid. Big picture, eh, DI Halloran?'

Halloran sighed, wishing Theo didn't have a point. 'Fine. Frankly we're so short on time we don't have it to waste on an argument. Besides anything else, I can't force you to do as instructed. But we don't actually know how many people we're up against here. It could just be Meg, but there's a chance Mountjoy is with her if he's in on it. If you come across either of them, whatever you do, don't approach.'

'So what should I do?'

'With a possible gun in play, you should do nothing. Just call my mobile,' said Halloran, 'and keep track of where you are so I can come and rescue you.'

The darkening of Theo's face pleased Halloran more than it should, but after all the academic digs back at the museum, and his crack about the 'big picture', he couldn't help himself.

'Fine. The document indicated that the map was buried near the centre of one of the henges, but there are three and it didn't say which so I'll head to the central one.'

'Whatever your preference,' said Halloran, trying to sound as though he didn't care that Theo was attempting to call the shots. 'We'll head to the north henge, then, and if neither of us find anything, we can all move onto the south henge which is in a separate field.'

Halloran gave Theo his number and then they parted ways. Kitt walked at Halloran's side through the field towards the north henge. Halloran kept his pace quick. He would be much happier when they were in amongst the trees. Out in the open like this he and Kitt were sitting ducks if anyone with ill intentions happened to have a good vantage point. A few minutes later the pair were safe in the cool shade of the wood. Ahead, through the overgrowth, he could see the slight rise of the henge. It was difficult to see much in the shade of the wood and with plant life spiralling everywhere but this fact also meant that if Meg and Mountjoy were at the centre, they wouldn't be able to see him and Kitt easily either. As long as they used the trees and foliage to their advantage, they should have the element of surprise on their side.

At the edge of the henge Halloran grabbed Kitt's arm. 'Wait here.'

'Not likely.'

'Kitt, come on. They might be armed for all we know. Just stay here for a minute whilst I take a quick look.'

Kitt sighed. 'All right.'

Slowly, tentatively, Halloran walked up the bank of the henge. When he neared the top he lay outstretched on his belly against a mix of dirt, fallen leaves and balding grass and slowly, ever so slowly, poked his head over the rim of the henge. He scanned the circular structure in all directions. Theo had said the document had indicated the map was buried at the centre of one of the henges but as far as Halloran could see there was no movement except the gentle sway of branches and the flutter of the odd bird. Halloran climbed over the ridge and continued to scan the terrain. He circled several of the trees looking for disturbed earth. Being careful to look for any sign that he wasn't alone. But there were none to be found. From what he could make out, it was unlikely Meg or Mountjoy had been digging for the map here.

Halloran took Kitt's hand and walked back to the edge of the small wood. There, he looked south to see if any figures stood on the horizon, but from this far away and with the slight undulation of the land, he couldn't make out anything concrete.

'She doesn't seem to be here, but I can't see too well,' Halloran said. 'We'd best start walking back towards the central henge. If we haven't found her, that means Theo might come across her first. And that could mean real trouble for him.'

The pair had been walking less than a few minutes when, Halloran's phone buzzed in his pocket. Theo's name flashed up on the screen.

'Found her?' Halloran asked, quickening his step.

'Yes,' Theo hissed down the receiver. 'She's in the middle of the centre henge. She's been digging. Difficult to see exactly what she's doing now in the fading light but I think she's packing things up.'

'We are just a few minutes away. Don't approach her. It's better she gets away than you get injured.'

'Didn't know you cared, Mal.' Theo's voice was snide but Halloran wasn't about to get distracted from his task just then, and ignored the comment.

'Just hang tight. If she moves before we get there, call us back and let us know where she's headed.'

'Yeah, right.'

Halloran hung up the phone then relayed to Kitt what Theo had said. He grabbed her hand again and started to jog in the direction of the central henge.

'This is just your way of finally getting me out for a run, isn't it?' Kitt said as she huffed and puffed beside him.

He smiled. 'Well if you won't come the easy way this is what it leads to.'

'For the record, this is not my preferred investigative pace. Standing around in bookshops and tea rooms asking astute questions is really more my thing.'

'Noted,' Halloran said, squeezing her hand tighter. It took them five more minutes to reach the henge and there was no immediate sign of Theo. Halloran cursed under his breath. If that idiot had gone in there and confronted the suspects he didn't like his odds of survival.

Halloran approached the bank of the outer ditch with care but this time Kitt was not willing to wait behind and followed him up to the crest. Once again, the pair lay flat against the ridge of the henge and peered over the edge.

Halloran frowned.

'There's nobody here,' Kitt said. 'Theo definitely said Meg was in the central henge, right?'

'That's what he said,' Halloran said, scanning the circumference of the structure.

'Wait, Mal, over there,' Kitt said, pointing far over to the right, some distance from the henge itself. Halloran looked over just in time to see Meg disappear into a field of tall corn plants. Theo ran after her, about ten paces behind, and within a few seconds he too had disappeared into the crop.

'Bloody hell, why couldn't he have waited like I told him to?' said Halloran. 'Come on.'

Catching hold of Kitt's hand, Halloran ran towards the cornfield and soon the pair were themselves lost amongst the tall stalks, unable to see more than a foot ahead of their own noses. Their only clue as to where Meg and Theo had passed through before was a slight bend in the crops, a path beaten by a possible killer and the man who, if Halloran didn't find him in time, might be her next victim.

For the next three minutes Halloran could hear little more than the whip of corn stalks, Kitt's panting to keep up with him and the thunder of his own heartbeat. There was a good chance that he was going to lose one or both of his subjects here. Meg couldn't have chosen a better place to hide or double back on them than this. The fact that dusk was closing in didn't help matters either. He tried not to think about the less than favourable outcomes to this situation. After what he had put Kitt through, there was no love lost between him and Theo but Halloran did have a duty to protect the public and as such, the idea of anything happening to him was unacceptable. Kitt might be able to forgive him but if Meg got away with another murder before he apprehended her he would never forgive himself.

This thought caused Halloran to double his pace. Considering she thought jogging a form of self-inflicted torture, Kitt was doing a good job of keeping up with him. All he needed to do was get to Theo. Halloran had just about reassured himself that if he could do that, he could probably defuse whatever situation was unfurling between him and Meg when, out of nowhere, a head-splitting sound thundered across the field.

BANG!

The boom was followed by the din of what seemed like a hundred crows fluttering and cawing their low warning up into the darkening sky and after that an even darker silence.

THIRTY

Halloran would have recognized a bang like that anywhere. It was a sound that chilled him to the bone and seemed to reverberate around every ear of corn long after it should have faded away.

'Was that . . .' Kitt began but couldn't bring herself to finish the sentence.

'This way,' said Halloran. Despite the hot panic rising up inside him, he tried to focus on the memory of the sound and the place he felt it had carried from. Exactly what he would do if Meg was waiting for them when he was unarmed, Halloran couldn't say. He cursed himself for not packing protective vests on this trip. But he had no idea there would be firearms involved and there was a good chance that Meg had shot Theo, leaving him to bleed to death while she made her escape. They had to take the risk and at least try to help him, even if he had in part brought injury on himself by ignoring Halloran's cautions.

Less than a minute later, the pair pushed out into a small break in the corn at the other side of the field from which they had started. What they found there was not something Halloran could have predicted. In the short time he had been running he'd imagined every possible scenario, except this one.

Meg and Theo were standing side by side. Meg was wearing a rucksack but the more diverting detail was the gun she was holding. Both she and Theo had satisfied smiles on their faces that immediately sent Halloran's heart rate soaring even higher. Hoping he was somehow mistaken about what seemed to be going on, Halloran continued to approach slowly, until Meg raised the gun and pointed it at him. Then he instinctively raised his hands in the air.

'Told you a gunshot would get their attention,' said Theo. His face looked different. Thinner somehow. Meaner. There was a coldness to his words.

'Theo . . .?' Kitt said. He raised his eyebrows at her with a certain smugness but did not verbally reply. 'Oh, Theo, what have you done?'

'Get behind me,' Halloran muttered to Kitt.

'I will not. I'm not using you as a human shield. If we're going down we're going down together.'

There would have been something sweet about this statement if Halloran hadn't been so desperate to protect her from the bullets that were likely to fly their way at any second.

'Don't act so surprised,' said Theo. 'I've done what anyone else in my position would have done. I've put my own self-interests first and made a deal.'

'What kind of deal?' said Kitt.

'You didn't find the map, did you?' Halloran said to Meg.

'Still a bit of a needle in a haystack,' said Meg.

'But with my expertise it won't take us long to find it,' Theo said.

'Making deals with a wanted murderer? For all your studying you never really were that smart, were you, Theo?' Kitt said with a real bitterness to her voice.

'Come on Kitt-Kat, think it through,' Theo said.

Kitt flinched at the old nickname but did not otherwise respond.

'Making a deal was the only smart thing to do, given the situation,' Theo countered. 'The document, the map, they're the ticket to fortune and glory, kid.'

Kitt frowned. 'Stop quoting Indiana Jones, you idiot. Is any amount of fortune and glory worth your soul? Because that's what you're selling. How could you turn on us like this? Meg killed someone for that map. Strangled the life out of someone who had worked by her side without a second thought.'

'Shut up!' Meg shouted, levelling the gun at Kitt. 'I only did that because I had to. If Amber had been reasonable, it would never have come to that.'

'By being reasonable, I assume you mean let you sell

the document and the map for your own profit?' said Kitt, showing a considerable amount of pluck considering Meg was holding a gun.

Meg shook her head. 'It never had to be this way. She just kept on and on about how the document and the map didn't really belong to her or anyone else. How it belonged to the people. Whoever donated that box to the archive didn't even know what they had. The public only appreciate things because we tell them what to appreciate. So, shouldn't we get some credit?'

'You don't think Amber had a point? That it would have been unjust to profit from a document like that?' Halloran said. No matter what, he had to keep Meg talking. His only hope of making sure he and Kitt got out of this alive was by buying time until back-up arrived. Luckily for him, criminals, and murderers in particular, loved to talk at length about their own genius. One way or another, their egotism was always their downfall.

'I think that the real injustice is that a twit like Amber Downing made the biggest historical discovery in living memory. Just stumbled across it in a box some other oblivious twit donated. How is that fair?'

'Life's not about fairness,' said Kitt. 'It doesn't give you the right to go around killing people.'

'It's a shame she had to die but from what Meg says Amber was being unreasonable,' said Theo. 'Come on, Kitt, you and me know how the arts world works. Sure, a museum would pay a pretty penny for those documents but they'd put them on display, and from donations and merchandise and entrance fees to exhibitions, they'd make back what they paid ten times over. Everybody could have won.'

'So Amber deserved to die because she didn't want to profiteer from our shared history, is that what you're saying, Theo?'

'Sounds like it to me,' said Halloran. 'Sounds like Amber wanted to do the honourable thing and Meg killed her for it.'

'Well, we didn't all have the luxury of going to private school and having a wealthy family to bail us out,' Meg almost screeched.

'Spare me,' said Halloran. 'You think you're the only person in Britain who knows what it means to go without? It's not an excuse for murder, Meg. Nothing is.'

'What you think of the situation isn't that important, to be honest,' said Meg, her eyes flashing with anticipation. 'Neither of you are getting out of this field alive.'

Halloran swallowed hard. When he'd enrolled in the police force, he'd known and accepted that it heightened the odds of him dying at the hands of a criminal. He'd often wondered if it would be at the end of a knife or a gun. Whatever the end looked like for him, he'd always promised himself he would go out fighting to his last breath for what he believed in. He could accept that kind of fate for himself. But not for Kitt. All she had done was try to help him put his past behind him, and now it looked like they would both soon be history. He had to stall Meg some more, any way he could.

'So you want to spend your life in prison?' he said. 'Murdering a police officer is frowned upon by most judges and courts, just so you know.'

Meg laughed. 'The thing is, we didn't shoot you, DI Halloran. You shot Kitt and then yourself.'

'Nobody who knows me is going to believe a tall tale like that for a second,' said Halloran.

'Won't they? Won't people believe that investigating a case almost identical to the one surrounding the death of your ex-wife drove you over the edge? When we come out of this field bloody and dishevelled as hostages freed from an overworked, overstressed police officer and tell them that story, won't people start to gossip about how hard you'd taken the death of your wife? Won't people believe that you started ranting and raving about her before shooting your now-girlfriend and then yourself? I think that's a story I can sell.'

'And I'll help you sell it,' said Theo.

'It'll never stick,' said Halloran. 'For a start, that gun belongs to Amber. I don't own any firearms. How would I have got hold of it?'

'Oh, you found it at some point during your little covert investigation amongst Amber's belongings, and you never told anyone you'd found it. Not even Kitt. You thought it might come in handy, especially if Jeremy Kerr ended up having played some kind of part in this murder. And maybe he did.'

Halloran narrowed his eyes. She was just taunting him. It didn't make sense for Kerr to be tangled up in something like this. 'How did you plan this? You couldn't have known I would come up here and investigate.'

'Truth be told, I didn't plan any of this,' said Meg. 'My only plan was to get the document from Amber, no matter what, and make sure someone else took the fall for anything I had to do to make that happen.'

'Someone like Max Dunwell,' said Kitt.

Meg scoffed. 'Yes, the village idiot. It was almost too easy to frame him. The way he mooned after Amber was ridiculous.'

'If all you wanted was the document then why did you vandalize the wall near the cottage? And why did you attack Kitt?' said Halloran. 'I assume it was you who stole the box containing the second clue from us too, and that I understand, but why all the scare tactics?'

'When I first heard word that the inspector who solved the murders five years ago had come back to the village, I didn't think it was good news. The idea was that the local plods would find the evidence that linked to Dunwell and assume it was a copycat murder. I thought maybe they might have a go at solving the clue Amber left behind. That they might unwittingly lead me to the document if I had trouble solving whatever stupid riddle she'd set. But other than that I expected it to be case closed within the week. Then you came sniffing around.'

'So you tried to scare us off,' said Halloran.

'Actually, I was just trying to do as many things as I could to confuse the police. It seemed if I sent them round in circles long enough they'd get tired or bored and just arrest Max – the most obvious suspect,' said Meg.

'I can't believe you killed an innocent woman over this,' said Kitt.

'Amber wasn't so innocent,' Meg snarled. 'She slept with Mountjoy for her job, you know.'

'And you used that fact to blackmail her, didn't you?' said Halloran. 'When she threatened to go public with her discovery and ensure the documents were displayed freely at the archives.'

'Why she would tell someone like you a secret like that I don't know,' said Kitt. 'But somehow you managed to gain her trust.'

'Not really. The stupid cow had one too many glasses of wine at the office Christmas party and spilled her guts about what a mistake she'd made. I had no idea then that the information would ever come in useful. I just thought she was pathetic for letting someone like Mountjoy compromise her like that. Still, she can at least rest in peace. Her secret is going to stay safe. Mountjoy will never breathe a word about it and you won't be breathing long enough to tell anyone what you know.'

'Give it up, Meg, there's just no way you're going to get away with this,' said Halloran.

'Only one way to find out,' said Meg, cocking the gun.

Halloran braced himself for the impact. He'd never been shot before but he did what he always did when he anticipated pain: he fixed his mind on something else. A clear vision of anything not related to what he was about to endure. And right now, playing in his mind, was a clear picture of Kitt running towards a police car. Bailey was inside and had arrived to take her away. Somewhere safe. Somewhere far from here.

'I want to shoot them,' Theo blurted out.

Meg looked at Theo. It wasn't quite a look of suspicion but she hesitated over his request.

'Well, it's up to you, of course. You can rob me of the satisfaction,' said Theo. 'But then I won't be in it anywhere near as deep as you are. You'll have killed three people and I won't have a body count against my name. If you at least let me put a bullet through Halloran's skull, which by the way I've been fantasizing about ever since we met, I'll be in it as deep as you which ensures a certain loyalty, don't you agree?'

Meg looked from Halloran, to Kitt and then to Theo. He sidled up to her, looked deep into Meg's eyes and stroked her cheek. 'I have no problem with the idea of needing to stick around you for the foreseeable. Let me prove to you just how on board I am.'

'Actually, I think it's best that I shoot Halloran. If you want a job doing well, and all that. But if you really want to prove your loyalty, once I'm finished with him, you can shoot her,' Meg said, indicating Kitt.

Theo looked over at her, his eyes hard brown marbles. How had Halloran not seen this coming? He should have at least suspected when he saw just how excited Theo was about the discovery of the document that he might want a slice of the profits for himself.

A sly smile snaked across Theo's lips. 'Shooting her won't be a problem.'

Halloran could see Kitt was doing all she could to keep her face straight and stern but the slight wobble of her mouth betrayed the fact those words cut her deeper than she had expected them to.

'Glad to hear it. But first, let me get Halloran out the way,' Meg said, advancing towards him.

Halloran tried to think quickly, desperate to formulate a plan. If Meg got close enough, within reaching distance, he could wrestle the gun off her. He would likely be shot somewhere vital but it might just buy Kitt enough time to run away. To reach safety, just as he had imagined.

'Mal, I'm sorry,' said Kitt. 'I should have known Theo couldn't be trusted.'

Halloran turned to her and, part out of desire and part out of fear this might really be it, pulled her close to him and delivered a deep kiss. A kiss he hoped she would never forget, even if he didn't make it out of this field. Of all the places to go out, a field on the outskirts of Thornborough wouldn't have been his preference.

'Listen to me,' he said, brushing a stray strand of hair out of her face, 'none of this is your fault. You were just trying to help me. I never should have let you get involved.'

'Let me?' Kitt said, forcing a smile. 'Just because we're about to die, that doesn't mean you're within your rights to get ideas above your station.'

'Come on, Inspector,' said Meg. She was still a few paces away. Not close enough for Halloran to make his move. He needed to somehow draw her closer. 'Be thankful that I'm killing you first. It means you won't have to watch Kitt die. Of course, she'll have to watch you die but that's just how this works.'

An ache rose in him at the thought of her enduring even half the pain he had when Kamala had been killed. He tried to shake it off. The only thing that mattered was that Kitt lived on. That he saved her in a way that he never could Kamala. He gestured for Kitt to stand back. Reluctantly she obliged before slowly placing her hands behind her back. It was an unusual gesture but he didn't have time to dwell on that; he had to focus on Meg and draw her attention away from Kitt. If she wanted to make this even vaguely look like a suicide, she'd have to shoot him from pretty close range, and that would be his moment to strike.

'Stop blabbering and get it over with,' Halloran said to Meg. 'I'd rather not look at your face any longer than I have to.'

Meg blinked hard, slightly stunned by Halloran's sudden coarseness. 'Well, well, I knew you'd come out scratching eventually.'

'What are you waiting for? Or don't you have what it takes to pull the trigger?' Halloran almost barked.

'Oh, don't worry, I'm going to give you exactly what you've got coming to you,' said Meg. With that, she marched towards Halloran, pointing the gun straight at his heart.

THIRTY-ONE

The gun barrel couldn't have been more than three feet away from Halloran when the world around him slipped into slow motion mode. He frowned, trying to get a grip on the sickness that was taking hold of him. There was only one other time he'd ever experienced this feeling and that was when he had come home from work five years ago to find Kamala lying in the master bedroom of their cottage, her skin pale, her body limp and breathless. Though he knew by the carvings on her hand and the marks around her neck she couldn't possibly be alive, his eyes wouldn't accept the sight of her, lying there and lost to him for ever. How long had it taken him to call for an ambulance? Probably only a few seconds but it had felt so much longer.

Seconds were stretching out now as they did then. Halloran could see every small movement Meg made. Her face contorting into a hard grimace. Her raven hair billowing in the low breeze as she marched towards him. Her fingers clenching around the gun by degrees as they prepared to pull the trigger.

Tears threatened as a singular thought pounded in his mind: whatever happened next to him and Kitt was on his head. If his bitterness hadn't got the better of him, they wouldn't even be here. In some alternate dimension that probably only the likes of Ruby Barnett had a window into, the pair were still back in York and had never ventured up onto the moorland to solve a mystery that wasn't even by rights theirs to investigate. In that blissfully oblivious world, they were watching the sun set over the Ouse. They were curled up in each other's arms, dreaming of all the sunrises and sunsets ahead. In coming here, without even realizing it, he had jeopardized all of that.

At last, Meg took a step that brought her within reach. Halloran tensed his muscles, preparing to make a grab for his assailant, when something unexpected happened.

Without warning, Kitt lunged towards Meg, her arm outstretched.

'Kitt! No!' Halloran shouted, fearing Kitt was going to do something stupidly selfless like throw herself in front of him to take the bullet. It was this blinding fear that for a moment prevented him from noticing that Kitt had something in her hand. What was that? A bottle of some kind? Perfume?

Shocked by Kitt's assault, Meg went to point the gun at her but before she had the chance to fire, Kitt sprayed the substance into Meg's widened eyes.

Meg staggered backwards, screaming out in pain and surprise. Before Halloran even had time to react, Theo leapt on Meg from behind and tackled her down into the grass. Though Meg's eyes were red raw and streaming from Kitt's attack, her survival instincts had clearly kicked in as she jolted and pushed furiously against Theo's attempts to restrain her.

'Let me go,' Meg screamed over and over. 'Let me go or I'll shoot you.'

Despite Theo's efforts, she wasn't going to go down easy. She still had the gun clutched firmly in her hand and was waving it every which way as she writhed and twisted against her opponent. Halloran had to put an end to this, now. Before anyone else got hurt.

Leaping into action, Halloran caught hold of Meg's gun arm and tried to point it away from all human beings in the near vicinity. He managed to do this just before Meg's finger squeezed the trigger and a bullet blasted into the nearby corn, scattering yet more crows. The shot startled Halloran and Theo enough for them to momentarily loosen their grip on Meg. Not missing a beat, she kicked Halloran in the stomach, winding him badly. Somehow he managed to hold onto her arm but not quite tight enough as she manoeuvred herself into a sitting position, jerked out of his grip and fired the gun a second time.

Theo flew backwards with the impact of the bullet and let out a pained groan.

'Theo!' Kitt cried out, and was at his side in seconds.

Meg paused for just a moment, possibly in shock of what she'd managed to do in the struggle even though she had threatened to shoot them but seconds ago. Making the most of the chance, Halloran seized Meg by the collar, pushed her to the ground and swiped the gun out of her hand, throwing it off into the grass near Kitt so that Meg wouldn't get the chance to snatch it off him again.

'Stay down,' he barked at her. He pulled the cuffs out from his pocket but as he did so a pained moan loud enough to momentarily distract him sounded out. Halloran turned back to where Kitt was tending to Theo. Running a hand through his hair, he watched the lush green grass turn red.

THIRTY-TWO

Kitt had taken off her cardigan and was tearing the sleeves off it to wrap around Theo's arm, tying the fabric tight to slow the bleeding.

Holding Meg's wrist with one hand and whipping out his phone with the other, Halloran dialled 999.

'This is Detective Inspector Malcolm Halloran, officer number 9969,' Halloran said once he had been connected with the ambulance service. 'A man has been shot and we need immediate medical assistance. We are currently at Thornborough Henges, approximately seven miles north of Ripon.'

The operator asked how bad the wound was and Halloran was about to explain when out of nowhere, a sharp, excruciating pain pulsed through him. Looking down, he saw Meg releasing her grip on a small kitchen knife that was now sticking into his right thigh. He couldn't tell just how long the knife was, but it was sharp. It had sliced straight through his jeans with ease and blood was starting to pool at either side of the handle.

Halloran dropped the phone to the ground and fell to his knees. He lost his grip on Meg and watched as she made a break for it, diving back into the corn. Breathless from the hard throbbing of his wound, Halloran took a closer look at the knife. Bloody idiot. Why hadn't he searched Meg to make sure she wasn't carrying any other weapons? He reached down, winced and slowly inched the blade out of his leg. A ragged, desperate groan escaped him as he did so.

'Mal!' Kitt screamed over at him.

'I'm fine,' he lied. He had to compartmentalise the pain. He couldn't let Meg get too much of a head start on him. That corn field was as good as a maze. 'Throw me your scarf.'

'My new scarf?' said Kitt.

'Yes!'

Kitt quickly unwound the scarf from her neck and brought it over to him. Within seconds, Halloran had wrapped it tight around the wound and tied the makeshift bandage off with a tight knot.

'Here,' Halloran said, picking up his phone and pushing it into Kitt's hands. 'Hold onto this, and put that gun somewhere safe in case she heads back this way.'

'What? Wait! Mal!' Kitt tried but it was too late. He was already limping into the corn, trying to trace Meg's path by the broken stalks that she had beaten back in her haste.

This worked for a couple of minutes until he came to a patch of corn that had been beaten down in two directions. He took the path that looked least trodden. The one that looked as though it had been made by someone who didn't want to be detected. He was only a few paces down this route when he tripped and fell flat on his face. He groaned at the impact and looked down at his feet, expecting to see an offending scrap of gnarled root, instead, however, he saw Meg standing over him, bedraggled and huffing. She was holding a large rock high above her head and with a scream she brought it down with full force, aiming for Halloran's temple. He crossed his arms, forearms up, to defend against the blow. The rock hit bone with a sickening thud, but missed his head. He grabbed the rock and threw it off into the crop. Meg tried to leap over him and make another run for it but Halloran grabbed her ankle as she passed over him and tripped her. She tried to kick him off, aiming her heavy walking boots square at Halloran's face and kicking up dust from the sun-parched field, making it difficult for him to see. Still, Halloran kept his grip tight until at last, seemingly exhausted, she stopped struggling. She let out a final exasperated screech and sat there gasping and panting.

Brushing the dust off his face, Halloran rose to his knees and got his handcuffs out. Meg responded with nothing more than a grimace. As he leaned in to cuff her, however, she grabbed his hand and sank her teeth into the skin.

Halloran cried out but used his good hand to push her

backwards. She was disorientated for a moment, but then shoved Halloran backwards in return and straddled his chest before clamping her hands around his throat. The unexpected pressure on his windpipe panicked him for a moment. His hand was smarting, his leg was throbbing and he was tired from the struggle but, of all ways, he wasn't going out that way. The same way Amber had. The same way Kamala had.

Using every ounce of might he had left, Halloran pushed himself onto his front so that Meg had no choice but to fall beneath him. He ripped her hands away from his throat and tried once again to restrain her. She clawed and kicked at him for all she was worth and at any one time, Halloran couldn't get hold of more than one wrist to stop her assault. She went to bite him again, on the arm this time, but just as her teeth met his flesh a loud bang sounded out just behind them.

Meg and Halloran both jolted at the sound. He jumped away from Meg and spun around to see Kitt standing with the gun, pointed squarely at her. Theo stood just behind her, bent and pale, his arm wrapped up in a makeshift sling Kitt had devised with what was left of her cardigan. Meg made a move as if she was going to try and run.

'I wouldn't move, if I were you,' said Kitt. 'I don't take kindly to women rolling around in the cornfields with my boyfriend. And I've not had any experience in firing guns so if I have to shoot you, I can't promise it will be in a place that you'll survive.'

Meg glared at Kitt and slumped to the ground, weeping and trying to catch her breath all at once.

'Come on,' Halloran said, picking his handcuffs up from where they had fallen, getting to his feet and pulling Meg to hers with his one remaining good hand. 'Meg Crampton, you are under arrest for the murder of Amber Downing.' He continued to caution her and they began the slow walk back to the car. Kitt helped Theo all the way, draping his strong arm around her bared shoulders to support him as he limped along. A fact Halloran tried not to focus too much on. It helped that he had to keep a close eye on Meg. Given how much of a fight she had put up, he wouldn't have put it past her to make one last break for it, even in handcuffs. The wound in his leg was still throbbing and the last thing he needed was another chase. As it turned out, if she was silently plotting to escape, this wasn't a problem he would have to deal with alone as by the time they were approaching the car, Halloran could hear sirens wailing in the distance.

THIRTY-THREE

Halloran tried not to wince as the paramedic wrapped a bandage around his hand where Meg had done her best to take a chunk out of him. Kitt watched on in the closing dusk, biting her lower lip and rubbing Halloran's back as he leant against a stretch of drystone wall trying to get his energy back after a gruelling evening. At least his leg had been properly bandaged now and some pain relief had been administered. In this kind of scenario it paid to be grateful for small mercies.

'You are an absolute nuisance, you know,' Kitt said, her tone betraying her concern even if her words didn't.

'Oh I know, I would have warned you about that before we got together but since you're so learned I thought you had already understood that about me and decided to take a chance anyway.'

'Maybe I did,' said Kitt, with a knowing smile.

'You're all good to go, sir,' said the paramedic. 'Just make sure you rest the hand and the leg as much as possible over the next week or so. No weightlifting or running any marathons.'

Kitt smiled at the paramedic as she walked away and then turned back to Halloran with a glint in her eye. 'Looks like you won't be putting me over your knee any time soon.'

'Don't be so sure. In case it escaped your notice, I do have a good hand and one good knee left to my name,' Halloran returned with a slow smile. '*Fifty Shades of Lady Grey*, that'll be the title of your autobiography if I get my way.'

'Oh, very droll,' said Kitt, her nose crinkling. 'That sounds more like an unauthorized biography written by Grace Edwards. Don't you dare say anything like that in front of her or Evie, I'll never hear the end of it. And did you have to remind me that I haven't had time to stop for a cuppa all day?'

'Yes, you're right, I'm sorry. That is the worst thing about being held up at gunpoint. Not having time to stop for tea.'

'True story,' Kitt said with a smile. Halloran chuckled but all too soon his good humour dissolved as he looked over to the ambulance and saw the paramedics preparing to load Theo into the vehicle.

'Do you think Theo was on our side all along?'

Kitt shook her head. 'We'll never know for sure. But I think so. As soon as Meg started walking towards you, he began signalling to me in a way that made it clear he was going to try and get the better of her. I had already started to rummage in my satchel for something – anything – that could be used as a weapon. All I could find of any use was my bottle of perfume. It was behind my back but maybe he saw or guessed what I was up to and recognized that the tables were likely to turn. I can't say for certain, even though I'd like to believe the best in him. Maybe we should talk to him before he goes to the hospital. Make sure there's nothing that went on between him and Meg that we don't know about.'

Halloran nodded and the pair walked over to where Theo lay on a stretcher.

'How are you feeling?' Kitt asked him.

'Like I've been shot in the arm,' said Theo with a grimace. 'But I suppose the main thing is we caught the killer in the end, and recovered that document. I'm sorry I . . . you know, that I had to trick you like that.'

'You had us worried,' said Halloran. 'It was a convincing performance.'

'It had to be,' said Theo. 'All our lives were riding on it.'

'How did you convince her you were on her side? What deal did you make?' asked Kitt.

'I know Halloran said to wait but when I saw Meg head for that field I panicked that we were going to lose her, and the map, for good. So I ran after her. I was trying to keep my distance but she must have heard me and known there was someone following her because when I came out at the other side, she turned on me and pulled out the gun.'

'You're lucky she didn't shoot you dead on the spot,' said Halloran.

'She nearly did, but I shouted at her not to. I had to think quick, so I explained who I was and told her I wasn't chasing her to stop her, that I wanted to help her and take a cut of the money and prestige the map would bring. I told her that there were police officers on her trail but that I would help her get away and offer my expertise to help her find the map. I told her to fire the gun to draw you to us and pretended that I'd help her get rid of you. What I was actually hoping for was a window to grab the gun off her but she kept quite a close eye on me so it was a while before she was distracted enough for me to make my move.'

Halloran stared at Theo and wondered if that was the truth. Kitt had said he'd signalled to her before he made his attack on Meg, so although he'd prefer to make out Theo was a traitor in this case, it seemed he was going to have to give him the benefit of the doubt.

'Given the way she responded to you while we were there, it looked as though she liked the sound of your offer,' Kitt said, her tone arid.

'Not going to lie, I turned on the charm as far as I knew how,' said Theo. 'I had to work pretty quick, Kitt-Kat.'

Kitt glared at him. Halloran followed her lead. When Theo had used that nickname before, there had been bigger things to focus on. Bullets to avoid. A killer to take down. But Theo needn't think he could slide into overfamiliarity just because he had played a part in saving Halloran's life that afternoon.

'Er, Kitt,' he corrected himself after a moment. 'I'm sorry I couldn't give you some kind of hint that I was playing her. I had hoped some part of you would know that I could never do something like that.'

Theo was looking just at Kitt now, and she was avoiding his eye. 'I don't know you, Theo,' she said, at last looking back at him. 'So I couldn't say what you're capable of, but on today's showing it seems you are capable of quick thinking and a great deal of courage.'

Halloran cleared his throat and reached out his hand for Theo to shake. 'I'd be forced to agree with Kitt on this one. Not everyone could have thought that quickly with a gun pointed at them. We're grateful for your help.'

Theo managed to give Halloran's hand a weak shake with his good arm and smiled. 'I'm glad I was able to decipher the text but if you ever need my help again, I'd prefer it if we left guns out of it.'

'We'll see what we can do,' said Halloran, secretly hoping this would be the last time he would ever have cause to call on Theo's services.

'Sorry to interrupt, sir,' a paramedic said, 'but now that we've got him stabilized we need to get him to the hospital.'

Kitt and Halloran stood back so the paramedics had room to work.

'Don't be a stranger, Kitt,' Theo said, as he was lifted into the back of the ambulance.

Kitt managed to offer him a smile and a firm nod. Even after the way he had treated her, it seemed she couldn't bring herself to be short or mean with Theo when he had taken a bullet to help them, and as the ambulance doors closed Halloran realized how much he loved Kitt for that measure of kindness alone.

'DI Halloran!' Bailey called over from his car. He had parked in front of Halloran's vehicle at the side of the road. In the back seat, Meg sat with her head slumped against the window. It was difficult to tell if she was moping or sleeping. After all the physical struggle they had both endured that afternoon, Halloran wouldn't have been surprised if it was the latter. The night was closing in on them and he couldn't wait for his own head to hit the pillow.

'Does she seem like she'll be in the mood for talking when you get her back to the nick?' Halloran said, nodding over at Meg.

'Difficult to say. I haven't drawn more than a lengthy glower out of her as yet but the interrogation room is often a – how should it put it? – sobering experience so maybe she'll say more when her legal representation arrives. Whether she speaks or not, I've just had word from the coppers searching her house and from the sound of things it's not going to be a difficult conviction.'

'Let me guess, she thought she was so smart, she didn't bother to cover her tracks,' said Halloran.

'She had a bit of a go,' said Bailey. 'But she wasn't very thorough. She'd thrown the balaclava she wore in the bottom of her laundry basket and with it a door key.'

'To what door?' said Kitt.

'We're not certain as we haven't tried it out yet but we think it's going to fit Amber Downing's front door. It's the same shape and size as the key we've got in evidence for her flat.'

'If it is a fit for Amber's door that would explain why there was no forced entry,' said Kitt. 'But why would Amber give Meg a key if she'd threatened her?'

'I don't think she did,' said Halloran. 'If there's one thing we know about Meg from the way she's carried on, it's that she's sly. I think she made a copy of Amber's key without her knowing, maybe went into her handbag at work one day. It would have to be before she threatened Amber, otherwise Amber would be suspicious of her. But if she's got a key to Amber's front door in her possession, that's probably how she got it.'

'We also found the spray paint she used to vandalize the wall outside the cottage and the car in Liam Long's forecourt in her outside dustbin.'

'She confessed her involvement in Amber's murder and the framing of Dunwell to us also,' said Halloran. 'You've got the witness statements from myself, Kitt and Theo, so between that and the evidence you've found – no matter what she says in the interrogation room – it's pretty much case closed.'

Bailey nodded and looked Halloran up and down for a moment. 'Sir, I'm sorry that I tried to shut you down about the clues Amber left.'

Halloran held a hand up to signal Bailey should stop talking. 'You've no need to apologize, Damian, you were doing your job the best way you knew how and I didn't give you much reason to trust my judgement.'

'Well, I'm not going to pretend like that helped us. But in the end we might not have cracked the case without you so I think we can forgive that you lost it at one point with a person responsible for the death of someone you loved.'

'But you and I know in this line of work you can't afford to "lose it". I've bent the rules on a few occasions in the last five years because of what happened back then, and after everything that's gone on here it's made me wonder if the force is still the right place for me.'

'Mal, are you saying you're thinking of leaving the police?' Kitt said, a note of surprise in her voice.

'I don't know,' said Halloran. 'I just know I'm only willing to stay if I can do things by the book. My recent track record hasn't been pristine on that score.'

'It's not like there aren't mitigating circumstances, sir,' said Bailey. 'It would be a great loss to the service if you left us. Maybe wait until all the dust has settled from this before you make any big career decisions, eh?'

'Sounds like sense,' Halloran said with a nod. 'There is one thing that is still bothering me about Meg's case, though.'

'Only one thing?' said Bailey. 'I've got a list a mile long.'

Halloran smiled. 'How the hell did Meg get around the moorland roads without passing a traffic camera? If she was responsible for the vandalism on the wall, the attack on Kitt, the theft from the car and the paint on Liam Long's vehicle then surely her vehicle would have shown up on a camera somewhere – more than once.'

'I don't know that yet, sir, but if it comes out in the wash over the next few days, you'll be the first to know.'

'Without wishing to be rude, can we go home now?' said Kitt. 'As pointed out previously, I'm well overdue a cup of Lady Grey.'

'Get yourselves home,' said Bailey. 'If we need anything else from you we'll be in touch. And thanks again for solving Amber's riddle. I really wouldn't have liked my chances of working that one out on my own.'

Laughing, Bailey made his way back over to the car where another officer was waiting, standing watch over Meg.

Halloran and Kitt began walking back to their car too. As they did so, Halloran noticed a sneaky little smile at the corner of Kitt's mouth.

'What's that look about?' said Halloran.

'Well, I think it's worth pointing out that technically speaking I saved your life today,' Kitt said.

'Do you now? I suppose that is true,' said Halloran.

'I saved your life even though I caught you rolling around in a cornfield with another woman.'

'That . . . wasn't exactly my preferred version of rough play,' Halloran said, raising an eyebrow.

Kitt's smiled broadened. 'Still, I think that after everything, you've got some making up to do, don't you?'

'I'd be more than happy to make it up to you,' Halloran said, his mind starting to race.

'I have a few ideas about how you might do that,' said Kitt, before opening the car door and sliding into the passenger seat.

Halloran frowned to himself. There was something teasing about Kitt's tone that spelled trouble. Opening the door, he got into the car and examined her face. Her eyes sparkled in amusement.

'Why do I get the feeling, my pet, that what you have in mind and what I have in mind are very, very different?'

THIRTY-FOUR

Halloran took a big gulp of his pint and set it back down on the table at Thomas's in York. He should have arrived earlier so he could down a few more. He should have done anything in his power to steel his nerves for the task ahead.

Kitt, Banks, Evie and Grace sat around the table, chattering over the background murmur of some pop record he was definitely too advanced in years to recognize. Between the toys stuck to the wall, the enlarged photos of the royal family visiting the city of York hung all around and the joyously kitsch patchwork upholstery, to say this wasn't Halloran's natural habitat was an understatement. A visit to Thomas's on karaoke night, however, was all in the spirit of the promise he'd made to himself to try and embrace the lighter side of life. After the heaviness of the past couple of weeks, it seemed the right kind of promise. Kitt had brought out a playfulness in him that he thought long dead, but he couldn't deny that deep down he had been resistant to letting that new-found humour spill out into other areas of his life where it was much needed. Tonight, he hoped, was the first step of many in a new direction.

'Nervous?' said Kitt, nestling her mouth close to his ear as she spoke.

'A bit,' Halloran admitted.

'Nervous enough about this to take your mind off work?'

'Almost, pet,' Halloran said, stroking her hair.

It had been two weeks to the day that he and Kitt had ventured up onto the moorland and made their first visit to Irendale in search of Amber's killer. In that time Bailey and his team had discovered that Meg had indeed made a copy of Amber's door key without her knowledge. They had also continued to do the rounds at local music shops and uncovered that Meg had made a cash payment in Scarborough the day of Amber's murder for a pack of Brew Hound guitar strings. Meg's internet search history had also dredged up numerous news articles on the Irendale killings committed by Kerr five years previously. Perhaps it was unsurprising that a murdering archivist would be so thorough with their homework.

At first Meg hadn't talked but the reality of extended jail time gave her some incentive to cooperate and ultimately she confessed all of the things she'd confessed to Halloran, Kitt and Theo in the field, and a bit extra. Perhaps the most interesting titbits were firstly that the note that the police found on Amber's body had been placed there by Meg. She had found it propped up against the clock on the mantelpiece and, not realizing the significance of the clock to the puzzle, had placed it on Amber's person in the hope the police would think it of greater significance and unwittingly help her uncover the next clue or maybe even the document itself. Secondly, Meg had answered the question of how she had avoided detection by all the traffic cameras. She'd been getting about on her bicycle and using the cycle paths that cut across the moorland rather than keeping to the roads. A course of action that Halloran would never have guessed, as with its sharp inclines and deep valleys cycling across the moorland surely made murder much harder work than it needed to be.

According to Bailey, Theo's official statement had matched what he had said in the aftermath of Meg's arrest so there was little doubt that, all told, he'd tried to do the right thing. As far as he knew, Kitt had only heard once from Theo since they had apprehended Meg and it was simply to reassure her that his wound was healing well.

'Malcolm Galfrid Halloran,' Kitt said just as the music lulled.

Halloran cringed.

'Galfrid?' said Banks.

'It was my great-grandfather's name,' Halloran said, trying to sound proud even though he knew he wasn't kidding anyone.

'So your name could be shortened to Mal Gal Hal?' said Evie, starting to giggle.

'Not really any reason to do that though is there—' Halloran began but he was cut off mid-sentence.

'Mal Gal Hal,' Grace repeated with a sparkle of excitement in her eyes. 'It sounds like the name of an ancient knight who fights for truth and justice across the land.' As she said this, she mimed holding a sword in her hand and began to fence an invisible foe from the comfort of her seat.

Kitt stared hard at her assistant. 'Grace, how much have you had to drink? It's only eight thirty. You might want to pace yourself.'

'I'm not drinking,' Grace said. 'Why?'

Kitt opened her mouth to say something but then thought better of it. 'Never mind.'

'What exactly did I do to deserve the middle-naming you just gave me?' Halloran said, turning to Kitt. 'Which, by the way, I told you about in confidence.'

'I know that face. You were thinking about work. We're supposed to be having a fun night out.'

'You're right,' Halloran said with a small smile. 'I'm sorry, I should think of more light-hearted things. Like the fact that someone, some day, might find the map at Thornborough, discover the real location of Clovesho and share it with the public as Amber wanted.'

'And that Kerr hadn't managed to kill again, sir. You really did neutralize that threat when you put him away all those years ago,' said Banks.

'I still wish his legacy wasn't there for people to take inspiration from.'

'You did everything you could to stop him. Maybe that's all that can be asked of us, and maybe it's time to move on.'

'You might be right,' Halloran said.

'Oooh,' said Evie, putting her hands to her ears as a microphone screeched. The whole table followed her lead and directed pained glares towards the stage.

'Welcome to Monday night karaoke at Thomas's. If you haven't already signed up, there's still time to put your name down, but to kick off tonight's fun, can we all welcome to the stage Mal Halloran who's going to sing a bit of an old-school classic: "When You're In Love With A Beautiful Woman" by Dr Hook.'

'Old-school classic, just like you,' Kitt teased, pinching Halloran's chin.

'I still can't believe you're making me do this,' said Halloran.

'Give it a chance, you might enjoy yourself,' said Kitt. 'Just be thankful I'm not making you go up there in a cowboy hat and an eye patch for the full Dr Hook aesthetic.'

'You don't know that I can't pull that off.'

Kitt looked him up and down. 'I think I do.'

'That song is a proper vintage tune,' Evie said with a beam.

'I got to pick the song,' said Kitt. 'I said he could sing that or "Close to You" by the Carpenters.'

'So in other words, I really wasn't given a choice at all . . . er, Banks? What are you doing with that phone?'

'Videoing your big moment, sir,' said Banks, holding the phone up so she could get a better view of Halloran's unimpressed expression. 'Gotta have something to project at next year's work Christmas party . . . assuming you'll be there, that is?'

'Ricci said I could start back tomorrow,' Halloran assured his colleague. 'Though long-term I'm keeping an open mind. Maybe I've got hidden singing talents and will wind up winning *The X Factor*.'

Banks scrunched up her nose in response. 'Not one to kill dreams lightly but I can't see it, sir.'

'Mal Halloran, are you here, lad?' said the MC over the microphone.

Halloran cringed but accepting his fate, stood and walked over to the mic. As he did so he could hear wolf whistling coming from his table that he thought it better not to acknowledge.

The music started, and so did Halloran's singing. He was unsteady at first, just about carrying the tune but not with any degree of confidence. After a few lines he looked over at Kitt and through the dimness of the pub lighting, he noticed a smile on her face as she watched him making an utter fool of himself. Something about her smile made the foolishness seem worthwhile.

He hadn't had much reason to smile over the last couple of weeks and if he was honest, even with Kitt in the picture, after all that went down at Irendale five years ago he had found it difficult to find joy. He used to find joy in police work. In serving others. He'd lost sight of that somehow, after all the loss and betrayal.

A loud whooping sound came from Kitt's table. Evie, Banks, Grace and Kitt were all clapping along to his uneven performance. And something about their light-heartedness gave him faith that even though he was still recovering from the trauma he'd experienced five years ago, and even though he was still learning to trust again, if he kept trying he would find his way back to joy.

In some strange way, he felt he had been given a second chance to make the most of the life he had now and glancing over again at Kitt he knew that was one second chance he wasn't going to waste.

ACKNOWLEDGEMENTS

Much appreciation is due to my agent Jo Swainson, without whom these books would not exist. Thank you so much for all you've done to make Kitt Hartley a reality.

Thanks also to my editor Therese Keating who has helped to sculpt the first three books in this series with great sensitivity.

Gratitude is also due to my specialist reader Hazel Nicholson for offering her keen editorial eye on matters of police procedure.

My enduring thanks goes to those people who read my work and otherwise encourage my creativity: Ann Leander, Claudine Mussuto and Dean Cummings. All you have done to help me believe in my work and myself cannot, frustratingly for a writer, be put into words.

I also want to say thank you to my family. Mam, Dad, Elaine, Sheena, Steven, Phil, Barbara, Ray, Christine, John, Tom, Gigi, Janet, Peter and Katie for all of the support you offer throughout the strange experience that is writing a book.

As always, heartfelt thanks to my husband Jo who offers more kindness and love than I ever could have hoped for.